More Laughter, Sweat & Fears

Life in the F

"Another humorous look at over thirty years of life inside a factory environment."

By

Trevor Whitehead

Chapters

Chapter 1: The early years

Chapter 2: The union in its heyday

Chapter 3: Time for a comeback

Chapter 4: Onwards and upwards

Chapter 5: Rise of the foot soldier

Chapter 6: A born comedian

Chapter 7: The Elstree experiences

Chapter 8: Opening a can of worms!

Chapter 9: Outsourced and another comeback

Chapter 10: Brussels

Chapter 11: Gone, but not forgotten

Chapter 12: New beginnings

All rights of distribution, including via film, radio and television, photomechanical reproduction, audio storage media, electronic data storage media, and the reprinting of portions of the text are reserved.

I dedicate this book to the hundreds if not thousands of people I crossed paths with throughout my time at the factory.

Geoffrey Martin-Smith, for his helping in jogging my memory of some of the characters and comical moments we encountered.

Warren Gibson, for revealing the real reason for the sudden departure of a certain convenor.

Roy Burton for his help in confirming the names of certain security personnel.

Last but not least, Gordon Beattie, Steve Battle, Steve Beavis, Mark Clothier, the late Brian Crease, Rob Fellows, Steve Jarvis, John Levey, Mark Lewin, John Manning and Terry Watts. I have the fondest of memories of you guys.

Last but not least my wife Su.

Authors disclaimer.

The events regarding any outsourcing, the involvement of any management, and the staff of the H/R at the time are alleged.

By the same author:

The Curry Affect

Arthur Ascot P.I

Ascot & Plunket

The UK's Number 1 Private Investigation Agency

Pattaya Dangerous

Laughter sweat & Fears

Housemates

3 Nights in Thailand

The Magnificent 3

The Bomb Hoax

July 13th

Birdie or Bust

Friends Reunited

A note from the author:

I first released this book back in 2017, and to be honest with you, I was never entirely happy with it. I read it recently and I know it's not one of my better works; in fact, some phrases and errors horrify me.
Plus, the shortness of the book always concerned me. I'd had the book printed in a larger print than normal to add a few pages.
So, I hope this time round I can do it justice.
This is a revamp of the original book; I've smoothed it out, reduced the large print size, and added some 50 pages along with another 24,000 words to the original manuscript.
I've added new stories and characters for you to enjoy.
Again I state that all the content in this book I know to be true.
It's a major improvement from the first book.

I was very happy to receive so many positive emails thanking me for the book at the time, some from family members of people I mention.
I received a very complementary email from a certain manager who I wasn't very kind to in the book, quite the opposite in fact.
He's retired now and living by the sea.
I didn't receive all complementary feedback though, I had an email from John Levy's wife Valerie letting me know in no uncertain terms that I'd spelt their name wrong and in fact, they were not Jewish!!
I guess I learned a lesson from writing this book, be careful what you say, it can come back and haunt you.
I should have learned my lesson by now; in my book "The Bomb Hoax" I refer to one of my school friend's fathers. When I wrote the book, I didn't give it a thought that a friend I'd not seen or heard of for fifty years would be sitting reading it.

She told me off and rightly so.
So, when I wrote this book it didn't cross my mind that some of the characters, I mention would one day be sitting at home reading about themselves.
So, John, I will amend your name as I relive the tales. "Toda."

Of course, in the four years since I first released this book a lot has changed. Unfortunately, a few more colleagues have passed away. It was when one of my close friends Brian Crease passed away, shortly followed by a close trade union colleague Richard Llewellyn that prompted me to write this book.
Plus this year's formation of the Tractor Plant Facebook group, largely thanks to Dennis Bailey. Like thousands of others, I crossed paths with, I never really knew Dennis at work, I think I played against him a few times in the inter-department cricket league. But can't recall a conversation I had with him in all my years there.
But the formation of this group which is just shy of 500 members has put me in touch with a lot of old colleagues, including my old foreman Tony Lynch who features on various occasions throughout my working journey.
When I mentioned the book to him, he said as long as I write the truth, he didn't care what was written about him.
Well, he's never complained to me since, so I guess he is okay with the content.
A couple of my old managers I have linked up on Facebook too.
So, once again I'll try and write and do justice about my time in the factory.

I will put on the book cover that this is the original book with added stories; I don't want people to think they are being diddled.
As I've mentioned before somewhere, all these tales and characters are true.
So, sit back and enjoy the Journey.

This book will cover my working life at the Tractor Plant, from the mid-1970s through to 2010. I will try and keep it in some form of chronicle order, however, at times, this may not always be possible. I will also venture away from the factory to my life outside and my involvement with the Labour Party and Trade Union activities. I will try and keep it as accuRate and humorous as I can.

I aim to make it a fun read.

I will use nicknames when I think fit, real names when appropriate and false names to protect a few from vigilantes. All that you read are based on true events, there is going to be no fiction in this book. Certain individuals will come across in a bad light, well, what can I say? I'm not sorry.

This is a light-hearted look at working in a manufacturing factory, 99% of my time in the factory was enjoyable, just the odd arsehole would occasionally cause a bump in the road.

For me, my working life at the factory was one hell of a journey. I met thousands of people over thirty plus years. Many of these characters will feature in this book. It's funny because I knew hundreds of people there, some for donkey years, but didn't know them by their name.

So, let's go right back to the beginning, not 1974 when I started at the plant, but much earlier when my father moved from Dagenham to Basildon.

My father worked at the factory right from the beginning in the early sixties. He was transferred down from Dagenham in 1963. He once told me when he started there, he could see from one corner at the back of the building to a corner at the front. Before a single machine was in place. Well, all of us who have been inside the Factory know that's a huge area. The place is the size of a mini town. The days before Health and Safety went OTT, people used to get around on pushbikes.

I can remember when I started and watched in amazement as a single-engine block would eventually be driven off the end of the assembly line an all singing and dancing tractor. That block had all the necessary parts added to it. Crankshaft, pistons, camshaft and all the other parts that eventually made it a fully working engine. Then moved over to the assembly line where throughout a couple of days of weaving up and down the lines, a tractor was slowly put together. It was some feat I can tell you, and at one point we were building more than a hundred tractors a day.

Not quite as long as Coronation Street, the factory has provided employment for many. Through all the plant's ups and downs, I loved working there. Of course, over that period of time, I had my moments when I wanted to jack it all in. But I will never speak badly of the place. It's still churning out tractors to this day, getting close to sixty years now. Something I and many others should be proud to have been a part of.

The factory has a great reputation for building a quality product. That's why it's survived for so many years. Long may it continue.

"A little taster."

You know, in every factory you'll find a village idiot. Well in my time as a trade union representative, I came across two. Now, since I wrote the first book, both have retired, one, Pat Brown, will feature later in this book. The other Mick McManus rose to be the prominent position of Trade Union Convenor at the time I published the first edition of this book.

When I was still at the factory as a lowly shop steward, for some unknown reason, the "Munch" as he was known became the factory's union, health and safety representative. When I found out about this appointment, I thought the convenor at the time had lost his marbles? Not one of your better moments, Geoff? (Ex Convenor)

Desperation came to mind when I heard. You see I was known as a bit of a maverick in that period. So any chance of a higher position was never going to happen. A few years before I'd left the T&G trade union and joined the then AEEU. This was frowned upon by the then Convenor who I will call the Rat, but as you'll read further into this book, you'll see it was a very good move for me.

Now, back to Mick the Munch.

He was if anything, enthusiastic and to be fair to the guy he tried his best.

This comical encounter I can remember as if it was yesterday. There had been a near-miss accident on the final assembly line. If my memory serves me correctly I believe a rear wheel had come off one of the tow tractor-trailers that was destined to be fitted to a tractor currently making its way along the production line. As the wheel flew off the trailer it took aim at an employee and resulted in a slightly grazed assembly worker. Admittedly it could have been nasty; luckily the guy involved was quick on his feet and managed to dodge the bullet so to speak.

I can remember being called over to that area to look at a faulty hoist, the guy involved with the wheel was, as James Bond would say, "Shaken, but not stirred."

So, in the aftermath of this incident, the "Munch" called all the stewards in for a meeting. When I say all the stewards, we were down to a handful by then. I don't know what it was, maybe I had a touch of wind. But I walked into the meeting smiling. Now, there was one thing that always went against the "Munch."

He came from Bristol. So, he spoke with a broad West Country accent that to the Essex man, well, not to put a too finer point on it, sounded thick.

The "Munch" took one look at me and pointed.

'This is no laughing matter, Trevor. That man could have been killed!! Worst still, he could have broken a leg!!'

Just a taster of what's to come.

If this is your first read, enjoy the book.
If this is your second read, I hope you enjoy the book a tad more this time.

Chapter 1

The early years.

To be honest, I have one vivid memory of my father's time at Dagenham Fords, and that was going to a Christmas party there, Ironic now as I write this because some forty-odd years later, I was organizing Christmas parties for the employee's children at the plant.
When I got involved in things like that, I'd often ask myself "why."
This was the period at the plant when doing anything that might cost the company money was a big no.
I often wondered if Charles Dickens got the idea of "Scrooge," from our H/R manager at the time.
Anyway, by hook *and a crook*, we'd somehow raised the funds and a good time was had by all.
It was at these parties that I found out how satisfying a thank you could be when the children set off home.

I guess my first memories of the factory date back to the late sixties. I must have been around twelve at the time. We were living in a tiny village called Stow Maries, you know, one of those blink and you'll miss it type of places. My mum and dad moved there from Rainham in 1963. My nan had lived in the village for most of her life and my mum had attended the tiny village hall school back in the 1930s.
A beautiful village, but not much to do for a teenager. However, that story is in another book.
My dad had completed twenty-five years with the company and was going on a night out to London's Talk of the Town.

I can remember the build-up as dad treated himself to a new suit. When I think back, my dad would only have been thirty-nine, he started work at fourteen.

Now, these were the days before you could take your wife to these long service dinners. We lived down a very small lane and I remember standing next to my mum as this big coach manoeuvred along and pulled up outside our bungalow. Dad, in his new suit, climbed aboard and we waved him off.

As I write this it crossed my mind about my theory of my dad being a snob.

We lived about fifty meters from a bigger main road, I guess dad wanted to show off our posh bungalow to the other long service guys who were on the coach.

The next morning, I woke up and could straight away smell vomit. Walking in the kitchen, mum was clearing up the aftermath of the boozy night out. Sat on the kitchen table was a vomit-stained Engelbert Humperdinck LP. Signed by the man himself. Strangely, my dad, had it framed, and for years that vomit stained LP hung on the wall.

A couple of years before Engelbert hung on the wall my granddad passed away, on my mum's side. They lived in the same small lane as us. My nan gave my dad, granddad's old moped. It was one of those 49cc pedal to start types. I say 49cc, it could have been a lot less. This was because the top end reached roughly 20mph. I say this with some authority as I had a go on it myself when my parents were out.

I only managed one ride as I'd been spotted by a nosy neighbour and they told my dad.

Now, Stow Maries was a good thirteen miles away from the factory, doesn't sound a lot, but on a moped that had a top speed of about twenty miles an hour, it was far enough. I'm guessing it did a lot of miles to the gallon, so that was enough to get dad peddling. I remember the afternoon we had really bad snow, dad had rung and said it was bad at work. He left work early but unbeknown to mum and me, the moped wouldn't start.

So, he peddled home the thirteen miles. Bad enough on a normal bike, on a moped it must have been a killer. He arrived home about three hours later, dripping wet and knackered. I think after that encounter the romance of the moped died. He was soon back to driving his Vauxhall Viva.

For some reason, and it's something I should check out really. I seem to think a man from work turned up and bought the moped off my dad. I have an inkling it was a guy called Laurie Heath, who I met years later.

He was a hoist man at the plant when I started, a job I would do for my last twenty years working there.

I contacted his son Les to enquire about Laurie and was sad to find out that he had passed away in his sleep in March 2021. He had a claim to fame, his younger brother was a well-known singer in the early 1960s. He performed under the name of Johnny Kidd, more widely known as Johnny Kidd and the pirates. Their original name was Freddie Heath and the Nutters?

Johnny was killed in a car crash in 1966.

Laurie must have been a good age when he passed as his younger brother would have been eighty-five had he still been with us.

So, I started at the plant in 1974. Once I passed the medical and escaped the clutches of this strange man who I think was called Ralph. He was what was known at the time as a medical officer? I haven't a clue what qualifications he held, but he held onto my balls and made me cough for far too long for my liking.

I was deemed fit to work, well apart from my ears.

Now, my first week at the plant was done in near-total deafness. Ralph told me I needed to have my ears syringed.

There was no way I was letting him loose on my ears, not with those wandering hands. Instead, I went to my local doctor. Unfortunately, they agreed with Ralph and I was dispatched with a prescription for ear drops that I needed to squirt in my ears twice a day for a week.

The morning after the first dose I woke up deaf and for the long week that followed I struggled to hear and near the end had started to learn the art of lip-reading.

The following Friday evening a nurse did the syringing.

Christ, I was shocked and embarrassed by the amount of wax that came out. Needless to say, I felt like I was walking around with bionic ears after that little episode.

I hadn't been working at the plant long when I found out my dad was a bit of a terror. I don't have to look far to find where I get my mischievous nature from.

This behaviour was a bit of a shock to me, he'd never displayed this side of him to me before.

He was a tinsmith at the plant, a highly-skilled trade. I used to watch in awe at some of the things he and his colleagues made from sheet metal. I wouldn't imagine there are many of his creations left in the plant now. He made many of the guards and like for engine machining, sadly that side of the factory has long gone.

In my early years working there, I used to have my tea break with him in the morning.

Now a small fact, never argue with your dad, he's always right. The classic example, sugar! My dad never took sugar in his tea. I used to take three. He'd make me a cuppa, then I'd have to go to one of his mates and scrounge some sugar. He said if you can drink tea with no sugar for one week, I'll never take sugar again. So, for a week I suffered, I was a bit of a teapot, so maybe six to eight cups a day. After a week, I made a cup and put three sugars in, and as dad predicted, I couldn't drink it.

I sat with him one-morning tea break and it must have been around early November time. I say this with a bit of confidence because all of a sudden, he stood up and pulled this huge firework out of his bag.

'Loudest banger on the market,' he informed me. The other two tinsmiths, Ernie and Bob came over and inspected the firework that looked like a stick of dynamite.

Now, unbeknown to me, the tinsmiths were in dispute with a certain General Foreman, who was, unfortunately, sitting in his office right next to the tinsmith's area of work. After watching Bob and Ernie scarper, I thought it was a good idea to follow suit. The three of us watched from a safe distance as my dad proceeded to light the banger and throw it on the roof of the office.

Fair play to him, he just sat there with his fingers in his ears and literally waited for the fireworks to follow the explosion.

You can imagine the noise as it went off on the metal roof. My ears were ringing some thirty feet away. The foreman ran out followed by the clerk who also worked in the office with him. I can see him now, tea dripping from his shirt throwing a right tantrum at my dad.

For the life of me, I can't remember General foreman's name, if it comes to me, I'll put it in. (Could be Sid Miller)

The clerk I can remember, Mick Moody, will feature at a later date. He and my dad put a joint suggestion into the company once and won a new car between them.

My dad was a compulsive suggestion scheme contributor. He'd stick an idea in at least once a week. He used the phrase "got to be in it to win it" thirty years before the lottery slogan came out. I have a feeling the suggestion scheme died when we were taken over by Fiat.

For some reason, my dad always went to work in a collar and tie and carried a briefcase. A bit over the top to carry cheese sandwiches? I never asked him why,? Thinking back now I'm assuming it was to impress the neighbours. I guess that's why I think of him as a bit of a snob back then.

He had some strange habits, Including his name? When I started at the factory, I had people coming up to me saying, "Your George Whitehead's son, aren't you?"

My dad's name was Edward, mum called him Ted. So not sure where this other name came from. But at work, everybody knew him as George.

He was well known in the Ford wine making circle, and I can honestly say after sampling many of his homemade concoctions that the wine was crap.

In fact, a glass of Elderflower gave me the Rodney Trotters. Each to their own.

A few memories always come to mind when I think of my late father.

The first one that comes to mind was when I got myself chucked off the school bus for fighting.

I'm ashamed to admit I was a bit of a handful at school, I would take anyone on, and if they were bigger, I'd tool up with my sister's rounders bat, well that was until it was confiscated.

Now, because we lived in the middle of nowhere, I used to get a bus to ferry me back and forth to school.

This particular day I had a set too with a lad called Michael Friend. A real gobshite with a big mouth at the time.

Things came to a head on the journey home from school one day.

The driver stopped the coach and chucked us out in the middle of nowhere. Deciding to be clever, I thought the quickest way to get home was a straight line.

So, I headed through fields and all sorts. Unbeknown to me my dad had come out in the car to look for me, so he wasn't best pleased when he saw me walking up the lane, covered in mud.

My mum went mad and sent me to bed without any tea. Bless my dad, he sneaked in a while later with a sandwich for me.

So, the next day I thought no more of it. The afternoon's journey home all seemed normal. No fighting, well I couldn't face another night without chips.

The school bus used to drop me off in a pub car park. The pub was called the Stow Bullocks. Unfortunately, a few years later it closed and is now a private residence.

As the bus pulled into the car park, I could see my dad's car parked up, something he'd never done before. As I stepped off the bus my dad appeared.

'Wait in the car,' he instructed me. Now what I should mention, we Whitehead's are a solid breed. My dad was over six feet and had arms the size of an average man's legs. His brother, my uncle Barry is a colossus of a man. Six foot-six, and not the type you'd want to mess with.

As I reached the car and looked around, I could see my dad pummeling the bus driver.

Let's just say I never had to walk home again.

I'm not sure if my dad got into trouble over that incident. I never saw the driver again, the next day a different man was sitting in the driver's seat.

Chocolate Angel Delight. My god, I could never eat one of those again.

I can only liken it to my dislike of vodka, I got badly drunk on vodka once, even to this day I couldn't drink a glass for the life of me. Just the smell makes me want to vomit.

My dad came home from work one day and marched in carrying a huge box containing the popular dessert, Angel Delight. There had been an accident on his way home from work and a trailer had tipped over carrying loads of these boxes.

He said they had been scattered all over the place.

Knowing my dad, he would have aided the scattering and dad being dad, had one away.

Now, to begin with, I loved them, each night after dinner, mum would pop out a bowl of this chocolate dessert out of the fridge, and I mean each night.
I never counted how many of these small boxes were packed into the huge box, but after about a year I couldn't face another one.
Now, people that know me can certify I'm a chocoholic, but even to this day, like the vodka I couldn't face another chocolate Angel Delight.

The Pig.
No, I'm not talking about someone at work, although a Rather large Shop Steward comes to mind as I write this.
I'm talking about the pig my dad knocked down on the way to work. We were living in Maldon at the time this happened, some eighteen miles from work.
Occasionally my dad and I would travel to work together, usually on a weekend.
Now, another strange habit of his, he would never buy a Ford car, even with the lure of the company discount voucher.
For some reason, he loved the Datsun. He would trade it in every couple of years for a new one. I found this strange because he was not saving any money? The Datsun's were cheap, but once you knocked the discount off the equivalent size Ford the difference was minimal.
I know this because he tried to convince me to buy a Datsun Cherry once.
So, this particular morning we're on our way to work, dad was driving and I wasn't taking any particular attention to the road ahead.
Suddenly he hit the brakes as out of nowhere came this pig. Bang, he hit the front of the car with a hell of a thud. We were on a country road, it was early morning, there was no one about, and the pig was dead.

Thinking we'd drag him to the side of the road; my dad had a different idea.

He didn't want to leave him behind, so, somehow, we managed to stick him in the back of my dad's hatchback. We had a real struggle trying to lift the poor thing in I can tell you. Luckily, he wasn't a huge pig, but I would imagine he weighed around 80 kilos. And lifting a dead weight while trying not to get pig shit all over you is no easy task.

I can remember the smell, I was surprised my dad would put this smelly animal in his pride and joy.

Bizarrely, he covered the pig with a travel blanket? However, the head was poking out. Not sure why he did that? He had his reasons and I didn't ask. Thinking about it now maybe that was a tactic to reduce the smell?

'What on earth are you going to do with it? He bloody stinks,' I naturally asked.

'Going to make bacon,' my dad replied. He informed me that he was going to have a word with the works canteen manager. Not sure my dad had thought this through? How he expected to get the pig past the security, only he knew. Luckily, or unluckily for my dad, that problem as it turned out never materialized.

Unfortunately for us, ten minutes further along the road, a grunting sound signalled that by some miracle the pig had come back to life.

Trust me when I tell you, he was one unhappy pig.

One thing that will stick with me forever was when my dad told me to calm down. That the pig was trapped in the hatchback boot and couldn't escape.

Well, that prediction lasted all of five seconds, for as I turned round and could see the head of the pig appearing through the back seat.

Now, I'm not going to knock the Japanese made Datsun range of cars as they were then back in the early eighties, but the word flimsy came to mind that day.

The time my dad had pulled up on the side of the road the pig was running riot on the back seat. I was out of that car faster than Usain Bolt on speed.

The next couple of minutes were spent trying to get it out of the car. He kept snapping at me like a crocodile and I was wary of being bitten. Pigs make a hell of a noise when there frightened, this added to the drama we were now experiencing.

Eventually, with some pure pulling and pushing, we got it out. The pig never looked back, he ran off, in the direction of Wickford High Street.

When we checked the interior of my dad's car, it was wrecked. The back seat had a big hole in it. There was shit and piss everywhere. And you can imagine the smell. The ten-minute drive to the factory and the thirty-minute drive home was done with all the windows open. This was the time before car valeting became popular.

So, my dad would be out with a bucket of hot soapy water and disinfectant for the next few nights trying to kill the smell.

It cost him a lot of money to put the car right in the end. The pig had made holes in the back seat and ripped the headlining. I'd love to know what excuse he used at the garage who repaired it.

Just to wind him up, the morning it happened I sent him over a couple of bacon rolls for his morning tea break.

Later that morning I was called over by a Wickford guy by the name of Peter Bell.

Now Peter and his work partner, Bill, had the best jobs in the factory. They were in charge of the scrap compound outside at the back of the plant.

Now, I can say with certainty that they had the best job because I was sent out to work there while Peter recovered from a heart attack.

'I'm not going to hang myself, but I soon discovered there were a lot of "Perks," that went with the job.

It will come as no surprise that the pair of them drove new cars and had a nice property each. These are two men that had never done a day of shift work or overtime. I only saw a small amount of what went on there, but there were big perks to be made.

I can remember Bill being well put out that Peter had gone off sick with a heart attack. He made it very obvious that he didn't want me working with him.

Well, that was something that had come back to bite him, he and Peter had insisted it was a two-man job when being watched by the dreaded works study guy.

Luckily all his moaning was water off the back as I'm thick-skinned and decided I'd branch out on my own while I was posted there.

Bill didn't like it, but there was nothing he could do. I think he nearly had a heart attack himself when he heard Peter had a setback in his recovery and would be off work for at least another three months. On hearing that news I will admit I did break into a smile.

To be fair to Peter, he was a decent bloke, I know for a fact he'd lectured Bill on his behaviour towards me.

One thing I will say about him, he was like an old woman when it came to gossip, so it was no surprise that the morning of the pig incident, he spotted me and called me over.

'Here, Trevor, never guess what I saw this morning on my way to work.'

'A pig? Running down Wickford High Street.'

'How'd you know? Did you see him?'

'See him? We gave him a lift, we picked him up from his house, dropped him off near the High Street. I can tell you one thing, he lived in a right pigsty.'

I can only remember dad being upset with me once. Not because of what I'd done, but because I was plastered all over the front page of our local paper "The Maldon & Burnham Standard" for two weeks. I say two weeks because it was a weekly newspaper. Let me condense the tale.
I used to go to a youth club in a little village not far from Maldon, a village called Cock Clarkes.
My girlfriend at the time lived there. We used to go to the village hall on a Wednesday night, meet friends and it was just a place to hang out. I had just turned seventeen, still riding about on my scooter, but taking driving lessons. We went one night and were informed that it was the last time the youth club would be open.
Shock horror! Turned out a man who lived next to the hall kept complaining to the council about the noise and mess.
So, between a few of us, we hatched a plan to teach this man a lesson, We were out to get revenge.
Now, with a couple of mates, we decided how funny it would be if we placed a pretend bomb on this guy's doorstep.
So, over the next couple of evenings, in my friend's dad's shed, the three of us built what we thought a bomb would look like.
I can still see the finished article now. One of those big square type 9-volt batteries, three plastic toilet roll holders, painted to look like TNT. Wires going from the battery into the putty that we hoped resembled gelignite.
A large alarm clock and all finished off by making a plinth for it to sit on.
The three of us stood back and admired our work.
So off I went to Cock Clarkes that evening. The homemade bomb was placed on his doorstep, covered by a cardboard box.

I walked over to the phone box, found his number, and rang him.

'Hello.'

'Listen arsehole, I'll teach you to get our youth club closed. Open your front door, I've left you a present.' With that, the three of us scarpered.

At 3 am, there is a banging on my mum and dad's front door. I could see the blue flashing light reflecting on my bedroom ceiling. I heard my dad thumping down the stairs and utter the words most dads would say after a policeman asked if I lived there.

'He's been in all night.'

Needless to say, the shit had hit the fan. We'd made the phoney bomb look too real. The police wouldn't touch it, they called in the bomb disposal unit. I think it was safe to say, they weren't happy.

Our timing was bad because of the troubles linked to the IRA, which had been going for a couple of years by then.

It went to court and because I made the phone call, I was labelled as the ringleader. What didn't help was I was seventeen and the other two were still sixteen. So, the papers could only print my name. We went to court on a Wednesday. Because the local paper had a cut-off time for printing, I was on the front page, a photo of me arriving in court, and those famous words at the end of the article …. "Case continues."

I ended up on probation for a year. The paper picked up the story the following week. I think my mum got the brunt of, "I saw your Trevor in the paper." She served in a little High Street bakers shop. When mum was unhappy, dad was unhappy. I think it's fair to say life was a bit fragile in the Whitehead household for a few weeks after that.

The full story of this outrageous act and the lead up to the incident is covered in another book, "The Bomb Hoax."

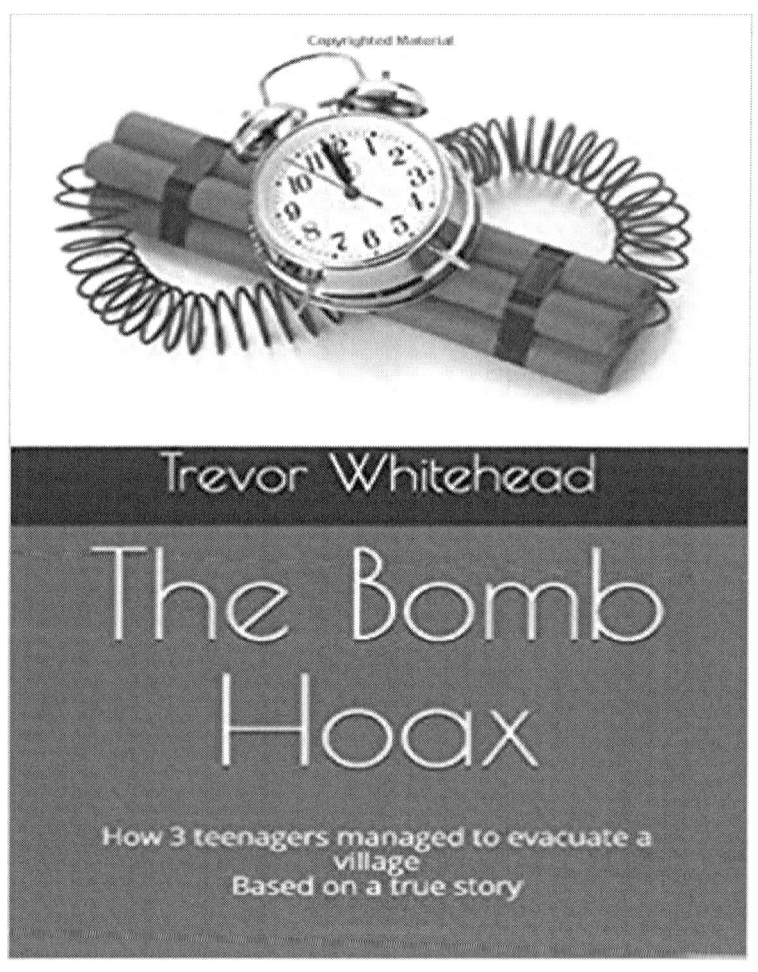

I guess through my teenage years I gave him some eye-rolling moments, but he let me learn by my own mistakes. I can only ever remember him giving me one piece of advice.
'Never go out with a girl with big hands?'

So, let's get back to the factory. It was a time when you could get anything. There was always somebody selling something. I heard a rumour that a man walked around carrying a clipboard for years selling insurance. Apparently, he didn't even work for the company!

There were certain sellers spread across the factory. I'm not sure how the territories were marked out or who sold what, but you could get most things in the factory without having to go to a shop.

I can remember buying a cheap digital watch, a few months later I went back to the guy because the battery had run out. He informed me he didn't sell batteries, that I needed to see a guy in engine machining.

Way before the national lottery, the big thing was the football pools.

Now, you'd get your pools coupon collected on a Thursday. Oily Joe, fork truck driver out of the stores. He must have made a killing collecting the football pools in the plant. Christ knows how he ever got any work done on a Thursday, he'd be busy collecting the coupons and money all day. The supervision turned a blind eye because they used his service too.

You could get anything at work, from cheap cigarettes and whiskey to shell suits and trainers.

I was working for Central Maintenance. A wide range of skills and ages, at the time I was one of the youngest.

I was a Labour Party man back then. Not sure what to say about them now? I certainly wouldn't vote for them now.

As I took an interest in politics it was a natural development to support the Trade Union.

Now, my first Shop Steward was an Irishman named Peter Maloney. Stout, cloth cap and a roll-up permanently hanging from his lip.

I had a lot of time for Peter, if you've ever seen the classic film, "I'm alright Jack," starring Peter Sellars as the Trade Union leader "Fred Kite." I think a lot of "Fred Kite" was in Peter.

Peter Maloney second left, customary fag hanging out of his mouth.
Far-right, ex convenor George Catton.

Unfortunately, we had a new manager arrive. Albert Mustoo was the only manager I'd worked under at that point. To be honest, I hadn't had a lot of dealings with him, he was the type to let the foreman do their job.

The only time he spoke to me was to thank me for using my jumper in putting an engine fire out on the road sweeping lorry.

I had been told to drive it around the Plants estate for the day. Not sure why I kept getting these different jobs, but when I was asked to drive the road sweeper, I thought great. Outside in the fresh air, what could be better.

However, after a couple of hours driving around the same route it was getting very monotonous.

It's not like you could listen to a radio, this road sweeper was hot and very noisy.

I started to notice people pointing at me as I drove along, what I couldn't see straight away was the smoke coming out of the engine area. I stopped the truck and jumped out, grabbing my jumper on the way.

As I searched for the lever to open the engine compartment, Albert arrived.

He found the lever and grabbed my jumper and threw it on top of the smoking engine.

He then went inside the cab and pulled out a fire extinguisher and proceeded to put white foam all over the engine area.

When I mentioned the remains of my jumper to him, he just smiled, said thanks and walked off.

Needless to say, I liked him, my dad had spoken highly of him. Not sure if he retired or was moved but he was replaced by a fly by night character by the name of, Gerry Bomando.

A fiery character, who looked like an ageing gigolo. Not sure where his roots lie, he had a continental type face, and with that surname, he certainly didn't come across as English blood. Fat, with his shirt tucked into his trousers. Smelling of cheap aftershave and was boosted in height by built-up shoes, a receding hairline bulked up with the aid of a perm. He looked like he was ready to audition for a part in Only Fools and Horses.

I'm not sure how on earth this type of character became a manager of a maintenance department?

I think he was a manager of material handling before we inherited him.

He was one of the guys I spoke about as selling goods on the side, he had a stall at a market in the poor man's travel resort of Canvey Island.

Unfortunately for Peter Maloney, Bomando took an instant dislike to him and very quickly put an end to Peter's reign. Peter made the mistake of taking him on and got his arse smacked.

What happened to Peter was something I would make sure wouldn't happen to me in the future.

Don't take your position for granted. Being a shop steward had certain perks, time off work for courses, meetings, little junkets away if you were lucky.

Now, by doing all this you needed to make sure you kept your workmates happy. If they had a complaint, you needed to be seen as doing something about it.

If you didn't, then the perks you were getting became a target of hate.

In other words, if the manager didn't get you, the guys you represented would.

It didn't take long for things between Peter and Bomando to come to a head.

Bomando bided his time then ridiculed Peter in front of many of us.

Peter had been neglecting his shop steward duties, something that would often happen if you had been a steward for several years. They get lazy and think they have the job for life. Over the years I saw it many times.

So, Peter had lost the confidence of the guys he was representing.

As soon as Bomando came in as our manager he tried to make a name for himself by making the Central Maintenance department huge.

It seemed every time I came off a week of nights and on to the day shift, they'd be three or four new faces.

It wasn't like we had taken on more work to justify this increase, so in a matter of weeks, he'd added about twenty-five new guys into the department?

This was only going to end one way, badly.

Of course, in the end, I think our budget was well over, so in an attempt to pull it back he slashed all overtime.

To be fair to Peter, he tried to reason with him, but Bomando wasn't having any of it. Bomando had got wind of Peter's precarious position with the guys and used it to his advantage. Peter made the fatal mistake of having a shouting match with Bomando outside the office.

A group had gathered to watch proceedings and it was soon obvious that Peter didn't have what it takes to tackle this joke of a manager. He should have, it was obvious he'd gone mad by increasing the headcount. Peter should have taken him on as soon as the increase in heads started. There are procedures he could have used to bring this to the H/R.

But being old school, he decided to have this slanging match in front of us. Bomando had an answer to everything Peter threw at him.

It was painful to watch, to be honest.

Unfortunately for Peter, the respect and support dwindled even further and it wasn't long before the Shop Stewards election came.

Peter's reign was finished, and after the ballot count, up stepped Bobby Graham.

I'm not sure how he became our steward, I suppose when it's a two-horse race and one of them is an also-ran, you're not left with a lot of choices.

Now, here was a character who could bamboozle just about everybody.

Bobby Graham was a stocky little Irishman who waltzed around in a white boiler suit and smelt of body odour. However, he came with a fearful reputation.

I'd heard many a story of his exploits at the Irish club. I can picture him now, five feet four, grey greased back grey hair. Now Bobby had one particular flaw that wasn't good if you were a shop steward, no one could understand him. Not ideal when you're the elected representative of men.

It was a trait that got worse if he got excited.

Wanting to make an early name for himself as our union rep, he had a public clash with Bomando. He hadn't learned from Peter Maloney's mistake.

He launched an attack on the manager. Unfortunately, none of us, including Bomando couldn't understand what the hell he was ranting about.

It was around this time that I felt I wanted to be the shop steward. The only thing I had against me was my youth, Peter Maloney and Bobby Graham must have been around the fifty-plus mark at that time.

The first thing I had to do was belittle Bobby Graham, followed by a stand against Bomando, I needed to show the lads I wasn't scared to speak up.

So, when Bobby had another stand up with Bomando, it was time to step forward.

I bided my time until Bobby had scathed Bomando, I knew what would come next, I'd seen and heard it before. Bomando, who loved to play to an audience would hold his arms out and say 'I haven't a clue what you're on about, Bobby?'

This would prompt Bobby to have a go again, but of course, he was more excited and I'm not sure if any Irishman would be able to translate what on earth he was saying.

Once again Bomando played to the audience, however, this time I was waiting.

Once Bobby had finished I turned to Bomando.

'He said you're a c***.' Both looked around at me.

'No, he didn't.' Answered Bomando, shocked by my intervention.

'Yes, he did, I understand Gaelic and he said you're a c*** and a useless prick. If you don't start dishing out the overtime, he's going to knock you out.' With that statement I walked off leaving them to it, my reputation had started to rocket.

I made sure I kept a wide berth from Bobby for a while, the guys who saw my little intervention were saying it was the funniest thing they'd seen.

However, I wasn't after a cabaret spot, I wanted to be their shop steward.

We suffered Bobby for a few more weeks until things started to get ugly.

Nothing worse than men not getting any overtime. We'd not been back at work long after a strike, so we were keen to try and recover the lost money.

Bomando wouldn't budge, something had to give. I'd personally had my fill with Bobby, I couldn't avoid him forever and had a set-to with him one morning.

He still was sulking over my translation moment with him and Bomando. I didn't know if this confrontation was going to lead to blows, I had the upper hand as he was at least eight inches shorter than me and I must have been four stone heavier.

Plus, he was giving away about thirty years. I was still wary though because I'd heard his nickname was one punch.

I tried my best to hide my fear and stand my ground expecting the worse, but after another rant, he stormed off.

He didn't know it at the time, but it was over for him. We needed a steward that we could understand, someone with a bit more brain as well as brawn.

I did a petition for a vote of no confidence in Bobby. Something you could do if you were unhappy with the current steward.

As long as you could get over fifty percent to sign you could force an election. It show's what his reputation was like when a few colleagues were scared to sign.

Luckily, we had enough signatures to force another Shop Steward Election.

Cometh the moment, cometh the man. I stood against Bobby and had a landslide victory. I was voted in and became a Shop Steward at twenty-two.

Getting the job was the easy part; I now had to show my men I was capable of dealing with Bomando.

Now, someone was looking down on me, because within a week of me becoming the Shop Steward for Central Maintenance, Bomando was gone. At last, the hierarchy had seen through the then managers ridiculous way of running a maintenance department.
Of course, I did what any Shop Steward would do, I put a rumour out that I'd been to see the H/R Manager to get Bomando removed.

Far-left the imposing figure of Derek West. In front of Derek is the talkative Irishman "One Punch" Bobby Graham. The front row next to Bobby is my first convenor Bill Cleary.

For a while, I was the best thing since sliced bread. Still wet behind the ears, I was brash and cocky. Little did I know this would lead to my first of many showdowns with the Plant

Convenor at that time. My first encounter was with the fearful Bill Cleary didn't go well. In fact, it was nearly all over before it started

Chapter 2

The Union in its heyday.

In the late nineteen-seventies, the trade unions were at their peak. These were the days of walkouts, long strikes, big pay rises. I've been on a nine-week strike, a seven-week strike and numerous shorter ones, and let me tell you, it was very harsh. The latest I've heard from the tractor plant is the union is just about non-existent? They'll be a lot of old shop stewards turning in their graves with what has happened over the last few years.

So, the first strike I was involved in stretched out for nine weeks. Now, when you went on strike in those days you knew it might be for some time. It was a game of holding your nerve. If you didn't hold your nerve, then the union held it for you, as I'll explain later.

Although finding work was quite easy back then. It became a shock to the system to do real manual work. I found an advert for a hod carrier, cash in hand. Eleven pounds a day was more than I was getting paid working at the factory. I did my usual, it can't be that hard and applied for the position.

There was a housing estate being built in Chelmsford, so I went along.

'You done hod work before?' The guy in charge looked at me suspiciously.

'Of course, I have.' I thought how hard can carrying a few bricks and a bit of cement be?

'Okay, start tomorrow at eight.' I went home, stopped on the way and bought a hod from ironmongers and a broom handle. I asked the bloke in the shop to fit the handle, which he did. I stand with the hod and broom handle over my shoulder and ask the bloke if I had it right.

'You look, good mate, you carried a hod before?'

'Yes, many times,' I lied as I left the shop.

'Just so you know it's not sale and return.' He holliers after me. Strange man, I thought to myself as I reached my car.

The next morning, I turned up at the building site, I take the hod out of the boot of my mark 2 Cortina and march over to the guy who hired me. His welcome left a bit to be desired.

'C***.'

Not sure if this was the usual welcome for a new guy, so I just smiled.

'What you got there?' He pointed to my sparkling brand new hod.

'Well it's not a nine iron, is it?' This remark caused a repeat of his welcome.

He grabbed my hod and walked over to a bench and sawed at least two-thirds of the handle off. I felt a right cock, and realised what the sale and return remark meant.

To be fair after a shaky start, I got the hang of things. Bloody hard work I can tell you. I was only 21 at the time and thought I was fit, but I had two bricklayers to keep up with, no easy task. Bricks and mortar flew up the ladder all day. Keeping the mixer going and taking up bricks to keep two men going was tough. In my mind, I kept going by telling myself to stick it for a week. My mum sewed some padding in my shirt to ease the pain in my shoulder.

I somehow managed it to the end of the week and picked a cheque up for fifty-five pounds. That was enough encouragement for me to turn up the following week. I kept thinking, "It's only for a few more days." Fords being on strike was big news and each evening on the TV it looked like the strike would soon be over.

The hell it was. Nine long weeks. At one point, I did consider taking up the hod full-time, fifty-five quid for four and a half days work was tempting.

However, I had started in the middle of September, come late November it was a different ball game. Cold and wet, hard graft, any thoughts of a career change soon disappeared.

We'd been on strike for seven weeks when on the news my dad and I thought the strike would be over.

We'd been offered a 17% pay rise. Dad went to the mass meeting as I was still working on the building site.

As I drove home that night and listened to the news on the radio, I couldn't believe the offer had been turned down? It was done on a show of hands, my dad said there was a near riot when after the vote the convenor stood on a back of a Transit and said the voters rejected the deal.

By all accounts, the vote was two to one in favour of acceptance. However, the union asked for a rejection and no way was the then convenor, Bill Cleary going to look a fool to his other Ford counterparts by voting to accept the deal.

As I mentioned earlier, the union was always there to help you hold your nerve!!

So, another two weeks went by and we finally accepted a rise of 23%. The days of a hands shown vote would disappear a few years later along with the strength of the union, largely due to the iron lady Margaret Thatcher.

The good old days of a mass meeting. Addressing the troops Derek West. To Derek's left is the convenor at the time Bill Cleary.

Before Thatcher got her hands on the top job, we were on strike again.
Not fancying bringing the hod out of retirement, I saw an advert for delivery drivers at the Corona depot in Chelmsford. I'm sure you've heard of them, they were one of the largest soft drink's companies at the time.
I went for an interview and told them the truth. Well, not all the truth obviously, I didn't mention I was already employed. I spun a tale about wanting to try the job out for a month to see if it was for me.
I said I could only work cash in hand for the month. They must have been desperate because they offered me eight pounds a day cash in hand.
Not very good money, but when you're on six pounds a week strike pay, trust me, it felt like a fortune.

So, the first morning I turn up. The delivery trucks were of a size that you could drive them with a normal driving licence. This so-called depot supervisor threw me a book with the day's deliveries. He told me it was up to me to load the truck and find the delivery addresses.

It's funny, as I think back, I now realise where some of the characters in my first book have come from. This depot supervisor didn't like me and was the most unhelpful person I've met.

In other circumstances, I think I would have had a set too with this little shit, but I need the work so let it go.

I checked how much stock I needed, and I start loading up all different types of the then famous fizzy drink.

Now here's the thing, the first morning I loaded what I needed, I drive to the gate and the security guard waved me through. Now whether this guard eventually got the job at Heathrow looking after Brink's – Mat gold bullion, I can't possibly comment. He never checked a thing.

The back of the truck was fitted with a type of tarpaulin curtain, so you would load the truck and pull the curtains along each side, that way you couldn't see the crates of drinks.

I thought straight away I was on a good thing here. Especially as I had a close relative living in Chelmsford at the time.

The first few days were a bit of a nightmare as I didn't know Chelmsford that well.

I would do a delivery and ask the shop where the next shop on my list was. Sometimes I'd drive across Chelmsford to do the next delivery, only to find the next one was one minute away from the shop I'd been to before.

I soon started adding more crates of drinks to my load each morning, drive out with a cheery wave to the security guy. On route, I would do a drop off a few crates at my relative's house, after work I'd pick a few cases up and take them home.

I think my whole family, apart from my dad were sad when the strike was over.

My relative in Chelmsford was happy though, he hadn't been able to park his car in his garage for weeks.

When I first became a shop steward, the convenor was a man called Bill Cleary. Odd-looking fellow, smoked a pipe wore thick-rimmed glasses and a goatee beard. I think I will be kind and call him stout. When I look at the old photos of him he has an uncanny resemblance to Vladimir Lenin.
He ran the stewards with an iron fist. He didn't suffer fools gladly. I can't remember how many Shop Stewards there were at that time, over thirty I would imagine.
This was a time where we had close to 5000 guys working at the plant.
The man I mention next if he is still alive should be in prison. He will feature later in the book, for legal reasons I'm wary of naming him. The majority of people who read this book will know exactly who I mean. I think the name that suits him best is *Rat.*
The *Rat*, who would eventually become convenor, was also fearful of Bill, as were most of the stewards.
I never understood why, I certainly wasn't. I guess I didn't think of myself as a career shop steward back then.
Being a member of the Labour Party was compulsory, as was attending a monthly branch meeting outside of the plant.
Honestly, I went along to my first branch meeting and I couldn't believe what a waste of a couple of hours it was.
The meeting lasted less than twenty minutes, the chessboard would come out and old Lenin would play whoever. I was reasonably good at chess, but he wouldn't play me, I'd already had my card marked at my first shop steward's meeting.
The meeting I refer to was an eye-opener in many ways.
I decided my best policy was to keep quiet, watch and learn, however it didn't go quite to plan.
Now I didn't know a lot of the steward's, like I mentioned earlier there was a load of them, so many in fact that at least

ten would be sat on chairs away from the long conference table.

I was sat at the table, a mistake as it turned out.

One steward I did know was a guy called Roy Carsons, he worked in the lab. A nicer guy you wouldn't meet, always pleasant.

He was the union rep looking after the canteen. A job I fancied as he got a free breakfast and lunch each day. No wonder after a few months he was beginning to resemble Billy Bunter.

Anyway, Roy announced to the convenor that he'd agreed with the canteen management to have piped music in the canteen. Roy sat there all smug, thinking he'd done a good thing, as did at the time. Big mistake as it turned out.

Bill Cleary decided to bring him down a peg or two.

He shouted across to Roy making me jump and me to pay attention.

'How dare you agree to something like this without bringing it back to this table. We, the shop stewards committee are the ones who will say yes or no to piped music. Now get up and go and tell the canteen management that you have overstepped your position Don't you ever agree to anything until you bring it here, to the table. Do you understand?'

'What about the piped music?' Asked Roy.

'Fuck the piped music,' hollered back Cleary.

Poor Roy, he sat there white-faced and glassy-eyed for a minute, then stood up and left the meeting. Not only had he been well and truly bollocked, but it had also been done in front of all the stewards present. A lesson learned.

The meeting continued until Bill decided to flex his muscles towards me. After a gentle introduction to the other stewards, I thought the meeting would be a breeze.

So, when Bill turned on me, I was a bit surprised and like Roy unprepared, to say the least.

'I have to say, Trevor, I don't like these votes of no confidence in a Shop Steward. If there was a problem with Bobby Graham, you could have least spoken to me.'

Now having witnessed poor Roy's humiliation, I decided attack was the best form of defence. Of course, being green behind the ears I didn't think of the consequences.

'Sorry Bill, but when a manager has the steward in his pocket, it's time for action. I don't give a fuck if you like a vote of no confidence or not, it had to be done. No way was we prepared to have another two years with a steward we needed a translator to understand.'

I sat down and nothing more was said. However, I'd blotted my copybook and I think it's fair to say my stint as a shop steward wouldn't last long while Bill Cleary remained the convenor.

I missed out on all the trips and was given the cold shoulder. I was even told to sit away from the conference table at meetings. He was a vindictive little shit that I often thought I should give a slap.

However, like Bomando, one minute he was there, then he was gone.

I never knew the reason behind Bill's departure. For some reason in the back of my mind, I have a feeling he did surface a few years later. Like me, he had his fifteen minutes of fame in the local paper. Something to do with dodgy diet pills if my memory serves me correct.

I'll pick up the convenor story later in the book.

Those early years I had some good foremen.
Alf Nicolson comes to mind. What a storyteller, he'd hold Council many a night and give us some of his navy stories. However, the other foreman Johnny Teague was an utter cock in my opinion.

He didn't like me and was constantly on my back. But, just like Bomando and Cleary, I saw him off. Little did I know what was coming.

The worst kind of foreman is an ex-shop steward. Step forward, Jimmy Ferris.

Now, before I start on Jimmy Ferris, I need to say something. This Tractor plant group on Facebook is marvellous, one of my old managers Keith Davis has been kind enough to share numerous photos with the group. Majority of employees receiving awards or retirement photos. One photo he shared was of Jimmy Ferris's retirement.

Someone, I know posted "Great Foreman?" Now, I had to question this remark. The guy had never worked under Ferris, so I asked why he thought he was a great foreman? He couldn't answer.

For the record, Jimmy Ferris was a shit, and the majority who worked under him would agree. I know he's passed on, but I'm not going to be nice about a man who for over a decade treated me and others with disdain.

When I first started at the plant, Jimmy Ferris was a Vehicle Repair fitter and a Shop Steward. When I eventually started doing night work it was a known joke that if a vehicle went down after midnight, it would have to wait for the day shift to repair. The foreman wouldn't wake him *allegedly.*

So, one Monday morning I walked in and saw him prancing about in a shirt and tie, and a foreman's green jacket.

I knew things were about to get worse.

In the early weeks, he'd run around like a blue arse fly trying to impress. We had a running battle for several years. It was around this time that I discovered I could impersonate our top maintenance manager at the time, Albert Musto. Oh, I had some fun on the phone taking him off.

I'd only heard Albert speak once, but he had the gruffest of voices, a voice I soon perfected.

I could see Ferris in the office just about to have his lunch, I had just done a repair job and was going to log it off after my lunch. So, feeling mischievous I walked next door to the heat treatment department and used their phone. Mick Moody answered and in my gruffest Musto voice, I barked.
'Put Ferris on.' I could hear Moody whispering, 'It's Albert.' As he passed the phone over.
'Yes sir,' Christ I nearly gave the game away on hearing Ferris grovel.
'Listen Ferris, this job, so and so.' I spoke about the repair I'd just finished.
'If it's not completed in the next ten minutes, you'll find yourself back on hourly pay putting the wheels on the tractors.'
'Don't you worry sir, I'll get straight on it.' The phone went dead. I was laughing my head off as I walked back out onto the aisle just as Ferris came running out.
'Whitehead,' he shouted. I pretended I didn't hear and kept walking.
'Whitehead,' he screamed a second time. I stopped and shouted that I was just about to go to the canteen. He came running over.
'This job you're on. How are you getting on?'
'I've just this second finished it.' I could see the wave of relief come over him.
'That's good. I've just had Albert on the phone chasing me up about it. But I told him, don't you go worrying about my boys, Albert. It will be repaired when it's repaired.'
What a Bullshitter.
Mick Moody said something sarcastic to me one day, so I thought you can have some of the Musto treatment too.
I phoned the office near lunchtime.
'Hello Moody, it's Albert.'
'Hello Albert, what can I do for you?'
'I tell you what you can do for me, go over to the canteen and eat my steak dinner.'

'What?'
'I ordered a nice steak lunch, but my gout is playing up. The doctor told me to lay off the steak.'
'I thought it was chicken that did that?'
'No, it's a steak that does it to me. Anyway, Jim Ferris told me how well you've been running things in the office, so have the steak as a thank you.'
'Well, if you're sure Albert.'
'Of course, I'm sure. Get yourself over to the canteen now. Tell the chef you've come to eat Albert's steak.' I hung up, and as I walked towards the office he came bounding out.
'Enjoy your sandwiches, I'm just going for a nice steak.' I watched him flounce off. Sucker.
These phone calls became a welcome outlet, but unfortunately, all good things come to an end.
Albert Musto left or retired and in stepped Les Clemmie. Now, Clemmie was a man of few words, I don't think I heard a word from him for about five years, I used to call him whispering Les. This put an end to my impersonations …. For a while, at least. Clemmie thought it a good idea to have a reshuffle of maintenance staff.
It was decided to put us on a 3-shift system. Now the extra money was welcome, but it was the most unsociable type of shift work. 7am-3pm, 3pm-11pm, 11pm to 7am. Friday's were the worst; Friday late shift and Friday nights were a killer.
Along with this announcement came a promotion for Jim Ferris, he was now our general Foreman. I couldn't believe it, but at least that would keep him away from me, or so I thought.
A foreman was brought in for each shift. On one shift came the Irishman *Tony Lynch*.
Now Tony will feature later on in the book. If you can imagine the Irish comedian Dave Allan, he was a lot like him. Had the Irish dry sense of humour, and wouldn't take any nonsense from anybody, including Jim Ferris.

The next shift had a guy called *Ricky Hunt*. Not sure how I can describe Ricky? Hyper comes to mind. Always rushing about, chasing his men, I was glad he wasn't my foreman.
Our supervisor was a guy called *Ken Lawrence*. Now I did have contact with Ken, albeit only the occasional email. He was a Facebook friend, but unfortunately, he took me off. I can only think he read the first edition of this book and didn't like how I portrayed him?
Truth hurts sometimes, Ken.
There was certainly no love lost between Ken and Jim Ferris, I can safely say Ken hated Ferris.
I had seen Ken around the plant occasionally, to be honest, I thought he was a clerk. He used to wear these largely flared trousers that must have been fashionable once, so once he became our foreman, he was referred to as "Baggy trousers." Poor old Ken, he certainly went from the fat into the frying pan when he took the job as foreman of our motley crew. What I will say is he was way too nice a guy to be a foreman. He was an avid stamp collector. Many a night shift I'd walk into the office and he'd have all these different stamps laid out on his desk.
Unfortunately for Ken, he was way too laid back. He didn't bollock any of us on his shift. He became known as "Easy Ken," on the other shifts.
Something Jim Ferris soon picked up on. I'd given being a Shop Steward a rest for a while, it was the time when Bill Cleary still held this grudge against me and I had other things going on in my life at that time.
Now, I was friendly with a few of the security guards, and good job I was. They became our early warning system. Jim Ferris, for reasons I can't explain started coming in and checking up on us in the middle of the night. He wouldn't dare do it on the two other shifts, I know that Tony Lynch would have said to him, 'Well you're here now; I'm going home to my bed'.

Jim Ferris had it in for Ken and hated our shift, so he would come in at 3 am and try and catch us asleep, *allegedly*. But luckily as Jim drove through the gate, one of the security guards would ring Ken, and he'd shoot around making sure we were hard at it. Many a time Ferris would check on me. I might have been a bit bleary-eyed, but I was working.

Only once did Ken let me down, and it caused a near riot. I am pretty placid these days, but back then it didn't take a lot for me to blow up.

We used to work 37.5 hours weekly shifts, so each week I'd get my payslip and if I hadn't done any weekend overtime, that's what I got paid for. We used to get our payslips on a Thursday. This particular day I strolled in and Ken handed it to me. I opened it and couldn't work out why it showed 37.25? I'd been docked 15 minutes. I stood there trying to work out if I'd been late the previous week. I knew I hadn't, I was never late. These were the days when we still clocked in and out. So, I questioned Ken.

'I'm fifteen minutes short here, Ken.'

'Oh …. Don't worry about it, I'll give you a no break.' This meant he'd mark down that I'd worked through my lunch break and would get 30 minutes overtime. To most people, they would have accepted this and let it go.

Not me.

'Why am I fifteen minutes short, Ken? I wasn't late last week, I didn't clock out early?'

Ken sat there all flustered, then the truth came out. The week before we were on the late shift. Jim Ferris had done one of his surprise visits. How sad, he wanted to come in and check up on us on a Friday evening. So about fifteen minutes before going home time I walked past Ken and Ferris and said goodnight. Went upstairs, washed up, came down and clocked out at 11 pm.

Now Ken let me down. Ferris told him to dock me fifteen minutes for going off in his eyes early. This is a Friday late shift when we had no production working.

Ken being Ken, didn't like confrontation, docked my time and didn't tell me. I guess he was hoping I wouldn't notice. To say I lost it was an understatement. I can honestly say it was the only time I fell out with Ken, I felt really pissed off. Trying to hide it made it worse.

Jim Ferris office was directly above; Usain Bolt wouldn't have got up those stairs quicker. I burst through the door and his clerk Maltese Joe said he was busy. Busy my arse, I went through without knocking and Ferris absolutely shit himself when he saw the anger on my face. I was so angry. Of course, he tried to justify it, but he knew if I took it further, he was on a loser. I won't write down what was said, let's just say we had a heated debate that ended with him giving my time back.

So, if our relationship was already fragile, it was the straw that broke the camel's back that day.

After that fracas, life for Ken became even more difficult. If there was a problem, Ferris would stick the blame on Ken and our shift.

I can remember an incident with some white cellulose paint. Because our shift was weak in his eyes, Jim Ferris gave us all the shit jobs. I came in on a late shift and Ken told me we had to paint the white on the Zebra crossing outside the plant.

'What, in the dark?' I enquired. It couldn't be done till all production had gone home, so after 6 pm.

Ken was always reluctant to say no to Ferris. In the end, Ken agreed and said he would leave Ferris a note saying we couldn't paint in the dark.

'Let's at least get the paint out of the stores.' He suggested.

So, I went with him in our little electric buggy to the stores and got the last four cans of white cellulose paint that was in stock. Now I think we were cursed never to get this zebra crossing painted. As we drove back to the office, two cans flew off the buggy and the contents flew everywhere. The next few hours were spent mopping the mess up. Trust me when I tell you the paint fumes made you high. This wasn't going to be the last time I got high on paint fumes.

Anyway, I eventually cleaned it up best I could, I had to get some black spray paint and go over the area again. End of the matter as far as I was concerned.

Wrong.

Next afternoon I go to work and immediately I'm summoned to Ferris's office.

Ken was already there looking like a naughty schoolboy.

'Where's the paint, Whitehead?'

'Good afternoon to you, too.'

'Where's the paint?'

'What paint?'

'You drew four cans of white cellulose paint out yesterday, where are they?' I smelt a Rat, and I looked at Ken.

'Tell him, Ken.'

'I've already said we had an accident and lost two cans.'

'Where're the other two cans, Whitehead?' Oh my god, I stood there and the penny dropped. I won't write what happened to the other two cans because, to be honest, I don't know. They had mysteriously disappeared? Let's just say the supervision in those days were allowed to park their cars behind the office. I won't point the finger!

I kept quiet and pleaded my innocence. In the end, I took Ferris's advice and I went off and multiplied.

Let's say things between Ken and me were a bit fragile for a few days after that incident.

Now I thought that was the end of the affair. But I should have known better, Ferris wouldn't let it go. One Friday morning he asks me to accompany him to a local builder's merchant. He buys a large can of white cellulose paint.

'They still haven't got any in the stores,' he informed me.

'Get that bloody zebra crossing painted tomorrow, I'm getting my arse chewed by the plant manager.' Now the zebra crossing was directly outside the main foyer.
'Block half and paint it, then block and paint the other half. Lock this paint in your locker until tomorrow.'
As far as I was concerned, I had an easy Saturday morning's overtime coming up …. Or so I thought.
The next morning, I get everything prepared. I sorted out the paintbrushes, some masking tape and then loosened the lid off the paint tin then set it back on the can. Now the Central maintenance office and workshop were located at the back of the factory, so I had a bit of a walk carrying the full tin of paint to the front entrance.
Enter Roy English. Mr Toot, I used to call him. He was one of the wooden rubbish guys, he drove a small tractor and pulled all the rubbish trailers from around various areas of the plant. We had big rubbish bins on wheels. So, Roy would collect and replace them. Now, these tow tractors had a small cab as they had to tow these bins outside to the back of the plant, where they were emptied.
So, just as I started to make my way to the front of the factory, Roy, pulled up next to me.
'Where you going, Ginger?'
'Outside the foyer, I'm repainting the zebra crossing.'
'Jump in, I'll give you a lift.' I hand Roy the can of paint.
'Just be careful with the paint, I've loosened the lid.' Roy took the tin of paint off me and sat it down between his legs, behind the gear levers. I climbed into the cab and tucked myself just to one side of him.
We start off, and we're having a general chit chat when he turned a sharp left by the engine assembly. You can guess what's coming. The whole tin tipped over, the paint emptied all over his foot and went everywhere over the floor of the cab.

I didn't know whether to laugh or cry. I had Roy saying, 'I don't believe you, Ginger.' As he spoke his voice started to get higher as the fumes engulfed the cab.
'Stop for Christ sake,' I shouted.
Roy pulled up and I climbed out. I took the tin out and it had about half an inch left in the bottom. It was then that I saw the white paint dribbling out from under the tractor cab.
'Take the tractor outside,' I shouted to Roy.
He drove off and proceeded to leave a white line behind him as he went along.
I ended up going off and getting a couple of tins of black spray paint and blackout the trail Roy had left behind. I eventually follow this white line outside to where Roy had parked up on a grass verge. He stood there, one leg looking like he had a white wellington boot on. High as a kite from the fumes, giggling and smoking a roll-up. Again, he shouted, 'I don't believe you, Ginger.'
Anyway, I went and collected some rags and between us, we mopped up the paint in the cab. I then give it a coat of black spray and it looked okay to me.
Enter, Vehicle Repair fitter Ronnie Wood.
Dear old Ron, what a nice man he was, I say was because this story is going back at least thirty-five years. He'd be pushing ninety now. Having said that, so would Roy. I can't believe he'd still be alive, not after he'd got himself hooked on paint fumes.
Ron told Roy to bring the tractor to the Vehicle Repair shop. 'I have some stuff that will clean that all up.' Now bear in mind we're talking about a battered old tractor, anyway it was Roy's pride and joy, so off he went.
I continued my way back inside and checked I'd covered all the trail of paint. I got back to base and saw Roy and Ronnie with the said tractor. As I approached, I can see that Ron has cleaned all the paint off! The black paint, the cab was now

back to showing all the white paint. I think that's the first time I used the word Muppet. In fact, they were a pair of muppets. I was more concerned about facing Jim Ferris on the Monday. The zebra crossing was still not done, I expected the worst. Just about my luck, I was on the early shift Monday. I clocked in and got changed. I walked into the office and straight away Ken informed me Ferris is wanting to see me. I looked at Ken, he had fear on his face.

'Calm down, Ken. I'm not facing a firing squad.'

'He's fuming, Trevor.'

'Fuck him, it was an accident.' Brave words from the condemned man.

So, I ambled upstairs, the clerk sat there, not Moody, he'd gone by then. Maltese Joe, he cheered me up no end.

Now Joe, as you may have guessed, originated from Malta. He had a Maltese accent and was a real doom and gloom merchant.

'He in da office waiting to see you, he, not a happy chappy. You gonna get your arse kicked.'

I made a mental note to do one of my speciality phone calls on him at a later date.

So, I walked in without knocking and Jim was sitting behind his desk.

'What is it with you and this bloody zebra crossing? What the hell happened this time?'

So, I relay the story, exactly as it happened. As I got to the bit of finding Roy with his white leg, Jim burst out laughing. I mean really laughing. It started me off and I struggle to finish the story. It must have taken me ten minutes to get to the end as I kept stopping because I was laughing so much. Jim Ferris, I not lie, he was crying with laughter. Eventually, we both settled down.

'I have to say, I was going to bollock the life out of you. But that is the funniest thing I've ever heard in a long time. Go on, get to work.'

I don't know, as I write about this incident, I've sort of softened a bit about Jim Ferris. Not that soft, mind. He'll always be known as a shit to me.
I guess outside of work he was a decent enough chap. Ken Lawrence wouldn't agree with me I know.

Jim disappeared soon after we got taken us over by Fiat. Right early on they started getting rid of a lot of the deadwood, so the General Foreman role ceased to exist.
He got offered a normal foreman's role, but I think his pride got in the way and he retired at fifty-three. I heard through the grapevine he passed away around 2016.
With Jim Ferris gone, Maltese Joe was shipped downstairs into the foreman's office. I bided my time and then an opportunity arose that I couldn't resist. Enter Colin Gittings, AKA, Elton.
Now Elton was a sludge king driver. He'd tow a large tank around and suck out all sorts of crap from machines, drains, all sorts. He had a cocky strut about him did our Elton, but one particular day I killed two birds with one stone.
We were on the late shift and impatient Elton was trying to squeeze his tractor and tank through a small gap. A contractor had parked his Transit van in the way. Elton sat there for a minute tooting his horn. I was watching from above, I was up a ladder checking a hoist. Next thing I see Elton attempt to drive through the gap. Not a wise choice, he drove off leaving a long dent in the side of the van. About twenty minutes later I watched the contractor return. He climbed straight into the van and drove off. He'd not seen the dent along the side.
"You lucky bastard Elton," I thought at the time.
Next afternoon I decided I could have some fun. So as soon as I was at work, I used an internal phone and called the office. Joe answered.
'Central maintenance.' In my best-disguised voice, I spoke to Joe.
'Yes, who's speaking?'

'It's Joe, the clerk.'
'Hello Joe, it's Fred from personnel.' There wasn't a Fred working there at this time, but Joe didn't have a clue.
'Hello Fred, what can I do for you?'
'You have a Colin Gittings working for you?'
'Yes, he is due at work shortly. He on da late shift.'
'Could you send him over to personnel as soon as he arrives?'
'Sure, what he do?'
'He's in a lot of trouble Joe, keep this to yourself, but he caused a lot of damage to a contractor's van last night. Caused hundreds of pounds worth of damage. Drove off and told the contractor to fuck off.'
'Jesus Christ. I'll send him over as soon as he gets here.' I hung up, walked around the corner and straight into the office. Joe was alone.
'You seen, Elton?'
'No, not yet. Why?'
'You ain't gonna believe this.' He then told me word for word about the conversation we just had on the phone. Of course, I played along.
'I don't believe it.'
'Don't believe it? I've just had Fred from personnel on the phone.'
Timing it just right, enter Elton.
'You mister, you in big trouble. Don't get changed, go straight to Personnel, Fred is waiting for you.'
'Fred?'
'Don't act stupid. Fred, he personnel officer.'
Elton stood there quiet.
Well, I've never seen the blood drain out of a person's face quicker than that day. The cockiness had gone as the realization of his previous night's exploits hit home.
'What you been up to, Elton?' I enquired.
'Nothing.'
'Nothing.' Shouted Joe.

In walked Ricky Hunt, early shift foreman about to go home.
'What's all the shouting about.'
'Ask him.' Joe points at Elton.
'He been summoned to personnel, he crashes into contractor's van, caused hundreds of pounds of damage. Then drives off and tell the contractor to fuck off.'
'No, I didn't,' pleaded Elton.
'Come on, I'll take you over on the buggy.' Fair play to Ricky Hunt, he would always try and defend his men, even though Elton's foreman was Ken Lawrence. I watched the pair drive off in the buggy. Mission accomplished.
I got myself changed, walked back to the office just in time to watch Joe have a hissy fit. Elton stood outside, back to his cocky self.
'How'd you get on, Elton?'
'It was a bloody wind-up. Ricky just had a go at Joe about it.'
I walked into the office as Joe slammed the phone on the floor. Ken had arrived by now and was standing with Ricky.
'You finished now, Joe?'
'These men, they taka the piss out of me.'
'What's happened?' I enquire.
'Don't ask,' answered Ricky.
I walked out smiling.

I once saved Elton from a guaranteed pummelling. He came into work one morning like Mr Angry. He was a bit tubby, Elton. A bit like his namesake. He had the classic "Drop gut." You know, the belly poking out from under your belt. Not like me who was just fat. So, not what you would describe as a highly tuned athlete.
'What's up with you?' I ask.
Turned out he had a bit of road rage at the traffic lights outside the factory the previous evening.
'I recognised the bloke, he works on engine machining.' Good luck with that I thought and left him to it. Heading over to the

hoist crib where I was now based, I bumped into a guy named Brian Harris. Now Brian was always okay with me, I'd often stop for a chat and a laugh. Now, Brian had a fearsome reputation. He had a boxer's nose and you could tell he kept himself fit. Now and again I'd hear a rumour about Brian's latest dust-up. The latest one I heard was where he stopped at some traffic lights and three guys stuck their fingers up at his wife. So, rumour has it he got out of his car and knocked the three of them out. Now, I'm not saying it didn't happen, but the time a story about him reached me the exaggeration level would have risen a few notches.

So, it was most probably one man. Always take things with a pinch of salt with stories like that. It's a bit like me when I told Barry Campagna I was in the original lineup of the Bay City Rollers. He believed that for about eighteen months until he realised, they were all Scottish.

This particular morning, Brian's like a raging bull.

'Hey, Trevor. You got a guy who works over your side called Elton John?'

Well, it didn't take a rocket scientist to work out who Elton's road rage was with. So, I tried to reason with him.

'Yes, in fact, he's looking for you.'

'Send him over, I'll knock him into next week.' I could see the veins in Brian's head protruding.

'Listen, Brian. He told me he had a bit of a road rage incident with you last night. He wants to come over and apologise, he's been having a few problems with his wife. You know how it is.'

'Well, we've all been there, Trev. Alright if he comes over and apologises that's the end of it.'

'Cheers Brian.' I then had to do an about-turn and head back and track down Elton. Luckily, I caught up with him on his way over to hunt down Brian Harris.

'Alright, Elton?'

'I will be once I find this bloke.'

'Oh, I know who it is, it's a guy called Brian Harris. I've just spoken to him and he's very keen to meet you.'
'That name rings a bell.'
'Bell being the operative word here, Elton. That's what you'll be hearing once he chins you. For Christ sake man, go and apologise before he rips your head off.' I watched him walk off, the strut had disappeared.

Another character I have fond memories of is John Levey. AKA Jolly Green.
Now John was a compulsive gossip and had an uncontrollable laugh.
Now when I say uncontrollable, I'm not joking.
One of our lads passed away, Ricky Redmond. Now Ricky was our overtime monitor. A job he took very seriously. Thursday mornings a sheet of paper would appear on the office window letting us know who was working the weekend. Ricky would study it and if there was a mistake, he'd tear into the office to get it corrected. At the time, he made it that if you weren't working the weekend, but managed to get overtime in another department, he'd still book you.
We had a guy in our department named Geoff Lilley, AKA Catweazel. Now Geoff loved to go touring America. So, he would go off and find overtime anywhere he could.
Ricky would find out and book him. This resulted over a period of time in Geoff being hundreds of hours in front of everybody else. Not a problem until a new guy would be transferred in.
The rule being he would go on the overtime rota plus one hour below the bottom man. Poor sod would have to wait at least a year before he would get any overtime.
Ricky wouldn't budge, our Shop Steward at the time was weak. It was nearing time for a comeback.
Anyway, let's not run off to that period yet.
Poor old Ricky had a heart attack and passed away. He'd had heart trouble for a while, so not too much of a shock.

I must add that some people never learn. No disrespect to Ricky, he'd had heart trouble for some time before he was pensioned off from the tractor plant.

Next thing I hear he was working on Ford's production line at Dagenham. It was the time when they had a mountain of orders and had advertised for some short-term staff. How he got past the medical I'll never know. It might have contributed to his death, it certainly was a strange thing to attempt considering his health issues.

So, we hear of his passing, which was only a few months after he retired. We get time off to attend Ricky's funeral, so a group of us go. Enter John Levey.

I'm standing next to Jolly, luckily near the back of the church. Up stepped foreman Ricky Hunt to say a few words on behalf of his former work colleagues. All was going well until he mentioned that Ricky had been a good organiser. I whispered to Jolly.

'He certainly was on that overtime rota.'

Well, big mistake. Jolly starts laughing, he starts a few of the others off. We then have to try and make it look like were crying. Unfortunately, by now, Jolly is down on his hands and knees. What a show he made of himself. We all tried to distance ourselves from him. I just hope Ricky was looking down and enjoying the show.

Having said that, I doubt it. He didn't take kindly to a little camera joke at his daughter's wedding.

He'd invited a few of us to the evening reception, about six of us attended. We and our wives were sat around a table. I'd noticed Ricky taking the odd photo. I blame the drink for what I did next. Ricky had hit the floor to dance with his daughter. While all that was going on, I walked past his table and whipped the camera into my pocket and head into the toilet. With the aid of a couple of others, we take photos of my arse and manhood. I walk back and slip the camera back on his table. Now, you have to remember this is the pre-digital age.

This is the Kodak Instamatic, a roll of film age. Take the film to Boots the chemist and come back the following week to look at your twenty-four exposures.

Exposure is the key word here. Now, Ricky Redmond must have been on the shift before mine, because I can still picture him now, Standing, at the bottom of the stairs, hands-on-hips, roll up in his mouth, looking Rather angry. Obviously waiting to speak to me, I tried to play it cool.

'Alright, Rick?'

'Alright ... You C***'

'Whoa, easy on the insults.' He pulled a photo out that showed my cock and balls.

'I knew it was you as soon as my daughter showed me. You're the only c*** I know with ginger pubes.'

Caught, bang to rights. The curse of the redhead. I think he was more upset because he'd given the film to his daughter to get developed. So, I guess it was a bit of a shock to her seen my arse and three-piece suite staring back at her.

Let's get back to Jolly, for some unknown reason, my dad had taken to Jolly. They remained friend's years after they had both retired. If ever he saw me, he would always start the conversation by asking me, 'What's the news?'

Followed by, 'How long so and so been dead?' He had this fascination with people's death.

He looked like an undertaker so maybe that's why. Jolly used to have his morning tea break with dad. Every third week when I was on the early shift, I'd join them. Many a time my dad would say something funny and we'd have Jolly rolling around the floor in hysterical laughter.

Now Jolly, as gormless as he looked, had married well later in life.

His wife Val was a top personnel officer at a large bank in the city. At the time, she earned three times what Jolly did. He had a nice house and both had new cars.

It was the time the video recorder had just come out. The early ones, the ones with the piano keys and the wired remote. It would set you back around three hundred pounds.
A lot of money back then, out of my price range at the time. But Jolly obviously could afford one and had great pleasure telling us about the wonders of this new gadget.
There weren't many video stores around at the beginning. Within a couple of years, the market exploded and video stores became a huge success. A few of the lads and I even ran our own mobile video store at work. I'll come to that story later in the book. Our mobile shop was named "The tug club." Might give you an idea of what taste we catered for.

Jolly told me that he'd got a free membership to a video store in Chelmsford, where he bought the video player and where he lived.
Time for a phone call.
That evening, armed with the name of the shop where he'd bought the video player and the video shop, I called his number.
'Hello, who's speaking?'
'Good evening Mr Lovy, it's Sid from the video store.'
'Hang on, I need to turn the TV down.' Typical Jolly.
'Right, I can hear you now. Did you say you're calling from the video shop?'
'That's right Mr Lovy.'
'Levey, my name is Levey.'
'Oh, I'm sorry about that Mr Levey. Now, because you purchased your video player from such and such, you get free membership to our video store, ten free films with free delivery.'
'That's a great deal.' Jolly loved a bargain.
'What sort of films do you like?'
'Well, I like thrillers.' He answeres.

'Don't we all, maybe I can send one of my colleague's round. He'll have a lot of films you can choose from. I have your address.'
'That would be great. How long can I keep the films for?'
'Maximum three nights, after that it's a pound a night.'
'That's fair.'
'Can I ask Mr Levey; would you like my colleague to bring round some adult films?'
'Err …… Do you mean porn?
'I certainly do, Mr Levey.'
'Can your colleague come around tomorrow evening, but before seven? My wife comes home around seven-thirty.'
'No problem, Mr Levey.'

The next day at tea break, Jolly tells my dad and me all about the video offer, even about the porn. He walked off and my dad said to me what a good deal Jolly had got.
'I doubt it, dad. That was me who phoned him.'
It didn't end there.
The next morning Jolly told us this video guy hadn't turned up.
'I'm going into that video shop on my way home this afternoon, ask them what their game is?'
The next day my dad asked Jolly how he'd got on?'
'Denied making the phone call. I told them to stuff their membership.'

It was amazing how gullible Jolly was. A few months later he told my dad and me the saga of his new 32" TV. He'd ordered it at an HMV store in Chelmsford. He'd waited in the previous evening and it never arrived.
'Val's going to ring them this morning.' Now the mighty Valerie according to Jolly was not a woman to mess with. Later in the day, I could see Jolly had the hump.

'What's up with you?' He then tells me he'd phoned Val and basically after what I could imagine was a one-way phone call, Valerie had told whoever to stuff their TV.

'I had my heart set on that TV, Sony 32". Time for another phone call.

I waited until six, I knew Jolly usually made it home by five-thirty.

'Mr Levey?'

'Yes, who's speaking?'

'Dave Smithers, customer services for HMV.'

'You've got a nerve ringing me after the way you spoke to my wife this morning.'

'That's why I'm ringing, Mr Levey. The assistant your wife spoke to has been fired. We at HMV pride ourselves on our customer service.'

'What service, we sat in last night waiting for the new TV to come. It didn't, and when my wife phoned the store all she got was abuse when she called again it was an answerphone!'

'Deep apologies Mr Levey. This isn't good enough.'

'Too true it's not.'

'How far from the Chelmsford store do you live, Mr Levey?'

'About ten minutes.'

'Do you drive, Mr Levey?'

'Yes.'

'Okay, I have a slight problem you see. All the drivers are out on deliveries. If you can get to the store before seven, I'll make sure your Sony 32" TV is there waiting for you. I'll instruct the shop to give you a two-hundred-pound discount.'

'I'm on my way.' Jolly hung up.

Now I knew the discount would be enough to reel him in. What with Jolly's surname and nose, I thought he had to be Jewish, allegedly.

I can remember when Nescafe coffee was promoting something or another.

Jolly started collecting the coffee labels.

One morning I was driving to work when I passed the big recycling bins. You know the type, different colours for different things. One for plastic, one for cardboard, one for bottles. Anyway, as I drove past, I noticed Jolly's car. I pulled up and as I looked, I could see Jolly's feet poking out from the glass bin. He wriggled back out with a triumphant look on his face. He had an empty jar of Nescafe in each hand. If he saw a newspaper in a bin, he'd scour it for any money off vouchers. You can imagine being stuck behind him in a supermarket check-out.

The next morning, I once again never mentioned anything to my dad. Jolly turned up for the morning tea break fuming.
'You won't believe this George.' Jolly went all through the phone call part. I sat and kept my eyes on the newspaper, but my ears pricked.
'Sounds like they offered you a real bargain, John.' My dad was oblivious to my involvement.
'Bargain George? Do you know I drove straight to the shop, and guess what? You won't believe it, George. The bloody shop was shut, they close for half day on a Wednesday.'
How I kept a straight face I'll never know.
'Val is going to roast the customer services this morning. I wrote the guy's name down, Dave Smithers.'
'That's a small world, our window cleaner is called Dave Smithers.' Dad looked at me and the penny dropped.
My finest hour with Jolly was the new car hoax.
Each month our company would do a raffle. Very good prizes at the time. We were a part of a big combine in the UK and the raffle was open to all plants.
I can't remember the exact prizes but the top three were normally a new car, followed by large holiday vouchers right down to fifty pounds. I'm sure there were at least thirty prizes each month.

Occasionally someone at our Plant would be lucky. I decided it was about time Jolly had a bit of luck.

I was on the night shift so waited until Ken went off somewhere and snuck in and took some company headed writing paper and a company stamped envelope. I headed into an empty office, remember this is years before the computer world. This was done by an old-fashioned typewriter.

So, I typed a letter informing Jolly he had won the top prize in this month's draw and there would be a presentation of the logbook and keys two days later outside the office.

I also added that a photographer would be present from the company newspaper. I read it back and was happy with the finished article. I squiggled a signature and typed the name of the guy who always featured on the sheet of paper that came out monthly with the raffle results.

I typed Jolly's name, his ID number and Central Maintenance on the envelope and slipped it into the internal post mail. I went home the next morning happy with life. In a way, I was sad not to see the fruits of my work, but in another way, I think I was better off being on nights as this letter to Jolly had worked better than expected.

I'm a firm believer that the fewer people that know about your involvement in a wind-up, the better. So, I never mentioned anything to my dad, even though he rang me the next evening.

'Heard about Jolly?'

'No.'

'He's only won the top prize in the raffle, a bloody new Escort.'

'Lucky bastard, well they say money goes to money.'

'There's a big presentation outside the office at ten 'o'clock tomorrow morning.'

'Pity I'm on nights, I would have liked to see that.'

'I'll let you know how it goes.'

So that night I go to work and the news on Jolly's win is a hot topic. I try and play it cool as I'm beginning to worry things have got slightly out of hand.

A phone call from my dad the next evening confirmed my fears.
'Was that you?'
'What?'
'Did you type that letter?' I couldn't lie to my dad.
'Yes, how'd it go?'
'Great. Jolly turned up in his best suit. Maltese Joe turned up in a suit too. Tony Lynch went and had a haircut and about fifty people were standing outside the office at ten.
About ten minutes went by and people were getting restless. Tony instructed Joe to ring up and find out where the raffle people and photographer were. Five minutes later he comes out of the office shouting.
"They don't know nothing about it, the raffle not been drawn for this month yet." Everybody booed.
The letter is now over in personnel. Don't worry, they haven't a clue who typed it.'
Luckily for me, they didn't want to fingerprint everybody. The time I was back on the early shift it had all just about been forgotten.
I don't think Jolly knew anybody's real name.
He had nicknames for all of us.
Some I can remember, Fred the feet, Freddie Laker, White socks, Bones, Brains of Britain, Ginger, Harry the nose, Maltese falcon, Jimmy Ferret, Trousers, Picasso, Second hand Roy, the Outlaw National Front, Billy Bullshitter, Whispering Les and Scissors.
I know when he retired the factory was a bleaker place without him, his infectious laughter, the wind-ups and his sense of humour I really missed.

I went to see Jolly a couple of years after he retired. He'd moved to Devon and I was on holiday for a week in the area. I went to see him and he looked well and still collecting the money off vouchers.

As I mentioned at the beginning, I get the occasional email from Jolly's wife, Val. He is 78 now and in good health and still enjoying the delights Devon has to offer. You were good entertainment, John.

Another guy I tormented around that time was an oiler named Bill McKay. Tall, grey-haired man who was mild-mannered until you wound him up. I had him chase me around the factory one late shift.
I can't remember where I got this false rubber cock from. But I had some fun with it. It was impressive and a good nine inches long. It looked the real deal.
You could fill it with water and if you squeezed it, it was like a water pistol. So, now and again I'd fill it up, follow someone into the toilet and when they were mid-stream, I'd whip it out and start to pretend to relieve myself. Then turn to the guy and say hi while squeezing some water down their leg. Of course, before they got angry, I'd whip it out and show them the joke penis. I must have been feeling a bit mischievous with Bill because I followed him in.
I proceeded to do a pretend piss, then turned and squeezed it. It came out with such a force that it not only hit his leg and arm, but the spray also hit his face and glasses.
'Yer dirty bastard,' he shouted in his broad Scottish tone.
For some reason, I decided to leg it.
I can honestly say, Bill McKay wanted to kill me. He chased me from one end of the factory to the other. I was only in my late twenties and he was pushing sixty. But he wasn't going to give up.
I don't think my giggling as I ran helped his mood. In the end, I surrendered. I stopped and held the rubber penis in the air. Poor Bill, he was knackered. But he just sat down and started laughing. Luckily for me, he'd seen the funny side of it. I had some laughs with that toy until it split, and I ended up with a crutch full of water.

I hit my thirties and a horrible thing happened at work. One of the tinsmiths dropped dead right in front of my dad and me. Wally Clarke had joined the tinsmiths late in life. There had been three tinsmiths since the plant opened, all around the same age. One of them, Ernie Hughes went to school with my dad, so they'd known each other a very long time.

The other tinsmith was Bob Kent. Then came Larry Minchin, maybe ten years younger than the other three. They were all very good at their trade. At the time, they had more work than they could cope with, so they had Kevin Gill, a seventeen-year-old apprentice start with them. Nice lad and a very good footballer. But he was just into the second year of his apprenticeship.

So, the company in their wisdom advertised on the notice boards for anyone with sheet metal skills. Wally Clarke joined the team. He fitted in well and enjoyed the banter that came his way. You see, although Wally was the new "boy," he was about seven years older than my dad. But he kept himself busy and you could tell he enjoyed the work. He'd been working in the hydraulics area for years, so I guess it was nice to get away from the production side of things.

One morning I went and joined my dad for a tea break. Wally sat by his workbench maybe six feet away.

My dad told me that Wally hadn't been feeling well and had been to the medical for "indigestion."

He felt that bad that my dad went upstairs and washed his tea mug for him.

None of us saw the following coming.

We sat there reading our newspapers when Wally suddenly groaned and started to slide off his chair. We rushed over to help him but he couldn't be saved. None of us had a clue what to do. By the time a first aider and the medical arrived Wally was dead. It was awful, I'd never seen a man die before and it shook me to my bones.

It took me a long time to come to terms with that morning. It made me worry about my dad. Wally was only sixty, dad must have been around fifty-three at the time.
I pestered the life out of him to get out.
There were opportunities for him to get early retirement. But he hung on for a while. Then one day he phoned me and said he was retiring on Friday.
I was half relieved, but the other half of me knew I'd miss him terribly. I wouldn't say we were close, but he'd been at the plant all the time I'd been there.
He had remarried, he and mum had divorced some years earlier. Not the normal sort of setup, my dad married the woman and my mum married the husband.
I won't go into all the gory details, but they did a bit of wife swapping and it went too far. My mum and her husband Peter moved to Manchester for a while before returning to Essex.
When Dad retired, he told me he was selling up and moving to Norfolk. So, I was a bit surprised when he phoned me and said he'd bought a new bungalow in a place called Burton upon Stather.
'Where's that?' I asked.
'North Lincolnshire.' So, I go out to my car and look this place up on my roadmap. Basically, he was moving to Scunthorpe, or to village six miles further on. He liked it up there, I hated the place. Cold and gloomy, and that was in July.
I never got on with his wife and over time my visits became less and less. We'd talk on the phone weekly, but that was about it. He was just coming up to eighty when he passed away.

The other tinsmiths all disappeared in time. Engine machining was on the way out. Bob and Ernie left within a year of my dad. Kevin stuck it out for a while but left in his late twenties. Larry retired at fifty-five and became a postman.
I bumped into him a few years later in Cardiff of all places. I'd gone to Wales to watch Southend United in a minor trophy

final. LDV vans, I think. We'd made it to the final along with Blackpool. It was billed as the battle of the Seasiders. It was played at the Millennium stadium because they were in the throes of building the new Wembley Stadium.

I was staying in the same hotel as Larry. He was down with his family and I hardly recognised him.

He had lost loads of weight and looked good.

He told me he was into fitness and with the amount of walking he was doing delivering mail, he was in the best shape he'd been for years.

So, it came as a great shock when I heard he had dropped dead in a gym a few weeks later. Turned out he'd had a massive heart attack while on a rowing machine.

Such a shame, he was a lovely guy Larry. I found out at his funeral that his daughter was expecting her first child when he passed away, tragic.

I think when you work at a place with a huge workforce, news of a death was inevitable. You'd hear of someone passing away quite often.

Now, this is meant to be a fun read, so let's not hang around on this subject for too long. Death is death, inevitable for all of us; we just don't want to be reminded of it.

Cue a little story of when I became a pension trustee with Mr Happy, AKA Paul Norris.

We were asked to make a small contribution and introduce ourselves in the yearly pension magazine. I can't remember what I wrote, most probably the importance of being in a well-run company pension scheme.

I never knew what Paul wrote until the magazine arrived through the post. He made such a great opening statement, it's up there with the "Could have been worse, he could have broken a leg, gaff."

I opened the page and there was a photo of Paul.

I'm sure he won't mind me saying, but he has the face for a radio presenter, so, not exactly photogenic. If I thought that was bad, I wasn't prepared for his opening statement emblazoned underneath the horror photo. In big letters, it read:

"We're all going to get old and die."

He resembled the grim reaper, come to think of it.

I suppose in his defence it could be argued that he didn't beat about the bush. I can't be too harsh with Paul. He studied hard for a degree and went on to better things. Good on you mate. But let's not get ahead of ourselves here; let's get back to the eighties.

Whispering Les Clemmie handing over a retirement tractor to an old working colleague, Russ Wright.
That's me standing just to his left looking like I'm auditioning for Quadrophenia. To the right of Russ is the overtime monitor, the late Ricky Redmond. One match cricket guru Steve Holman stands behind Ricky.
Sandwiched between Les and Russ are Rob Fellows and Mark Lewin, aka Bones.

Chapter 3

Time for a comeback

The eighties turned out to be a funny decade for me. For some reason, I became a bit accident-prone.
I don't know why, but one particular late shift Ricky Hunt was my foreman.
And not for the first time I was in the wrong place at the wrong time, he spotted me just as I was about to go for my lunch break. That would be 7 pm.
'Trevor, do me a favour. Could you drive this tractor and park it up outside the gardener's hut?'
Cursing under my breath I jumped aboard and drove this old tractor outside and up the hill to where the gardener's hut was situated.
I'd always fancied being one of the gardeners, in the summer they would be cutting grass or doing the verges, shirt off.
Much better than being inside the factory.
Now, being I was late for my lunch break I thought I would be clever. Instead of walking back to the main building on the road, I decided to take a shortcut and run down the steep grass bank.
What could go wrong, it was a nice light summers evening.
I never knew what idiot left the manhole cover off, but I managed to find it and suddenly I had dropped down and was saved only by my arms sticking out. I can remember the shock, followed by the pain as I heaved myself out. Sitting there I felt I was lucky not to have fallen right down, I might still be there now.
I could see it in the papers, "The mystery of the missing tractor plant worker. Clocked in and was never seen again."
A bit ironic that statement, as my last book is about a man's disappearance.

Anyway, the pain from my legs started and I pulled my trouser leg up and could see I had ripped all the skin off my shins, both legs.

'Bollocks,' I shouted. There was no one about, so I had to hobble back to the office. Ricky was sitting behind his desk, feet up and eating a sandwich.

'All done?'

'I've had an accident.'

'What happened?' So, I relay the story and he starts to laugh. 'Teach you to take a shortcut. Go and have your lunch break.'

'What about these?' I dropped my trousers and the bottom of my legs were now a bloody mess.

'Jesus Christ, Trevor.' We never had medical coverage on a late shift, just first aiders. I can't remember who our first aider was at that time, but I can remember him telling Ricky I should go to casualty.

So off we go and after the usual long wait I get seen and patched up. Ricky dropped me in the car park next to my car. 'Go home and rest, I'll pay you till eleven.' He drove off and I climbed into my car. I looked at my watch, it was 10.40 pm. You were all heart, Ricky.

Now a funny thing happened after that. The next morning, I woke up, I was feeling a bit groggy, my legs were sore and I was busting for a pee. So, I limped to the bathroom and while I'm relieving myself, I glanced at the mirror. Looking back at me was a Red Indian? I check myself and I'm covered in a rash from head to toe. Panicking I phone the doctors. Well as we know, the doctor's receptionists are a breed amongst themselves. It doesn't matter what you say, you can't seem to get past them and speak to an actual doctor. To cut a long story short after about ten minutes of a thorough grilling, she agreed to send a doctor round to see me after the surgery had closed.

Early afternoon he arrived, took one look at me and told me I had measles? I was twenty-five at the time. I had a bad couple of weeks, what with the symptoms that come with adult measles, and my legs were very tender. I was living on my own at that time, so good old mum came over and spent a few days nursing her Chocolate Soldier.

Back at work and things were changing on the union front. The self-proclaimed union governor, Convenor Bill Cleary had left the company. The potbellied, goatee-bearded, pipe-smoking, trilby hatted dwarf had gone. Praise the Lord.
At the time, it had been three or four years since I was last a shop steward.
I'm not going to fully name the guy who was our shop steward at the time, let's just say he was known as "Fred the Feet."
An unflattering name, but understandable as his large feet stuck out in the ten to two position. He wouldn't be the last in our department to have that affliction.
You had to be careful when talking to Fred as he spat a bit when he talked, not a nice trait, so you were in danger of getting wet or tripping over his feet if you spoke to him. Face wise he looked like Hardy, of Laurel and Hardy fame. So, not putting to finer point on it, he looked a bit of a joke. Add the fact he was a crap steward, I could feel a Bobby Graham moment coming my way again.
An unlikely person contacted me to consider standing at the forthcoming shop steward elections.
Enter the *Rat*. Now I've already made my feeling known about this despicable man.
He will feature heavily as we move along. But, fair play to the *Rat*, he encouraged me to stand as a steward again.
I would imagine there was a lot of pressure from maintenance colleagues who were fed up with the current situation. A lot of people encouraged me to stand, my home life was stable so I thought "why not."

So, I stood, and mainly because I was still well respected because of my past battles with Bobby Graham, Bomando and Ferris, I walked it.

I'm not sure why I always did well in elections? I'm couldn't tell you how many elections I stood in, but I never lost.

I would say it was my great personality, charisma, and the way I fought for my men. In reality, it is most probably whoever faced me in the elections were more unliked than me.

Before I move on I have a funny story about Fred, well it was his son actually.

Fred told me he had managed to wrangle his son into the plant. I was pleased for him, as a steward the H/R was always happy to help. Now Fred must have pulled some hierarchy strings as when I met his boy, Steve, I thought how the fuck did he manage that.

Steve Collins must have been around the twenty stone mark, and unfortunately for him, he inherited his dad's feet.

Well, I'm not sure how his dad had managed to get him in, how on earth had he ever passed a medical? Well, only the medical officer at the time and his bank manager could answer that one.

But fair play to the guy, he didn't let his weight get in the way of doing a day's graft.

He was working in engine machining in the head line department.

One day the hoist he was operating was playing up and I arrived to use my array of hoist skills to fix it. Nine times out of ten this would involve a hammer.

I chatted away to Steve and he came across as a very nice guy. He laughed about his weight and told me he was going to his first weight watchers meeting that evening.

Good on you, I thought.

A couple of days later I bumped into Fred and he was not looking happy.

'Alright, Fred. What's up?'

'What's up, my Stevie's in hospital.'
Straight away I thought the worst.
'Has he had a heart attack?'
'No, soppy bastard joined this slimming club, got his mum to boil this fish last night. Ended up getting a fishbone stuck right down his throat!!
I shouldn't laugh I know, it was quite serious as he had to be operated on to remove the said bone.
I don't think Steve lasted long at the factory and our paths didn't cross again until I went to his dad's funeral some years later. He was still huge but had got married and had a young son. When he introduced his son I will admit to checking the boy's feet out. Luckily he had taken after his mother!

So, I was back, the brash and cocky Trevor had returned. Jim Ferris was still General Foreman at that time, he hated the fact I was again the shop steward. He had to tread a tad more careful with me now; after all, I had the clout of the mighty union behind me.
Revenge is a dish served cold, so I didn't waste any time upsetting my nemesis.
I quickly informed Ferris that I wanted to do a safety audit of our department.
He shit a brick, it was the procedure for him to take note of my findings, a copy would go to the health and safety guys who in turn sent a copy to H/R.
He had 28 days to put things right.
There hadn't been an audit for years and in a couple of hours I chalked up well over a hundred problems that needed addressing. Ferris was fuming and gutted, he couldn't touch me now I was the union rep.
His reign of power over me was gone. It was that thought that kept me a shop steward for years. Not once did I take my eye off the ball. I knew if I did, he'd be back on my case.

George Catton was now the convenor. Old school, he was the deputy under Cleary, so the natural successor.

I found a lovely short news clip on YouTube, of the Plant in 1984. There's a brief interview with George Catton in the report. Certainly, worth a watch and you can see a bit of the eighties style of vehicles we were building at the time.

I didn't know much about George until I came back from the wilderness. He was one-half of the double act, George and George. I likened them to the Two Ronnie's, or Morecambe and Wise.

The other George I knew well. George Sharpe.

As I sit here and write this, I can visualise his face. He reminded me of the late American comic who played "Bilko." Phil Silvers. He may have had a resemblance to Phil, but he had the voice of the Carry-On actor, the late Bernard Bresslaw.

A great photo of the late George Sharpe being presented with the customary tractor and onion by his son Andy on his retirement.

I liked George immensely, he was glad I had come back into the shop steward's fold. He could tell the most entertaining stories, none I care to repeat in this book.

He was a great supporter of George Catton and it was rare to see one of them without the other.
One thing George Sharpe struggled with was staying awake. I can recall being sent to Boreham House for some seminar with a few other stewards, George being one of them.
The Manager running this seminar was Michael Law. I'm not sure how to describe Michael, he was a bit of an "Oh look at me, aren't I wonderful" type of person in my opinion. He used to pull me up regularly when I called him Mick.
"My name is Michael," he used to remind me.
He suffered from little man syndrome, he had the smallest feet I've ever seen on a man, size 4.
Obviously, he was well thought of by the company as he was sent to Brazil for several years. Unfortunately, they sent him back.
I was sitting on the other side of the room to George and as I watched I knew it wouldn't be long before his head would start rocking and the eyes rolling. The problem George had, he wasn't discreet about it. He'd eventually get his head comfortable and within minutes he would start to snore. My God, I don't know how many times Michael Law banged the table that day. He wasn't amused.
In defence of George, we all struggled with Michael Law's presentation.
Not sure if Michael is still with us, he must be nearing eighty if he is. If you read this Michael, sorry, but you were boring and monotonous.
He was a frustrated singer; he stood up and belted a few numbers with a band that was playing at the Rats wedding reception.

'Don't give up your day job, *Mick*,' I advised him in my drunken state.

It must have been around this time that the inter-departmental cricket league started.
I was a decent player at school but had not picked a ball up since. A notice went up about the formation of this league and an opportunity to register your team.
A few of us in Central Maintenance fancied this, so we entered our department. The crux of the team was, Bob Fagg, Bob Fellows, Brian Crease and myself. All we needed now was another seven players.
We managed to secure a foreman by the name of Harry Geering, he was a supervisor in the tool room. A very fit guy and adopted the stand in front of the stumps attitude when he went out to bat. My fellow hoist-man Steve Battle stepped forward.
I have some lovely stories about Steve later in the book. He was pigeon-toed but had a good eye for the ball.
Arthur Rixon said he would play. A skilful electrician and Tottenham Hotspur supporter. Over fifty, but could still bowl a decent delivery.
It was a wise move signing up Arthur. His wife Mary would come along to support us, armed with a tin of homemade cakes.
We recruited a guy called Gordon Beattie as our wicket-keeper. I'm sure Gordon won't mind me mentioning his stout frame. Ideal wicket-keeper build, we thought at the time. He failed to mention that his nickname at school was "Teflon."
With the allowance of two guest players, we just about scraped a team together for our first match. Our last player was a guy called Steve Holman. A figure and shape more suited to playing darts, he could walk, so he was in.
I must admit when I watched him run his pace was deceptive … He was a lot slower than he looked.

The games were played at the Fords Sports and Social Club situated next to the plant in the evenings. Equipment was supplied and we turned up a tad apprehensive.

Our first game was against a team from the offices, an unknown entity, but they looked impressive as they warmed up, a few of them were in cricket whites, so I didn't hold out a lot of expectation.

The format was twenty overs a team, each player except the wicketkeeper would bowl two overs. If you hit 25, you'd retire but could come out and bat again if everybody else was out. Although we looked like a motley crew, we gave it our best shot. Because we hadn't played before we didn't know who was capable of what. Arthur turned up in his whites. The only one of us that had actually played cricket for a club, albeit thirty years ago.

Bob Fagg was captain. Bob was a bigger version of the late 1966 World Cup winner Alan Ball. Same golden hair and the high-pitched voice. Unfortunately for Bob his voice never broke. He wore glasses those days.

Years later he decided to have his eyes lasered. There's a funny story of him about to drive a tractor out of the factory when someone shouted at him.

'Mind the axle stand.'

'Don't you worry about that, I have 20 – 20 vision.' He called back. He then proceeded to drive straight over the axle stand!

Since I wrote this book back in 2017, I have had messenger contact with Bob, he hasn't changed despite heading towards eighty. Still playing golf with a few of the other retirees, including my old foreman Ricky Hunt. He never read the first edition of this book so I won't hold my breath that he'll read this one.

Right, back to the cricket. Bob thought it would be a good idea to get Arthur to open the batting. As I mentioned, we didn't have a clue about our team members capabilities, but we were soon to find out.

Now Arthur was a bit like the Cockney comedian Tommy Trinder. He'd pout his lips and say, "Alright you lucky lads, let's be having you." Bandy-legs, he would never have made it as a goalkeeper.

It's funny how some things stick in your mind. I can remember this match as if it was yesterday.

We lost the toss and were put in to bat first. Bob Fagg decided to open the batting with Arthur. We sat at the boundary watching the game unfold and eating Mary's cakes. It soon became apparent that Arthur was pitched in for a five-day test match. He obviously had designs on being the Central Maintenance's "Geoffrey Boycott."

Unfortunately, we only had twenty overs. Arthur blocked the first five, then hit a single off the last ball. So, he had run to the other end to face the next over. The words déjà vu crossed my mind as Arthur adopted the blocking technique for the second over. After two overs, we were 2 for 0. At this rate, we would be setting our opposition a mighty total of twenty-one to win the match.

Over number three and at last Bob Fagg got the scoreboard moving. He had a good over, hit a couple of boundaries then did the team thing and ran Arthur out.

Something Arthur would never forget. Of course, when he marched off after Bob had given him no chance of getting to the other end, we were full of sympathy.

'Did you see that? I was just getting my eye in.'

'Yes, Arthur. Terrible call by Bob.' Bob Fellows went out and joined Bob and we were getting some decent runs on the board. I can't remember everyone's individual scores, but the two Bob's, Brian Crease and myself all had a swing. The last few batsmen added a few more runs and I think we ended up with around eighty runs. We were happy that we'd posted a score that wasn't too embarrassing.

(Funny, I did have found an old photo of some of our team holding a cricket Trophy. The photo was taken behind the factory. We're not all in it, but the two Bob's, Arthur, Brian, Harry, Gordon and I are standing to attention. I have some type of shell suit top, skinny jeans and brown shoes. Deidre Barlow glasses and swept-back hair. I look a right cock.) Unfortunately, I cannot find that photo anywhere.

Back to the game:

A bit like our batting, we didn't know who our better bowlers were. I knew I could bowl a fast ball, Bob Fagg could bowl a sort of mix between a spin and middle pace ball. Arthur said he could bowl and after lashing Bob about running him out, to appease him, Bob said he could open the bowling. I had a chat with Bob and suggested he hold himself and me back for a few overs, try and use some of the others first.
I didn't think it would be good to use up all our better bowlers at the beginning. So, we adopted the tactic of putting a better bowler on with a lesser bowler. To start with, it seemed to work. Hats off to Arthur Rixon. He had lost a bit of pace, but he was deadly accurate. He'd say he was fast to medium, I'd say he was medium to slow. But in his two overs, he skittled a couple of their players out and didn't give away many runs. Brian Crease could bowl a decent ball, Steve Battle, as expected had a good eye and bowled well. Bob Fellows who said he wasn't much of a bowler surprised himself and us by not giving much away and taking at least one wicket.
We had them Rattled a bit, their run rate was creeping up. At the time, they were around 40 for 5. We'd got through twelve overs, so we were certainly in with a shout. Bob knew he still had me and himself to bowl. He decided to hold us back for the final push. Enter Steve Holman, and the wheels started to come off. If I thought Steve was a slow runner, nothing prepared me for the dolly's he was bowling. His first over gave

away about thirty runs. I'm pretty certain all his six balls were boundaries, either a six or a four. The opposition was suddenly back in the driving seat. Bob threw me the ball. I walked down the other end to bowl. I then went about another ten feet down. The batsman must have wondered where the hell I was going, along with my teammates. One thing about me, I hate to lose. I ran into bowl like a demon-possessed, I thumped the ball down with such ferocity it cleared poor old Gordon Beattie's head by about ten feet. My attempted bouncer had given away four runs. Gordon walked up to me.

'Calm down big fella.' He handed me the ball as and as I walked back to bowl the batsman smirked. 'Same again mate.' 'I guess as I ran in, he expected another fast delivery, I think he was already swinging as I let go of the ball. The ball came down the wicket and passed the batsman at half the speed of my previous ball. The batsman had swung the bat far too early. Out you go. I think I skittled a couple out that over. Bob couldn't risk another Steve Holman over at that stage so bowled himself. He bowled well and took a wicket, I bowled my second over and took another scalp. The time it came to Bob to bowl his second over the match was on a knife-edge. We had somehow managed to remove nine of them. The last two batsmen were at the wicket. They had plenty of overs in hand. Bob had one over left to bowl, Steve Holman had one to bowl and someone else who I can't remember had two to bowl. They only needed ten runs to win. After two or three balls, they'd reduced that target to six.

The next moment will stay with me for the rest of my life. Bob ran down to bowl, I think the man facing wanted to end the match in glory. He swung the bat and the ball flew up high and long towards the boundary. The ten of us watched as the ball went sky high and towards Steve Holman. He of the slow-running technique. Arms pumping, he ran towards the fast dropping ball. Ten voices shouting out to him, "Catch it." Followed by eleven voices shouting "drop it."

After a little fumble that had ten hearts jumping, he held onto it.

My God, we had won.

What a night, you'd have thought we'd won the world cup the way we celebrated in the clubhouse after. None of us wanted to go home as we relived the game ball by ball. This motley crew had somehow managed to win a game. One of my fondest memories.

Of course, we soon came down with a bang in our next match where we got absolutely hammered. To be honest I'm not sure if we even won another game that season. It didn't matter, we had our glory night and we dined on that for years. Happy days.

We never thought of these evening games as dangerous, that was until we were playing an office team that included the H/R guy Ken Pocklington.

He was a nice man, Ken, very polite and fair, not like the mob that would follow him later in my working life.

He ran after the ball and tripped, I was batting and he fell and it looked fairly innocuous from where I was standing.

However, he screamed in agony and when I ran over you could see a very serious break to his arm.

We had to call an ambulance and Ken was off work for a long time.

It certainly made me more aware after that when chasing a ball.

Unfortunately, Ken is no longer with us.

I have a cricket related story regarding our captain Bob Fagg. Maybe twenty years after our cricketing exploits, I'd managed to get three tickets for an executive box at Lords. I had been tapped up by an insurance guy trying to make inroads at the plant.

He didn't have a hope in hell of ever getting his company in there; however, I wasn't going to tell him that.
He came good with the tickets and I asked Bob if he fancied it. For old times sake, I suppose.
My union colleague at the time was Mick McManus, so as long as he drove I said he could come.
Now, these were the days when you could get the use of a company car, pool cars as they were known.
Mick said he would sort the car with the H/R and pick us up.
Now at the time, I was living in Wickford and Bob in Benfleet. Neither of us was far from the plant.
So the Friday morning arrives and Mick pulls up in the tiniest car I'd ever been in. It was old as well, a Fiat Cinquecento.
Well, it looked no bigger than Noddy's car.
Well, we pulled up outside Bob's and he comes out and is horrified what we're travelling in.
I should mention here that Mick and I were Amicus the Union reps at the time and Bob was T&G.
There was a lot of rivalry between the Amicus and the T&G shop stewards. Friendly rivalry to be fair.
So I guess me inviting Bob was not only about him being a friend but also to rub the T&G guys noses in it by demonstrating the Amicus union had better junkets.

Squeezed in the back it didn't take Bob long to start wining.
'Wouldn't get this in the T&G, the H/R have taken the piss out of you.'
I must admit at the time I wasn't disagreeing.
A bit later he was at it again.
'I can't feel my legs, I can't stretch them out.'
'This car can carry five people,' reminded Mick.
'Bollocks, five dwarfs maybe.'
I told Bob to settle down because we were soon going to stop for a breakfast en route to London.
'As soon as you spot a place, pull in, Mick.' I asked him.

About another thirty minutes go by and we've still not stopped.
'I'm bloody starving when are we stopping?' Asked Bob.
'I've not seen anywhere yet?' Shouted back, Mick.
'Not seen anywhere? We've passed about six McDonalds.' Pointed out, Bob.
'You said to stop at a restaurant?' Countered Mick.
'We're Amicus, we don't eat breakfast in the likes of MacDonald's, that's for T&G guys.' I tell Bob just to wind the situation up a bit more.
'I didn't mention McDonald's, listen, next place just bloody stop will you.' Pleaded Bob.
I'm not good when I'm hungry at the best of times, so I with Bob on that request.
So another thirty minutes pass, and the three of us haven't a clue where we are.
Mick pulls up outside a shop that says "Breakfast rolls."
I get out and I can hardly walk as I wait for the blood to start pumping.
Bob somehow manages to extract himself out of the car and is walking around like a calf that's just been born.
'Jesus Christ, I need to eat,' he announces as he does a funny walk.
Eventually, he's straightened up enough to go into the shop. Mick and I follow.
'I don't believe it?' Cries out Bob, sounding like a higher voiced version of, Victor Meldrew.
I did think what the hell is he moaning at now as I stood behind him.
When I look up I see Mick has parked outside a vegan restaurant.
However, it's amazing what you can eat when you're hungry.
I'd never tried a vegan Sausage Egg and Cheese Roll before, and it's safe to say I won't be trying it again.
As we head outside the time is ticking by, we needed to find the cricket ground.

'Leave it to me,' announced Mick who stops the first person unlucky enough to be walking past at the time.
'Excuse me mate, any idea where the cricket ground is?'
The man looked at him as if he was mad.
'You blind?' He asked.
'No, I just need directions to the cricket ground.'
The man turns and points.
'Try ... There.'
We look across to where the man's pointing and sure enough, situated behind a Tesco's was the said cricket ground.
'Yeah, I thought we were close.' Announced Mick, as we climbed back into the Noddymobile.
We parked up at the back of this large Tesco's and start to leg it to the ground.
The insurance rep had arranged to meet us outside with the tickets and we didn't have long.
Our progress was hampered by us getting approached by a nasty looking homeless man.
He looked like he'd just strolled over from the set of the "Walking Dead."
'Can you spare some change guys?' He asked in a slurred voice.
'Get a job,' called out Mick.
Now, for some reason, (Most probably due to the meths.) The guy thought Bob had spoken to him.
'Come here and say that, you fucking arsehole.' The man started to head towards Bob.
Well, in true Benny Hill fashion the three of us start to run. Not sure why, because the man couldn't run a bath, let alone catch us.
So we get to the front of the ground panting and luckily our guy is there to meet us.
I do the introductions and follow the guy in.
Now, this wasn't my first time in an executive box, I'd been a couple of times to a box at Roots Hall, home of the once league team Southend United.

Fiat had purchased a box for the season and I won't lie, I used my union clout to get a couple of goes.

However, the difference between the two boxes was immense. Poor old Mick, he couldn't take advantage of the fine wines and beers that were flowing nicely.

Bob of course took full advantage of the drinks and nibbles and made a right pig of himself.

I can't remember the lunch menu or who was playing cricket, I can remember there were a few other guys who were hobnobbing in the box with us.

I will blame the drink for what happened next. But it was something Mick and I, and then the whole plant got to know. These other guys with who we were sharing the executive box were interested in what we did.

So I explained that Mick and I were Amicus union shop stewards at the Basildon Tractor Plant. I sort of explained our role of representing the workforce.

Surprisingly they were quite knowledgeable and we spoke of the demise of the union under Maggie Thatcher.

We had quite a lively debate I seem to recall.

Once we'd kicked Maggie Thatcher into touch, they turned their attention to Bob.

'So Bob, what do you do?'

A simple question that I thought would get a simple answer.

'I'm a union officer,' he announces.

I look at Mick, and I think it was the sheer embarrassment of that statement, that Mick and I kept quiet.

'Wow, does that mean your Trevor and Mick's boss?'

'Yes, you could say that.'

Bob's eyes kept darting between Mick and me, it was a look that said please don't drop me in it.

I'm sure to this day if Mick had been drinking he would have lashed Bob there and then. But he was sober and like me, he didn't want to embarrass our Bob.

Well luckily play resumed and we went back to watching the cricket.

It wasn't until we got back to the car that the piss-taking started.

'You sit in the front, Bob, can't have an officer crammed in the back like a lowly steward.'

Poor Bob, that slip of the tongue haunted him for the rest of his working life.

He was no longer known as Bob Fagg. From that day he was known as "Officer Bob."

I hope Bob doesn't mind me telling that story; it was so funny at the time.

We have the occasional messenger video call and it's always a pleasure to talk to him.

He's hardly changed. He gave up the pigeon racing a few years back, something he was very successful at.

I had settled back into my shop steward's role, I think I was always destined to be some form of representative. I loved to hammer my point of view across and take up any cases of wrongdoing. Plus the fact I was an augmentative bugger, helped.

The first thing I did when I was elected was to stick to my campaign promise and scrap the current overtime rota and introduce a fairer system. I wasn't happy with this booking people's hours if they found overtime in another department.

I also got rid of booking hours and just changed it to a simple rotation system. I gave the new layout to the three foremen and popped upstairs and gave one to Jimmy Ferris. For once he had something good to say.

'Thank God for this. That was a terrible system you had before. Have you given Ricky a copy?'

'I've given one to all three foremen.'

'Not Ricky Hunt, Ricky Redmond. He's the overtime monitor.'

I'd forgotten all about him.

'Not for much longer, I'm taking that role.' His days of "Book 'em Danno," had gone.

'Good luck with that.' Came the sarcastic response from the ferret.

That remark stoked me up and there was no way Ricky Redmond would survive by the time I had finished.

I left Ferris's office and knew I was going to have a little battle on my hands. Ricky Redmond had been the overtime monitor since the year dot.

He played merry hell when I told him. Went to see Ferris, who played the "Nothing to do with me," card. He went to personnel and eventually I was summoned over to see one of them.

I think this is a good point to mention the Personnel Department. I will be brief.

Ninety percent of them I didn't like. Especially later at work. Once they started bringing in these graduates with absolutely no life skills, I didn't have time for any of them. I liked and respected the likes of Carl Curbishley, Dennis Morley and Ken Pocklington.

Old school and world-wise. I can't remember who I dealt with, but I agreed to hold a ballot for the overtime monitor position. Honestly, I had serious issues to address and I was being sidetracked by Mr Angry. He was still smarting over the photos of my arse, cock and balls.

So, I stuck a notice up and I was expecting a two-horse race with Ricky Redmond. Elton tried to muddy the water by sticking his name in the hat.

After a few choice words with him, he withdrew. In the end, Ricky received only two votes. He'd made a lot of enemies over the years.

Mentioning Carl Curbishley reminds me of a nasty accident that befell him on a team-building exercise in my old neck of the woods, Maldon.

This was attended by H/R, some managers, a few stewards and a few brown noses who'd wrangled a weekend away on some old boat, all paid for by the company.

Poor Carl was having a great time until someone didn't close a floor hatch after them. Carl stepped into an empty space and had a nasty fall. A bit like Humpty Dumpty I suppose. I have experience of falling into empty space when I took that shortcut that time from the gardener's hut.

The difference being, I managed to save myself by having my arms out.

By all accounts, Carl shot down like a missile being fired out of a submarine.

Badly hurt as I recall.

In some respects I'm glad I wasn't there, my dislike of the H/R was well known and I'm sure the finger would have been pointing my way.

Once I had dealt with Ricky, life as a shop steward became easier. George Catton was doing a good job as far as I was concerned.

People like the *Rat*, Alan Phillips and Geoffrey Martin Smith were all senior stewards.

I didn't realize it at the time, but those three would become key figures in the union, I grew old with these guys. Stewards came and stewards went. Some didn't last long. They wanted to become a shop steward for their own gain. Normally a grudge against a supervisor.

Some were voted out by their membership. Any weakness was soon put to the test. Elections were always a tense time for a shop steward. We had an election every biennial. The notice would go up on the boards and if you wanted to stand you had to go and see the convenor and get a nomination form.

Now depending on who the guy was and what current steward he was wanting to replace, one of two things would happen. If it was a steward well-liked by the convenor, he would try and put the prospective candidate off. I know this because I heard it first hand when the *Rat* was the convenor.

'You sure you want to commit to this role for the next two years?'

'Well, I wouldn't be asking for a form if I didn't. That **** **** is beyond useless.'

'Really? And you think you can do better?'

'Well, I can try?'

'Trying's no-good mate, you go away and think about what you're doing.' Nine times out of ten the guy was never seen in the convenor's office again.

If the convenor didn't like the steward, a completely different approach came about.

'Come in mate, you want a cup of tea?'

'That would be nice, cheers.'

'Trevor, make ****** a cup of tea will you.'

'So, you want to become a steward?'

'Well, I'd like to give it a shot.'

'You're just the type of guy we're looking for. Here, take a nomination form, get two signatures and bring it back to me before Friday. So how you been?'

Of course, later on, the said Steward who was now facing an election had heard the news and come in to see the convenor.

'Has that bastard ****** come in for a nomination form?'

'Yes, he has, but don't worry. I can't see him standing. I gave him a good talking to. Told him the pitfalls of being a steward. I'll be very surprised if he takes it any further.'

Back to George Catton.

I'd not heard any grumblings about George. He was a long-standing steward who had served under Bill Cleary for many years.

To me he was a breath of fresh air after my time, I should add, a short time under Bill Cleary.

I liked him. He had a dry sense of humour and a sharp brain. I can only liken to what happened to George, by using the way Tony Blair took over leadership of the Labour Party. I was going to say that he took over from Neil Kinnock. But that's not factually true. For a brief time, we had John Smith (until he keeled over in the shower) then Margaret Beckett for two months before Tony Blair was elected.

Now, Neil Kinnock was a good opposition leader but wasn't well-liked by some of the MP's.

Being Welsh obviously didn't help. But I've met Neil Kinnock. He is a very nice man and very sharp. But Tony Blair was ambitious and soon started a campaign that would belittle Neil and lead him to the leadership.

George Catton was a very nice man, as I've already stated he had a sharp brain. But what led to his downfall was he wasn't a great public speaker. At least not in the eyes of some of the more prominent stewards that I have already mentioned. They were out to get him.

I should mention here that there was only one steward that stood out when it came to addressing the troops, Alan Phillips. He had a bit of Tony Benn in him. He was a far better speaker than the Rat ever was.

The *Rat's* ambitions couldn't wait any longer. A plan was hatched and I'm guessing each of those three senior stewards was targeted to get support from the junior stewards.

The *Rat* was making his bid to be the new convenor. Geoffrey Martin Smith had me in his sights.

He came to see me and told me the plan. I wasn't overjoyed about it in the beginning. My point of view was to let George see the remainder of his term out.

I honestly can't remember how long he had left, I'm sure it was less than a year. But the prince in waiting was growing ever more impatient.

Rumours started to leak out about George's inadequacies. The promise of a more active role in the shop stewards committee swung it for me.

I was ambitious, and I knew that if I went against the *Rat* in the vote and he got elected, then I'd be back in the Bill Cleary type scenario of having a pissed off convenor against me.

The meeting and vote of no confidence were awful to be involved in and witnessed. I had done it myself years previously with Bobby Graham. I wasn't overjoyed about doing it, but Bobby wasn't Steward material.

George Catton was. He'd been an engine machining steward for several years and knew his stuff. Being a convenor is a full-time role. You're transferred out of your department and I guess you come under the personnel department.

So, George was voted out. The *Rat* was voted in. Alan Phillips became the deputy. In a bid to curb George Sharp's anger he was elected as the plant Health and Safety Rep.

Truth be told, I don't think George Sharpe ever forgave the *Rat* for shoving his mate out.

George Catton didn't want to go back onto the shop floor. You can't blame him. He'd worked his way up in the union to the pinnacle.

Going back to being an operator in the engine machining area wasn't a move he relished. I'm not sure how old George was at this time, mid-fifties I would hazard a guess.

Remember, he wasn't even a shop steward now.

Personnel put him in a photocopying office for a while until they could work out what to do with him.

In the end to save everyone's blushes he took early retirement. He cut a forlorn figure and you couldn't help but feel sorry for him. I will say this for George. At least he walked out with his head held high. Not like a dirty Rat caught stealing the cheese. That moment was yet to come.

You have to remember, at this time I got on well with the Rat, his fraudulent times were still to come.
None of us realised the depths this man would sink to.

I would say the Rat was the vainest person I've ever met, and I've met a few in my time, I can tell you.
The first thing Rat organised was to have a large stewards office put up in the middle of the factory.
He called it a steward's office, but really it was for him. It was a big office sectioned off, so he kept out of sight with the workforce.
You always knew he was skulking in the back because as soon as you opened the door, a cloud of smoke would billow out.
It was a handy place for me; I could hide away in there on my own on late and night shifts.
For a man who was so unfit, he surprised us all by digging in for a works gym.
When I write this now, he must have been on an earner somewhere along the line. In fact, the gym was built right above his office in one of the old locker rooms.
It was nice when it first opened, with plenty of equipment, nice showers and a sauna.
I used the facilities many times.
The stewards had a tendency to look out for each other, something I will cover later in the book.
When I first started at the plant, you paid your union dues in cash to a union rep.
Not necessarily your shop steward, but a designated collector.
Enter Derek West into my life. A huge man who if you'd put in a babygrow, he'd give Big Daddy a run for his money.
He was a collector of union dues and despite his size, when he zoomed in on you there was no escape.

I was just about to write about the factory being a closed shop.
But I'm not 100% sure that statement is correct.

I know one of the first things that happened when you started, was to get a union membership thrust at you. If I remember correctly, this was done just about straight away.

Until I started at Ford's, I'd not had anything to do with unions. I knew all about them via my dad, especially when he was on strike.

Now my dad had a bad back, this was an ailment that would flair up on hearing of an industrial dispute.

I can recall a funny story about my dad's mysterious bad back. It must have been the mid-1960s and Fords must have been on strike. My dad was at home and unbeknown to me he was off work sick!

As I mentioned, my dad's back would play him up every time he was on strike.

Now there was a big thing in his favour, we were living in the tiny village of Stow Maries, a far cry from Basildon and the tractor plant.

So, he would phone the doctors and make an appointment. Something has just come to me as I write about this. My dad kept a walking stick in our garage, and he'd take it with him to the doctors.

Obviously, I'm just guessing what tales of woe he told the doctor, but he would arrive home with a note stating he wasn't fit to work for the next two weeks.

The doctors would have been in Maldon, I would think the doctor didn't have a clue my dad was working at Ford's and was currently on strike.

So, he could claim sick benefits from the social. Now, these were the days when you could claim sickness at work as well. You couldn't claim for the first three days, and I believe I'm right in saying that your sickness claim was frozen until the strike was over.

This didn't bother my dad because he could bullshit with the best of them.

The social and work payments were less than you could earn working, but it was enough to live on comfortably while sitting on your arse.

My dad's bad back would drag on for weeks, it was only the news of a return to work that would get him off his sickbed!

Now, I'm exaggerating with that last statement, which leads me nicely into this humorous tale.

Our garden in Stow Maries was big, it backed onto fields. It took a lot of time to upkeep, so an enforced break from work was just what the doctor ordered literally.

My dad had been off work sick for several weeks, it must have been one of the longest strikes.

This particular day he had me helping him lay some turf at the bottom of the garden.

I can picture the scene now; my dad stripped to the waist, pulling a heavy roller up and down the strip of grass. Standing to one side my mother and the doctor!

Well, I can't remember what excuse my dad used, I know the doctor bollocked my dad telling him that's the reason he's back wasn't getting any better.

When I asked my dad about this incident years later, he told me the doctor was horrified seeing him pulling the roller, told him to rest up indoors and he signed him off for a further four weeks.

Four days later the strike was over but my dad had another three weeks enforced sickness lay-off.

This tactic of my dad's meant I couldn't use that particular ploy. It would have look mightily suspicious had a father and son gone off sick at the same time of a strike looming.

Now back to Derek West.

His sheer size was enough to intimidate you into handing over the cash. Well, it did to start with, and then as I got more confident, I used to give Derek the run-around. Being the size he was he couldn't exactly stealth in towards you.

But a more determined collector you won't meet.
His headstone should have read, "Always gets his man."
The thing is, I had no problem paying, it was the number of weeks that built up between his visits I'd get the hump about. I can't remember what we paid back then, it was only a small amount, but a small amount would eventually become a large amount by the time he decided to waddle over for a collection. So as payback, I'd make him work for the money.
Many a time I'd spot him, and be on my toes.
Of course, eventually, he'd catch me and I'd plead poverty. But unless I wanted to be shaken by my ankles I'd pay up.
He caught me once in the toilet! I came out of a cubicle and there he was smiling away holding my union contribution card. He was a likeable fellow though. I'm not sure if he was ever the canteen steward, more than likely. He would eat these huge dinners, then sit and eat a diet yoghurt.

Derek West, partaking in his favourite hobby.

He liked his food and a beer. He used to ride a moped to work like my grandad's old one.
He looked so funny on it, luckily for the moped; Derek didn't live far from the plant.

Not sure why? But Derek was an Everton FC supporter, I know of no other man that supported that team.
He had his reasons I can tell you.
The biggest shock I had with Derek was when I turned up to play inter-departmental football and out waddled Derek wearing a referee's outfit.
Well, because of his size I knew he wasn't dressed like that to run the line.
To be fair to the guy he was a qualified referee. I'm guessing in his younger days, obviously.
It's safe to say throughout the match he never ventured far from the centre circle.
However, it took a brave man to question any of his decisions, even if he was fifty feet away from the action.
He might have been grossly overweight but I wouldn't have wanted to mess with him.

Derek was no fool; he knew how to play the system. He was steward of the tractor repair guys, all the years I knew him I never saw him get his hands dirty.
Although on one occasion his judgement let him down.
He needed some work done on his car. I didn't know he owned a car because I'd only ever seen him on the moped.
Anyway, he decides to use a guy that worked in our department, a guy Jolly nicknamed the Outlaw.
Enter former Grinding wheelman, and part-time car repair and welder, Brian Wales.
Now, he wasn't known as the outlaw for nothing, he was a cowboy, at work and home.

He got removed from his Grinding wheel position because he was slapdash, not a good trait when operators were expected to stand in front of grinding wheels.

If a grinding wheel exploded, it could cause you severe damage. His card was marked, I was his steward and I tipped him off he was being watched.

However, a few weeks later he was pulled in again about what the supervisor judged as unsafe practices.

He was a funny bloke, always had a chip on his shoulder.

He was lucky not to lose his job; instead, I managed to get him shifted outside to join the guys who took the wood and rubbish out of the plant. He lost a grade over it, so he didn't come out of it unscathed.

At the time I can remember quite a bit of hostility towards him, he wasn't a well-liked fellow.

However, things settled down and I thought that would be the end of any problems with him.

This was until Derek decided to use him to fix his car.

Apparently, the car needed some welding repairs.

I wasn't there at the time, but a few days after the event I went to see Brian at home.

He had third-degree burns on his arm, shoulder and side of his face.

Outside, his garage was burnt to cinders and Derek's car sat there completely burnt out.

Poor Derek, he got so much stick from the guys after it came out.

I bet he was sick to the core by the number of people hollering at him "Yee haa."

The outlaw returned some weeks later, looking slightly worse for wear. He was grateful he was working outside and could avoid all the ridicule.

As for Derek, he eventually retired and was replaced with one of the laziest stewards I ever crossed paths with, a funny little guy named Bo Varney.

I'm not sure how long Bo was a steward, but he thought it only right to follow Derek's example and do sod all.

The difference being, Derek had earned the right, he'd been involved in the union since the plant opened.

Bo went from being a repairman to a professional seat warmer in the convenors office.

I won't lie, I didn't like the bloke, the only time I saw him move was when there was an overtime cut in his area.

The rest of the time he spent sucking up to the convenor. It was embarrassing if I'm honest.

I was a working steward, along with a few others. This always held me in good stead with my work colleagues.

Of course, I'd be lying if I didn't say I had my fair share of time off due to different courses and meetings.

So, my trade union comeback was complete, at the time I thought the Rat was okay, he was full of himself but looked after his stewards.

His treachery was still years away.

Chapter 4

Onwards and upwards.

By the mid-nineteen eighties, things were settling down after the *Rat's* successful coup. As promised, I received my first responsibility within the union. I was now the canteen representative. Couldn't have happened to a more deserving steward than me. After all, I was a professional eater.

It was while I held this position that I had the taste of my first junket.

Times were changing in the canteen. The lack of customers put the late shift service at risk. Paying two women to come in and serve maybe a maximum of twenty dinners was never going to last.

The *Rat* was approached and I was sent with two other stewards to Bristol of all places to look at the freeze dry food machines.

We accompanied two managers from the Canteen Company and Ken Pocklington from Personnel who was also our driver. We travelled down in a people carrier, very popular in the 80s. We were put up in a very nice hotel in Bristol.

Now the two stewards who came with me were Barry Mansfield the paint steward and Bill Hammond from the Product Engineering side.

Now, Bill and I have been Facebook friends for some time and who was the canteen steward at this particular time is under debate.

However, one of us was so let me continue with the story.

On arrival in Bristol, we were left to our own devices the first night.

I can remember Barry and I for some reason, descended to Bill's room and proceeded to empty his fridge of every single miniature.

I can't remember much more about that night apart from a half recollection that we ended up in an Indian restaurant.
Badly hungover, we had breakfast the following morning in the hotel and then told to check out as we were travelling to a nearby factory to see these freeze-dried food machines in action.
We had left the champagne unopened in Bill's room. Something to do with it being twenty-five pounds, for half a bottle.
However, the three of us were undeterred by the price and decided to have the champagne away.
All feeling slightly guilty, we checked out and made our way to the car park.
We all said no when the checking out clerk asked if we'd touched the minibar.
Once we were in the safety of the people carrier we started to relax.
As Ken started to drive off, looking across we could see the manager from the hotel running out shouting.
'Keep driving', pleaded Bill who was sat next to Ken and gone into panic mode.
Ken, who was driving, pulled up and gave Bill a funny look.
'What's up with you?'
'Err … Nothing. I just want to get there, I'm hungry.'
'Hungry? You've just had your breakfast?' Bill tried to make himself smaller by pulling his parka hood up and sliding down his seat.
Ken wound his window down and the out of breath manager of the hotel gave him an envelope. I could hear Ken thanking the man.
The manager walked off and three of the men in the car gave a sigh of relief.
It turned out the manager had given us a discount voucher each for that particular chain of hotels. That little incident with Bill I reminded him of for years.

We ended up at this small factory where they made the machines for the freeze-dried food.
Although it tasted okay, it wasn't the same as freshly cooked food. Frozen microwaved food has never been appealing to me.
After plenty of samples, we headed home.
We gave our report at the next stewards meeting.
I always remembered my first shop stewards meeting and the way poor Roy Carsons was treated by that gnome Bill Cleary.
So, we put the findings to the shop stewards committee and no surprise when the freeze-dried food machines were soon prominent in the canteen.

Unfortunately, there's a sad note to this story.
Barry Mansfield, shop steward for the paint floor and was three or four years younger than me passed away a few years ago.
He'd left work after the paint floor came downstairs and became more automated. He was a big guy with a big heart, a very popular steward. I have the fondest of memories when I think of him.
The Christmas bucket collection always springs to mind when I think of Barry, a story I will cover later in the book.
I only saw him once after he left the plant.
He stood in front of me in a garage when I was queuing to pay for some petrol.
To be honest I didn't realise it was him until he turned around.
He was now a taxi driver and had piled a lot of weight on.
We stood outside and reminisced about the good old days at the factory. A few months later I found out he had passed away.
He was only around fifty when he left us.

It was around this time that I had to take on another responsibility, this time work-wise.

Someone higher up had decided he wanted me to be a backup Grinding Wheelman.

I was told Just to cover holidays and sickness. Always one to add another string to my bow, I accepted the challenge.

Now you may think that's a strange use of terminology, but I found it a challenge because the man who was going to train me was a notorious storyteller. He has been dead for several years, so I feel I can name him. Neil Connelly, aka Billy Bullshitter.

As I mentioned at the beginning, everything I write is how I remember things. Sometimes they seem outlandish, but the events I write about are to the best of my knowledge, true.

Now Neil as a bloke was a decent enough fellow, or so I thought at the time. A good union supporter and a skilful and knowledgeable, Grinding wheelman.

Unfortunately, he had a problem; a big problem. He would come out with the most outrageous stories.

I'd never had a lot to do with Neil up to that point, but I used to hear about his tales third hand.

So, I was relieved of hoist duties for a month and was under the tuition of Billy Bullshitter.

It didn't take long before the tales started. Now what I'm about to write may well be true, I'll let you decide.

I told Neil my AA membership was coming up for renewal. No, I hadn't succumbed to the dreaded drink, it was the Automobile Association.

I'd joined a few years before and I had used them on the odd occasion the car had let me down. After that, I was always afraid to give the membership up. I used to think as soon as I gave it up the bloody car would break down somewhere. The membership wasn't that expensive, but this time for some reason I was stalling on it.

This gave Neil an opening for one of his stories.

'I don't have that problem, I'm a lifetime member.'

'Really? What did that cost?'
'Nothing. I wrote to them a few years ago and told them I had a lot of AA memorabilia in my loft. They sent a guy to see me and he was amazed at my collection. He offered me money, but I said no. It's all on display at their headquarters in London. So, in gratitude, they gave me a lifetime membership. If you go there, Trevor, you'll see a plaque on the wall beside the display. "Kindly donated by Mr N Connelly."'
Only Billy Bullshitter could come out with that story.
I had a neighbour like him once, Tony.
I used to call him "Topper Tone." Didn't matter what I did, he had already done it, but much better.
It was only day two and it seemed like this was going to be a long month. He then topped the AA story.
He'd asked me something which would lead to an opening for another tale.
'You booked anywhere for your holidays this year?' He asked me.
'Not yet, I quite fancy Cornwall or Devon.'
'Nice part of the country, did I tell you about the time I was on holiday in Devon?'
'No, I think you must have missed me out with that story.'
'Well the wife was happy just reading on the beach, but I wanted to do something. We had rented a nice little cottage opposite a church. So, one morning I wandered over and I bumped into the vicar. What a nice man, getting on a bit in years. He told me he was sad to see the graveyard in such a sorry state. A lot of the headstones had moved because of subsidence over the years. I told him, don't worry about that vicar. I'll sort them out for you. So, the rest of the week I went around and straightened all the headstones out.'
'Christ, how many did you straighten?'
'About a hundred. I tell you, Trevor. When I finished the vicar came over, he was nearly in tears. Thank you so much, Neil, he said.'

'Another plaque?' I ask.
'What?'
'I Just wondered if the vicar did something for you in return? You know as a way of thanks?'
'He mentioned about putting a stain glass window in with my name on.'

I soon discovered that as soon as I mentioned something, it cued him up for another story.
'I thought I might go beach fishing, Sunday'
'I didn't know you fished?'
I sat down waiting, it didn't take long.
'I have some lovely beach casters in my loft, I often go to Southend and fish off the beach.'
'Do you? I didn't know that.'
'Yes, in fact, I used to give fishing lessons. How to set up a rig, the correct way to cast out.'
'Really? I didn't know there was a correct way?'
'Yes, it's all in the wrist, Trevor. With little effort and a flick of my wrist I could cast out as far as the car park from here.'
He was talking of a distance of at least 400 meters?

A story I was reminded of by Geoffrey Martin Smith is most probably my favourite.
Neil went to a concert in London. Before it could start an announcer came on the stage and said sadly the concert would have to be cancelled due to the conductor of the orchestra being taken ill. Unless of course there was anybody in the audience who had the experience of conducting.
Neil shot his hand up and he was invited onto the stage where he proceeded to conduct the orchestra with aplomb. At the end of the night, he was cheered to the rafters, so good, was he?

I'll stop here because I could fill this book up with his stories. I have an open mind regarding Neil.

He did me a bad turn sometime later and I never forgave him. We were in a busy period in the plant; it was the time when we had introduced temporary labour.

Neil wanted to get his daughter a job, so he tapped me up. That was the nice part of being a steward; you could help by pushing through someone's application, often a family member to get some temporary employment, often leading to a full-time job.

So, I went to Human Resources as it was known by then and I did the necessary. Within days his daughter was safely installed and was given an easy job.

But, within weeks he had forgotten that good deed and did a bad thing behind my back.

He contradicted himself, and went and told tales about me to my foreman.

When he was teaching me the do's and don'ts of changing a grinding wheel, he reminded me a couple of times not to start a wheel change if you couldn't finish it.

It was a safety issue, I guess if there was an issue then the wheelman couldn't blame anybody else.

Wise advice I thought at the time. So months later, I'm doing some holiday coverage and I get a job come in about forty minutes before I was due to clock out. So I went to the stores and got the grinding wheel and left it on the buggy for the night shift. (Neil.) He went and told the foreman I must have left work early because I'd left the job for him? I found out, had it out with him and hardly spoke to him again after that.

I can remember my foreman Tony Lynch finding out what he did and going over to Neil and lashing him about his behaviour towards me. Some people have the shortest of memories. I did mention to him after his betrayal that as easy as it was for me to help get someone a temporary job in the plant, it was just as easy to get them out.

Nothing as queer as folk.

Neil Connelly's retirement.
I'm the scruffy one far-right; I'm smiling away because I was glad to see the back of him. Next to me is Tony lynch. Then Mark Lewin, aka Bones. Next to Bones is Billy Bullshitter, then our manager at the time Michael Newman. Standing next to Michael is the late shop steward and local councillor Richard Llewellyn. Far-left in the red top is Barry Campagna, currently the Mayor of Canvey Island. There are a few other faces I recognise, but none more famous than me so why mention them.

Now a man who could give Billy Bullshitter a run for his money is Ian Shoulders, aka, Stretch.

Now before I start, let me say I'm fond of Ian. He's a Facebook friend and a thoroughly decent guy.

Now the difference between Ian and Neil Connelly is Ian's stories, outrageous as they sounded, were all true.

My favourite story, his brother's wedding.

Now before I start, for the benefit of people who don't know Ian, he has a certain way of talking.

Not sure who started it, because there was another guy who worked with Ian for years, Steve Macklin who did the same thing. They'd finish a sentence with the word's "Right" or "Yeah, Right," or "You know what I mean?" Often, they'd say, "Yeah right, you know what I mean," all in one go!!

Steve eventually left the company, moved down to Devon I believe. I think Ian was a bit heartbroken for a while, losing his buddy.

One morning he ambled into the Hoist crib. People often popped in for a chat.

'Alright Ian, wanna cuppa?'

'Go on then.' He plonked himself down and I could see he had something to tell me. A social call was rare from our Ian.

The following conversation went something like this:

'Did I tell you my brother got married?'
'No, when was that?'
'Saturday, a bloody disaster Trev, yeah, right.'
'Why, what happened?'
'Be quicker to tell you what didn't happen, yeah, right, you know what I mean?'

I made myself a cup of tea as well; I could feel Ian was going to be sitting there for some time.

I can't remember where the wedding was, it wasn't local because they were staying in a hotel somewhere.

'I told you my brother was marrying a girl from Canada, yeah right.'

'No, I don't recall you telling me that, Ian. In fact, you've never mentioned to me that you have a brother.'

'Doesn't matter, me and my brother stayed the night before the wedding in a hotel, right. We had a few beers and a laugh, you know what I mean?'

'I do.'

'Next morning, I get up, a bit worse for wear. Go down for breakfast and there's no sign of my brother? Right.'

'What's he done a runner?'

'What, no. Don't interrupt Trevor, yeah, right.'

'Sorry mate, carry on.'

'No, he's still in bed, yeah, right. So, I leave him to it, know what I mean?' This time I just nodded.

'I have a shower and I thought I'd better try my suit on, yeah. I'd not tried it on since I picked it up from Moss Bross, right. So, I try the jacket on, yeah, and the sleeves finish halfway up my arms, right. The trousers I can't get up over me arse and the top hat is perched on the top of my head, way too small, you know what I mean?'

'Shit Ian, what did you do?'

'What could I do, Trev. I panicked, right. My brother's wife-to-be had about thirty relatives coming over from Canada for the wedding. There was me, the best man dressed as a clown, yeah. I went down to reception and asked for help. They told me there was a Moss Bross in the High Street. I take the suit with me and drive there, you know what I mean? Thank my lucky stars, yeah, right. They said they could change it free of charge. Job done, yeah, right, you know what I mean?'

'That was lucky, I mean, you are an odd size.'

'What do you mean, odd size?' Bless, Ian. As a kid, he would have been called gangly. As an adult, he was known as that lanky bloke. (Amongst others) Ian towered over me, must be at least six feet four or five.

'I'm just saying, you're not the normal off the peg size, are you?'

'Yeah, right. Doesn't matter, because they did have my size. I was happy, I had my suit and went back to the hotel. I just got back to my room, yeah, right. When there's a knock on the door. I open it, right, guess who's standing there, yeah?'

'Room service?'

'No, my brother. Wearing his suit, yeah right. One problem, yeah. The sleeves are way too long, the jacket is hanging off him, the trousers are about a foot too long and the hat is covering his eyes, you know what I mean?'

'I do Ian, you mixed up the suits.'

'Correct. How do you know that?'

'Call it a lucky guess, Ian.'

So, another ten minutes pass as Ian tells me about another mad dash to this famous "Moss Bross," which without asking him I assumed he meant Moss Brothers suit hire. Thinking he was giving his closing speech I stood up.

'Sit down, Trev. I haven't got to the best bit yet, yeah, right.'

'What there's more?'

'More, you won't believe this next bit, yeah. We get ourselves ready, yeah, right. Drive to the church, right. Thought it was looking a bit quiet, just a couple of people standing outside. My brother tells me that's a couple from Canada. So, we walk into the church, right. On the left of the aisle sat about fifty people, thirty-odd, from Canada and the bride's friends and family. On the right, our family and friends, or I should say where our family and friends should be sitting. It's empty Trev, yeah, right.'

'Christ Ian, what did you do?'

'What could I do, Trev? I panicked, right.'

'Where were they?'

'I dunno. We have the bride's guests and family sitting there who have travelled over three thousand miles, and my lot who had to travel thirty miles and they weren't sitting there, yeah, right.'

'What happened to them? I'll tell you what happened to them, they were sitting in the wrong church, Trev, yeah, right.'

Well, I can't remember the last time I laughed so much. You see it wasn't just the funny story, it was the way Ian told me. He had this deadpan look and rarely smiled.

Even when I was laughing he didn't crack his face. It's characters like Ian I really miss. He moved on to better things and I'm pleased for him. He ended up marrying our little electrician Amanda. Although there is a huge height difference, they always look extremely happy. Good on you guys.

I think what I'm trying to get across here is when you're in a large factory environment you come across a real spectrum of characters. I'm only scratching the surface of some of the people I met during my time at the plant.

Ian told me another story that day that I can't fully remember, linked to the wedding. Something about women in bathrobes and naked swimming comes to mind.

I hit thirty, and I was not happy about it.
I know you can't stop the march of time, but I didn't want to be thirty. It was "Live Aid" day. Everybody was watching the bands playing at Wembley Stadium and America. I was slowly getting depressed. Can that really be over thirty-six years ago? Oh well with age comes maturity. Really!!!

Now, as seemed to be the way in my working life, as things were going along smoothly, I'd hit a little bump.
Enter a new foreman, Clive Gibson.

We must have had a reshuffle, I have a feeling our dear foreman Ken was shipped down to Product Engineering.
A good move for him in my eyes. I mentioned it before, he was too nice to be a foreman, so he was put out to see the rest of his time in a nicer atmosphere. I'd see him occasionally, he looked a lot happier.
However, I don't think he was there long before he had a heart attack. He came back to work for a while then took early retirement.
So, Clive took us over and my co-workers and I soon discovered he didn't trust us?
He couldn't help but keep checking you were where you should be and the job was being done.
He was Australian, so we called him Skippy.
An odd-looking man with a lump on his forehead which he couldn't hide with his receding hair, to make matters worse he had an "Amish" type beard.
To be honest, he looked like he had his head on upside down.
Now just as my luck went, Skippy quickly moved to Maldon and became my neighbour!
This became a problem because I had to drive past his house to get to mine. So, no more sneaky off from work early for me. Not that I ever did!
He had four kids and a wife called Mary.
Now I met Mary a few times and she was a compulsive smoker and like Ian Shoulders, she often finished a sentence with the word, yeah. (A little side note here. I used Mary as a character in my first book "The Curry Affect.")
Now Skippy had bought a Ford Granada, he was one of these guys that would take on major repairs or upgrades. So, the Granada was soon in bits, strewn all over the front garden. I would imagine he was the toast of the small close he lived in. All nice 4 bedroom detached houses with nice gardens, except Skippy's whose garden quickly resembled "Steptoe's" yard.

So, with the car in about a thousand bits it came as no surprise when he tapped me up for a lift to work.

'No problem,' I said. Secretly cursing away to myself. I decided it was time for a bit of fun with our new foreman.

It was the middle of the winter and bloody freezing. Skippy only ever wore a very lightweight jacket, more suited for summer. When I got home that evening I blocked off the heater pipe to my car.

The next morning a came out of my front door looking like I was setting off on an arctic expedition. Thermal vest and long johns. Two pairs of socks. Jogging bottoms with jeans over the top. T-shirt, sweatshirt and a jumper. Woollen hat and gloves and a big parka with a fur-lined hood. I put sunglasses on but felt that was a bit over the top so took them off.

I had trouble walking, so I waddled around to my garage and got the car out. I pulled up outside Skippy's and he hopped out and into my car.

'Jesus H Christ, you feeling the cold?'

'Just a tad, Clive. Didn't I mention my heater has stopped working?'

'No, you didn't.' As Clive spoke you could see the mist coming out of his mouth. It was a thirty-minute drive to work; I guess we had been going about ten minutes before his teeth started chattering.

'You alright there, Clive?'

'Just feeling a bit nippy,' he replied with a shiver. The time we arrived at work he was a light shade of blue. He didn't wait for me, he just ran into the plant for a defrosting session.

On the journey home that night he'd got himself a coat out of the stores. He was still cold, but not as much as he had been in the morning.

I couldn't keep it up as I could hardly see out of the window screen. I had to keep scraping the ice off.

So that evening I unblocked the pipe and in the morning, I had another bit of fun. I set the alarm clock fifteen minutes earlier.

That gave me time to start the car and warm it up. I put the heater on full blast and by the time I pulled up outside Skippy's the car was roasting. I had my coat in the back seat and sat there in just my jeans and a t-shirt. Out stepped, Skippy. Looking like I did the day before, I don't know how many layers he had on, but he resembled the "Michelin Man." He plonked himself in the car.

'Jesus H Christ, you could have told me you got the heater fixed.'

'I didn't know, Clive. It just started working once I started the car. Must have been a blockage.'

I hit the accelerator so he couldn't get out to strip off. He did manage to get his coat off, but I'm guessing the thermals were on and working because when I looked at him he was dripping in sweat …... In January.

Not sure if he wanted revenge, or he'd heard about my zebra crossing skills, but he sent me down the hill to paint some yellow lines in another building down.

I'd used the machine before to paint lines, so not a problem. Now, I should mention before I went off to do this job I had to report to the office with the others on my shift for a five-minute Health and Safety briefing.

I'm guessing another directive from the Health and Safety guys. So, Skippy reads out the weekly Health and Safety Item. This week it concentrated on the misuse of tractors.

'They're not a taxi, so I don't want to see them parked up outside the canteen.'

Skippy was directing this at the wooden rubbish guys, it was only them and the gardener that drove the tractors in the plant.

So off I go and soon knock the lines out. I wanted to get back for a tea break so had a bit of a hurry on. I got to the bottom of the hill and was just about to push the machine up when a tractor pulled up. Terry Watts, one of the wooden rubbish guys poked his head out.

'Want a tow back?'

'Thanks, Terry.' So, I get behind his tractor and step on the tow bar. I have one hand holding onto the back of the tractor and one hand hanging on to the machine handle.

I must have looked a bit like a surfer, knees bent and hanging on for dear life. To be fair, Terry didn't go mad, he chugged along and before no time I was back in the main plant.

Unbeknown to me at that time, I'd been spotted by Skippy. A work colleague and friend Mark Clothier, aka Marky Mark, came to see me after I had received a bollocking from Skippy.

'It was so funny, Trevor. Skippy stood there telling us that it was serious Health and Safety issue that he'd mentioned in the morning. When suddenly you came along standing on the back of a tractor hanging onto the yellow line machine.' Now Mark could do a wicked Australian accent.

'He just looked and said, "Jesus H Christ, I don't believe it, he's meant to be the health and safety rep."

I think it's fair to add that Clive wasn't best pleased with Terry and me.

Skippy had a love of cars, he would go on about them all the time, I listened in once when he reeled off a load of car part brands I'd never heard of.

One, Mark reminded me of was Skip brown suspension? He talked the talk, but that Granada didn't walk the walk, it was in bits for months.

By the summer it was starting to disappear by being hidden in the long grass.

I asked him once if the neighbours had complained about the junkyard he called a front garden.

He admitted that an anonymous note had been left on the car. I think it's safe enough now to admit to placing that note.

Marky Mark will feature further in this book.

Talking about Skippy has reminded me about "The Tug Club." That was the name of our mobile video porn club.

It all started when several porn videos were offered to us at a discount.

So, a few of us clubbed together and bought about thirty porn videos. Now, this was the time when videos were at their peak. I won't mention the other shareholders …. Certain stories I will protect the guilty.

Marky Mark designed the membership cards, I printed off the film list and we got to work.

We stuck some posters up on the notice boards, and you could ring the wooden rubbish number and order a film. Now these posters, like the membership cards were designed by Marky. The advert made me laugh. He was a talented artist so had drawn a man wanking.

The bit that made me laugh, he'd written all tastes catered for, along with Double Bunging, Spit Roast, Anal, Gangbang and Swallow.

At the bottom, Mark had put "Free Belly Wipe with Each Film." I was concerned we'd look like a load of perverts after reading the poster; however, the films literally flew off the shelf.

We used to have these blue paper towels in the toilets. So, we had a pack and when a film was ordered, it would go in a plain bag with a paper towel.

Why Skippy reminded me about the video enterprise was he tapped me up for a free film one day.

'You're involved with this tug club video business, aren't you?'

'I couldn't possibly say, Clive.' I answered.

'Listen you; I've turned a blind eye to you driving around on your buggy delivering films when you should be working.' I had a small electric buggy to carry the ladders and tools I needed for my hoist work.

'Get to the point, Clive.'

'Mary's going away with the kids this weekend, thought I might get a film, au gratis.'

'In other words, you want a freebie?'

'You've got it.'

'Okay, I see what I can do.' On my travels, I go and see the boys and pick up a film that Marky Mark and I thought would be perfect for him.

Not that I watched the film …. Well maybe once for quality control reasons.

What I can remember of the film was it started like any other porn film, (So I'm told.) A beautiful blond girl and a guy who are at it within minutes.

This is where the film deviates from the normal routine. Because they are shortly joined by a third man who starts pumping the other guy?

Not the sort of thing we red-hot males like to see.

So, I popped it in the bag, slipped in the belly wipe and gave it to Skippy.

Monday morning arrives and he marches into the hoist crib, video in hand to see me.

'What sort of film is this?' He asked.

'Porn Clive, what you asked for.'

'But there are two men shagging each other.'

'I don't believe you.'

'There is I tell you. Jesus H Christ, I nearly vomited.'

'I watched the first five minutes, you sure?'

'Watch ten minutes and then you'll see.'

'Sorry mate, Marky Mark told me you'd enjoy this film. This is a new film we just purchased.

'I might have guessed he'd be involved.' (Sorry Mark.)

'I'll get you another.'

'Don't bother, Mary's back.' He called out as he marched off.

He did get me back in a roundabout way, and he didn't do anything.

I'd grown tired of trying to get past his house unnoticed. His living there was a pain and curtailed any early finishes.

So, I sold my house in Maldon and moved to Wickford. A few months later out of the blue, he moved too.

I was gutted; I loved Maldon and didn't want to leave. Within months he followed suit and moved to a village called Southminster.
I guess his neighbours in Maldon had a party and put the flags up when they saw the sold sign.

Poor old Skippy, he was a bit of a square peg in a round hole. He didn't last long. Another management shakeup and he ended up like Bomando, clipboard in hand checking stock. He was too clever for stocktaking. He told me that many times!! Last I heard of him he was working for Vauxhall at Elsmere Port.

The "Tug Club" ran for a couple of years then fizzled out. Like any enterprise, at the start, we were all keen to participate. But over time it became a pain. There were too many of us involved which didn't help.
About six of us, so, not much profit. Of course, in any video rental business, you have to keep new films coming in, so the little money we were making was going into the purchase of new films.
Also, we'd have some of our customers taking the piss, they wouldn't return the films or telling us they'd been stolen. Anytime we thought we'd been had over, the next film they ordered we always slipped in the gay film.
Eventually, we agreed to call it a day. I was getting pressure from the supervision about my delivery and pick up runs. I was a hoist man, not a postman.
It was good while it lasted, and to be fair it wasn't long after that the videos became obsolete as the DVD format was soon amongst us.

I think I should write about my two close working colleagues at this point.

Johnny Manning became a good friend for most of my working life, and a joy to work with.
Well, that's when I could stop him talking and rolling a cigarette.
'Hang on, Trev. Let me just work up a bit of steam.' That was his favourite saying when he wanted to make a roll-up.
I'd hated sending him off to get something. He was a bloody nightmare.
'Pop to the stores and get this, John.' Off he'd go, I'd carry on with the repair until I couldn't do anymore. I'd walk to the stores and there he was, talking. Often accompanied with a cup of tea in his hand.
'Just on my way back, Trev.'
My god, he could talk for England. I more laid-back guy I've never met. He operated at one speed, slow to moderate.' I've been to his house many times; his wife Molly and the kids are a lovely family. I say kids, they're in their 40s now.
Always made to feel welcome. John's house is lovely, decorated nicely and very homely. Not overloaded with ornaments and such like.
Now, this surprised me on my first visit because, at work, John was a hoarder. He hated throwing anything away. The Hoist workshop was on the move, we had to downsize.
This was late in my time at the plant.
Engine machining and assembly had all been ripped out. 70% of our spare hoists were obsolete, as were thousands of lifting hooks. We were told to get rid of. There was only John and me working on the hoists. I'd have a right old chucking out session. The next morning I'd walk into the hoist crib and half what I chucked out was back? It got that bad I had to hide where I was throwing it.
For all his faults, John was a great guy to have as a work partner. Very good on a computer and always on hand to help. He knew I was strapped for cash one time, he waited to see me and said, 'You do the weekends Mate, I've got no mortgage so

I'm okay.' So, for a few months until I got myself straight he gave me his overtime. It tells you what a quality person John is. Unselfish and kind. He is one of the guys I miss the most from the plant.

Unfortunately, John's eating habits and smoking caught up with him. He had a heart attack in his mid-fifties.

A serious one by all accounts. John's wife Molly phoned me and told me what had happened. Luckily in the Basildon area, they have a wonderful hospital with a top-class cardiac department, fully manned 24 hours a day. John was literally wheeled off the ambulance and straight into the operating theatre where they fitted stents to his blocked arteries.

I phoned Molly and told her I would pop in and see him after work the next day.

Walking into his ward I expected to see him laid up hooked up to machines with all sorts of tubes coming out. So, I was shocked when he walked over to greet me looking better than I'd seen him for a long time.

He said something to me that I'll never forget.

'I'm never smoking again.' He'd obviously had a visit from some doctor or another telling him he was in there because of his smoking. He looked well; I couldn't believe he'd just had a heart attack. Luckily over time, John made a full recovery. I won't mention the smoking, John!

We still keep in contact and it's always a pleasure talking with him. He must be 70 now; last time I spoke with him he was happily retired and playing golf.

Now the other hoist man was Stephen Battle. AKA, Stevie as he liked to be called. I never called him Stevie, told him it sounded like a tarts name.

Now Steve must have joined us when he was in his mid-twenties. When I first met him he was lean and mean. He had a strong Birmingham accent.

His claim to fame was his uncle on his mother's side was none other than rock star Roy Wood, of The Move and Wizzard fame. Quite ironic when you think two of the hoist man had famous relatives.

I teamed up with Steve when we were both in our mid-thirties. By now the lean had turned to fat. Being a cider drinker was taking its toll on this once skinny man.

I had a lot of admiration for Steve. He was one of these characters that if he took up something he'd give it his all and try and become the best.

I can remember when he was trying to be a knight. He'd joined this bunch of people who dressed up at weekends and pretended it was 1066. He'd have the full metal suit and go into battle … literally.

He took up golf and was playing every bit of spare time he had. I think he near enough became a scratch golfer. But he bored easy, he'd get good at something and that was enough for him. Strangely, he wouldn't wear overalls at work. What he arrived in, he worked in. He'd go out in the same clothes at night. For a while, he adopted the string vest look. Jeans, string vest and his belly sticking out. The lads nicknamed him Onslow, from the character in "Keeping up appearances." I think Steve suffered a bit from dyslexia. Someone had written "Onslow" on his locker.

He said to me one day.

'Why are they calling me Oneslow, Trev? I'm not slow, am I?'

I can remember Tony Lynch coming into our crib and telling Steve he must wear an overall jacket. Tony went back to the office as Steve stripped off stark bollock naked and just put his boots back on and the jacket. He marched into the office and shouted. 'Happy now?'

I can remember coming into work one day and as I walked into the hoist crib, there was a foul smell. Steve and Tony Lynch were sat eating a bowl of soup each.

'We're on the cabbage food diet.' I think Steve lasted a few days. Tony Lynch did it for months.

However, not the plan that was in the book. Tony would eat it Monday to Friday. Then knock back about thirty Guinness's over the weekend.

Steve and I were on opposite shifts but we used to see each other on the changeover. We'd work together some weekends and shutdowns.

One particular shutdown he brought in two pairs of funny buck teeth. They came with putty that would mould them to fit perfectly over your own teeth. We had such a laugh wearing them. The shutdown period signalled a lot of contractors in the plant. These guys had no Idea the teeth were fake. We'd walk up to them and say, 'Excuse me mate, any idea where the toilet is?' They used to give us the double-take look. Great fun. For some reason shut down signalled water fights. I have no idea why, but you'd go somewhere and someone would step out and launch a bucket of water over you? Of course, Steve and I decided to take revenge on anyone who dared to throw water at us.

'Not sure why, but I teamed up with two others to take on the Effluent Plant. They were situated at the bottom of the estate, away from everybody. I think they had sneaked up on us previously and given us a dowsing.

Joining me on the raid was Marky Mark and National Front, George, aka Tripod.

George was a funny looking man, had far-right views and the build of a porn star.

I can remember his daughter getting married. He had nothing but praise about the guy she was marrying. Of course, it wasn't long before he was a granddad.

I can remember bumping into him one day, he'd joined the gardening team and up to that day I always had a laugh and a joke with him. This particular day he had a right mood on.

I asked him what was up and he told me his daughter was getting a divorce.
When he told me the reason it took all my willpower not to burst out laughing.
It turned out that when his daughter left the house, her husband would dress up in her clothes. Apparently, as time progressed, he got more confident and ventured out!
All was good until a neighbour took photos and gave them to his daughter. She showed George and he decided to set a trap. I can't remember what his plan was, but basically, he waited in his car until the son-in-law came out the front door dressed as a woman.
Now George asked me not to say anything, but as the way of life in a large factory, it wasn't long before the scandal broke. To be fair to him, he took it on the chin and later used to joke about it.
So, back to the raid.
We armed ourselves with the water style fire extinguishers, stripped naked apart from boots and dustbin bags covering us. We tiptoed our way there. We could see them up on the roof painting. Not one of our better ideas because we had to climb up onto the roof. Mark and I agreed the best ploy would be to send George up.
'I don't know about that,' he complained.
'Just get up there George; we'll cover your back. When they chase you down Mark and I will be waiting for them.'
So, George made his way up this metal ladder that was bolted to the side of the building. It had safety hoops so you couldn't fall backwards, a good idea but would certainly hinder a quick evacuation, something George was about to find out.
Mark and I stood at the bottom of a ladder ready. Looking up what a sight to behold, George was big in the trouser department and Mark and I were hysterical watching him ascend. This jovial time cost us because before we knew it, we'd been spotted.

Some of the opposition had been working inside the building, had heard Mark and me laughing and came out aiming a fire hose at us.

Luckily, we legged it before this big hose came on.

Unfortunately for George, he had to get back down the ladder. I looked back and could see George now on the ground and running for his life.

George, like another guy I knew years earlier, had large ten to two feet. Stick a red nose on him and he'd pass as a clown.

I'll never forget that vision of George being blasted by that fire hose. The bin bags had been blown off and Mark and I watched as the full power of the water jettisoned him along the road.

'You pair of bastards,' he managed to splutter out as he shot past us.

Like I said earlier in this chapter, getting into your thirties came with a certain amount of maturity.

Steve and Tony Lynch loved to have a sauna. We had one at work, attached to the gym. We weren't meant to use it out of hours, but we did. I went up there one night and Steve and Tony were sitting there with hair dye on?

'You pair of tarts,' I called out.

I had a rather unsavoury sauna with Steve one night. We were both on nights for some reason; there must have been a two-man job that needed doing.

One night after we'd finished, he talked me into having a sauna with him. I don't think he liked going up there on his own in the middle of the night, neither would I come to think of it.

So, we get there, switch it on and strip off and get in.

After a few minutes Steve picks up the bucket and empty's the contents on the coals. The smell of piss hit us like a brick. Some bastard had pissed in the bucket. Christ that smell stayed with me for days. To make matters worse because Steve didn't close the door on the way out the steam hit the

fire alarm. Before we were dressed the alarm went off. We legged it pretty sharpish. It wasn't long before Roy Burton from security visited us.
'You pair of clowns, I saw you scurrying away from the sauna.'
'Not us, Roy.'
'Yes you, I have you on the camera.' Luckily Roy was a friend, still is to this day. He wiped the film off for us. I've always said that Roy Burton is a gentleman!

Steve broke up with his wife, it was a traumatic time for him, and every other poor sod that heard the story over the next few months. I did feel sorry for him; one Christmas his wife had asked him for a divorce and left him. The first day back to work after the Christmas, New Year break he told me he was so close to killing himself. He had the shotgun pointed in his mouth and his finger on the trigger.
I know it was a really bad time for him and I tried to be supportive.
The problem being he couldn't let it go. We'd be out in the plant somewhere doing a job and he'd see someone and call them over.
'You heard I split up with, Chrissie?'
'No, Steve, I hadn't.'
'Yeah, nearly shot myself, I'd had enough. Had the barrel in my mouth, just couldn't pull the trigger.'
A month later:
'Alright, Dave. 'You heard I split up with, Chris?'
'No, Steve, I hadn't. I'm sorry to hear that.'
'Yeah, nearly shot myself, I'd had enough. Had the barrel in my mouth.' I had the finger on the trigger, but luckily I couldn't pull it.'
This went on and on, I don't know how many more times I heard the story until I snapped.
I couldn't take it anymore, I had an outburst.

He was just getting to the punchline with another poor unsuspecting soul when my patience ran out.

'You mention the gun once more I'll pull the fucking trigger myself.'

He sulked for a few weeks then we kissed and made up.

He soon was up and running again. His next-door neighbour was a nice guy who worked in the plant. John Castles, aka, Forrest Gump.

We nicknamed him "Forrest" after we chased him through the plant in a car we had a water extinguisher aimed but couldn't catch him. It was amazing the speed people could run when they saw a guy with a fire extinguisher hanging out of a car window!

Anyway, John was married to a Canadian girl. I'm still friends with John now, He lives in Ontario and loves the Canadian way of life.

I'm not sure if it was a relation of John's wife but Steve had started to write to this Canadian woman. A romance blossomed and he was smitten. He came into work one morning and told me he was having the following week off.

'I see, bit short notice isn't it.' Steve was all sympathetic, but basically, the woman was flying over to see him for a week's visit.

Now, Steve would never do anything by half. So, he hired a stretch limousine to take him to Heathrow and bring them back to Basildon. He used my friend, Lee for the limousine trip.

I'd got Lee into the plant when they were taking on temporary labour. He ended up doing the limo work part-time. So, Steve booked him and on the day in question, I received a phone call from Lee.

'You won't believe what happened at the airport.'

'What?'

'I took him, and he asked me to stand next to him at the arrivals hall as I had the chauffeur's uniform on, so to make him look important. So, we're standing at arrivals, Steve's got a photo in his hand checking out any women that we're walking through on their own. He's looking and this big old woman who kept blocking the view. In the end, Steve shouted at her, "Can you move to one side please, I'm looking for my girlfriend." This woman turned around and shouts, Stevie.' Well, I couldn't stop laughing. Lee told me he looked at the photo and then said to her, 'I take it this is a very old photo.'

No one had seen him for the week. Tony Lynch had invited them both to dinner one evening but Steve cancelled last minute.
'Not like Steve to pass on a free dinner,' I remarked when Tony told me. I knew the real reason, but I kept it to myself.
The following week, he ambled into the hoist crib.
Slumping into a chair he looked all dejected.
I waited a couple of minutes then hit him with it.
'So, how was your week off?'
'Not good, Trev, not good at all.'
'Oh, sorry to hear that mate, did she not turn up?'
'No, she didn't. She sent someone who resembled her mother.'
He then proceeded to tell me the story.
'Christ, Steve, what a nightmare.'
Once again the Whitehead willpower was bought into question as I tried to keep a straight face.
'A whole week with her? What on earth did you do?'
'I only took her out in the dark. It's been the longest week of my life.'

It was around this time we were given a computer in the Hoist Crib. In the early days, there was no restriction on the internet, so we could near enough go to any website. This was all a bit alien to Steve, so he didn't get involved.
His love life was still non-excitant, so I thought I would help my mate.

'You know what you should do.'
'What.'
'Get yourself onto the internet dating game.'
'You reckon?'
'Without a doubt.'
I look at a well-known dating site and it starts showing some women in the Basildon area. Steve's eyes start to pop out.
'She's nice, that one's nice, look at her, she's nice.'
'Calm down mate.'
'She's nice, write to that one, Trev.'
'I can't, you have to join.'
'Sign me up then.'
'It's twenty-five pounds for a month.'
'Money well spent, Trev. Hang on.' He goes off to his locker and comes back with his bank card.
The next ten minutes we spend sorting out his personal details.
'Right they want to know your body shape?'
Steve stood up and tried to suck his belly in.'
'Average, Trev.'
'Interests?'
'Drinking, clay pigeon shooting, darts and golf.'
'You're going to be a real catch for someone, Steve.' John Manning had turned up and showed us how to put a photo in his profile. He was up and running. Steve went home, leaving John and me to make some what we felt were necessary adjustments.
I had kept a note of his internet dating password, so we went back into his profile. John played around with the photo and somehow managed to take about thirty pounds off his weight and ten years off his age.
'That's better, John. We need to make him more interesting. Ten minutes later Steve Battle was a teetotal, tri-athlete, whose hobbies included fitness training, travelling, ice skating, water skiing and mountain climbing. He'd run the London marathon in under four hours.

The next day I came into work on the late shift and Steve was smiling away.
'You'll never guess, I've had over thirty interests and eight messages of women wanting to meet me.'
'Never.'
It's true, Trev. I'm meeting one tonight.'
I must admit I did feel a tad bad, but it had gone past the point of no return. He went home a happy bunny and I logged into his account and put his profile back to what it was before.
The next afternoon I must admit I was a bit apprehensive, but a wave from Steve signalled normality.
'So, how did the date go?'
'Not good. I waited outside the pub but she never showed up. In the end, I went in and I pulled the barmaid. Happy days, Trev.'
Steve eventually settled down with a lovely Irish girl called Catherine. I think her sister was married to Steve's cousin, something like that anyway. She came over from Ireland and lived with Steve.
Steve and I are the same age all bar a day. It would account for our similar sense of humour. On one particular birthday, he came in looking very happy.
'Happy birthday, Steve. What did Catherine get you?'
'A hang-gliding course.'
Now what I can say about Steve, he was a bit adventurous, a bit like the factory's version of Bear Grills.
A few weeks later he tells me he won't be working the weekend.
'I'm going to Sussex to do my hang gliding course.'
'Good luck with that, mate.' Now I must admit I did have my doubts. Steve was at his biggest, he must have tipped the scales at seventeen plus stone. But he was going to a professional flying outfit, so I didn't give it another thought.

Monday morning, I didn't need to ask Steve how it went. He came in and slumped in the chair. A dead giveaway that things hadn't gone well.

He didn't even spike his hair which was unusual. Many a morning he'd walk in, wet his hair and stick his hand in the sugar jar and rub it in his hair. But this particular morning, he just sat there. So, I made him a cup of tea and tried to coax the problem out of him.

'How was your weekend?'

'Disastrous.'

'Oh, sorry to hear that. Hang gliding not go well then?'

'You could say that. I drove two hours to get to this place. Spent a whole morning watching videos, filling out insurance forms. We go outside and jump off a box to simulate a landing, there's only three of us on the course. We have lunch and then the problems start. First, they don't have a flying suit that fits me. I'm eventually squeezed into a suit that makes me look like Norman Wisdom. It wouldn't do up so they tied a string around me. Then they pull these scales out and ask me to get on. I could tell there was going to be a problem. The guy checks my weight and gets on a computer to make the calculations. This is followed by a lot of head nodding. Then they tell me, sorry, Steve. But, for you and our instructor to get enough speed to gain a lift-off you'll need to be running at 42mph.'

'Shit mate, what happened?'

'Do I look like Linford Christie, Trev? What do you think happened, I came home.'

I must admit I did feel sorry for him; he'd had his wings clipped. Talking of wings, he could talk to the birds.

Well, when I say birds I mean pigeons. He'd cup his hands and impersonate a pigeon mating call.

Christ, I used to laugh when all these pigeons were searching for the caller.

He could make the most amazing statues out of nuts and bolts. In fact, certain managers would order a statue off him.
He was a talented guy.
I went with him once to see his uncle Roy at the Cliffs Pavilion, Southend. I think he was billed as Roy Woods Big band at that time. Great concert and because of Steve's family connection we got backstage after and I met the great man himself.
Soon after, Steve was gone. His girlfriend Catherine owned a house in Ireland; I don't think she settled in England. Things at work were changing; we had to do a lot more computer work associated with the job. Steve was struggling to master the computer and that spelt the end for him. We were at that stage where the computer had to be used to log our work and all sorts of other things.
They sent him to a production line, he was too good to be wasted there, so, he took a small package and waved goodbye. Up to the release of this first factory book I'd not heard from him or heard anything about him since the day he left.
However, via a link with his girlfriend Catherine and John Castles we got in touch, and one evening in Thailand and Ireland about a year ago we had a messenger video chat.
Wow, we laughed so much, recounting all the mischief we got up to. Who had passed away and who was still with us He was still living in Ireland, doing well and hadn't changed. Still, that sense of humour I'd known since I first met him. He hadn't read the book but was going to get a copy.
I've not heard from him since. I guess I wasn't too kind about him as I told his story. He most probably read the book and was horrified.
Like John, I miss him. In a perfect world, the three of us would organise a meetup, relive the stories and get drunk. However, I'm 6000 miles away and Steve is somewhere in Ireland. But the beauty of fond memories, no one can take them away.

Chapter 5

The rise of the foot soldier.

I felt the need to get to the next level within the Shop Steward committee. I'd done several years as a junior steward and felt it was the right time to make a move upwards.

I was eyeing a JWC Position, being on the "Joint Works Council," was a prestigious position back in the day. Now my JWC steward was a guy called Eddie Edwards. Not the nutcase with the large glasses who jumped off snowy hills on skis. Our Eddie was a long-serving steward and well-liked within the union.

However, I was ambitious, and I'd had had dealings with stewards getting in my way in the past. I ended up having a major set to with him and something had to give.

The trouble with Eddie, he'd grown weak over the years. It's something I've mentioned before that can happen to a long-serving steward; you get a bit too comfortable.

The problem with Eddie as far as I could tell was that Jimmy Ferris and Les Clemmie had him in their pocket.

This was soon discovered by the *Rat* when he was asked to pay Ferris and Clemmie a visit.

You see the *Rat* was now the convenor, so they asked him, not summonsed like the rest of us.

Eddie had been to see Ferris and Clemmie and tipped them off that I was making a JWC challenge. What a tosser.

He sat and listened as Ferris and Clemmie put their case. They said it was ridiculous that Trevor Whitehead could be on the JWC.

Eddie had served that position well for many years. The Rat told me what was said at the meeting at a later date.

You see I was quietly confident I could take him out; I knew Eddie had backed George Catton when it came to the vote of no confidence.

As much as I was upset with the way they ousted George out, I had supported the *Rat* which meant I had the convenors support, although he kept it to himself.

I had great help from the likes of Geoffrey Martin Smith and another senior steward Alan Phillips.

I also had the backing from another steward who became a great friend. Tony Wilson. Now, Tony, as I mentioned earlier is today a very successful man. I have a lot of time for him and his lovely wife, Pat. They have been happily married for over thirty years now. A bit like Ian and Amanda, Tony being well over six feet and Pat just about five feet nothing. His early beginnings as a steward you would have thought he'd come from a trailer park. Bermuda shorts, boots and vest. He must have used the same tailor as Steve Battle at the time. Despite this, he soon rose up the ranks did our Tony. Despite his looks in those days, Tony was well-spoken; used words that sometimes made me think he'd swallowed a dictionary. The *Rat* kept on at him to smarten himself up, and eventually, he started to wear overalls. Through the *Rat's* help and guidance, Tony was removed from being a final assembly worker to being transferred to the garage repair.

Just by luck one day I was walking past and saw Tony standing by this brand-new toolbox on wheels and all these shiny tools inside. I'd not heard he'd been transferred, so it was a bit of a shock.

'Alright, Tony. What you got there?'

'I'm working in the garage now.'

'Really? They are going to let you loose on these expensive tractors?'

'What's wrong with that?'

'What's wrong with that? I had to come round and hang a pair of curtains for you. Now you're going to be repairing vehicles worth thousands of pounds?'

'Yeah, I know. Funny old world.'

To be fair, and in case a farmer is reading this and about to blame our Tony for his vehicle not starting. Tony never actually picked a tool up. It was just the *Rat's* way of getting him off the production line.

We became good friends and he was a great help getting me on the JWC. He'd seen the weakness in Eddie; it was time for the changing of the guard.

When I think back, Tony and I were lucky we didn't get fired one day.

At the time, the store's foreman was a guy named Alan Morley. Now Alan was born in the wrong era. He would have been the ideal spiv back in the fifties. The pencil moustache and the greased back hair, the strut and the wide boy image. In other words, he looked like a cock.

The stores was located next to the convenors office, so Alan was a frequent visitor. He was a joker, loved to tell a tale and was always ridiculing the store's steward, the one and only "We're all going to get old and die," Paul Norris.

Now as previously mentioned, Paul is another ex-steward who went on to better things. In actual fact, now I'm writing about him, he deserves a lot of credit. Because when I first got to know Paul, he could barely do joined-up writing. His spelling was littered with mistakes. I guess Paul felt like he'd won the lottery with the introduction of *spell-check*.

Now, it was alright for us stewards to mock each other, but we were a solid team, if someone from the outside tried, they'd do it at their peril.

For a while, Alan would come in and take the mickey out of Paul, often when he was sitting there.

The Rat was just as much to blame because he used to sit there laughing at Alan's continued ridiculing.

He did it one day and it was the straw that broke the camel's back as far as Tony and I were concerned.

Tony suggested and I agreed to pay Alan Mortimer a visit on his turf.

We must have looked like the Mitchell brothers on "EastEnders," only difference, we had hair. Marching into the stores, there was no sign of Alan. Undeterred we entered Alan's office and proceed to tip his desk upside down. I can still remember the opened mouth look on the store's guys as we walked away.

Alan came after us; he'd lost face with his men. The *Rat* made us go and apologise, which we did, half heartily.

Fair play to Alan, he could have reported us, but he was happy to see the pair of us apologising and kept it in-house.

Although I think there was a bit of shoving with him and Tony, plus they had a smarmy foreman at the time who I'd love to give a slap.

Anyway, the upshot being, he never took the piss again.

The meeting to elect the JWC members was electric, you could feel the tension. Eddie had underestimated me; he'd also crossed the line by bad-mouthing me behind the scenes.

Not a wise move. The *Rat* was different to Bill Cleary. Where Bill wanted to be the mouthpiece and everybody else keeps quiet, the *Rat* wanted stewards who would speak up. I had a big mouth, so I knew I was his type of steward. Eddie couldn't give me eye contact; it was at that point I knew I was in with a shout.

So, with the help of a few trusted comrades, they did the paper ballot and by a small margin, I had won. To be fair to Eddie, he shook my hand and said well done. He took early retirement soon after. A good shop steward in his day, but his day had gone, times were changing.

Oh, I would have loved to be a fly on the wall when the news filtered through to Ferris and Clemmie.

They'd lost their yes man; I was ready to do battle.
Whispering Les Clemmie had been the manager for about seven years and I could count on one hand the number of times he'd spoken to me. He had no choice now.
Sometimes I think I should ask Geoff what I was like back then. But, I might not like what they say. I know at the time I had a spring in my step and was looking forward to Rattling a few cages.
Unfortunately, I never really got stuck into either of them, within a month they'd both retired.
I couldn't believe it.
All those years of crap from these two characters and I didn't get a chance to give them a taste of their own medicine.
However, I was happy to see the back of Clemmie, he'd kept a tight rein on any overtime all the time he was manager. Must have been his Scottish heritage.
As for Jim Ferris, he left the company at 53?
Fiat didn't see the point of general foremen, so was offered a normal foreman's role but declined.
Pride got the better of him and he left. A strange decision, but I think you could get a full pension those days even at 53!!
He came to see me the day before he departed. I tried not to look too happy because of his imminent departure.
To be honest, I didn't like the bloke, I'd been having a running battle with him for at least fifteen years.
He expected me to forget all that and wish him a happy retirement. He could fuck off.
He gave me a voucher for a free dinner in the canteen.
That went straight in the bin.

As for Les Clemmie, like many others, he left and was never seen again.

Left to right. Me looking scruffy again, Geoffrey Martin Smith, Eddie Edwards, just before he was pensioned off, Paul "Were all going to die," Norris, and the late Richard Llewellyn. I would say this photo was taken in the early 1990s.

I could have written that once I was an elected JWC member they ran for the hills, but this is not a fictional book.
Now, a strange thing happened next.
For some reason, whoever had divvied up the constituencies many years previously had decided that the JWC position that I now held, meant that I now represented the security and fireman as well as a host of others.

I did know a few of the guards, and at the start, I didn't have much to do with them. They had their own steward, Roy Wood. Nice guy, polite and unassuming.
Not sure exactly what happened, but Roy decided to hang up his steward's badge.
The *Rat* put a notice up for a replacement. Unfortunately, as it turned out for me, no one stood.
The *Rat* called me over to his office and explained that they must have a steward. As nobody would volunteer, I'd have to take on the role, after all, I was their JWC member he explained.
'You can't cherry-pick, Trevor. Besides, there's only a few of them, a piece of cake.'
It didn't take long for me to be choking on the said cake.

So, an introduction meeting was arranged. I was a bit apprehensive as what I knew about security and firemen you could write on a back of a matchbox!
For the life of me, I can't remember what went wrong at the first meeting with the Security chief, a big white-haired, red-faced man called Jim McClure. I seemed to be cursed when a new Jim came into my life.
I'd never spoken to the man before. But he wanted to meet me and a time was for a meeting was set. Now big Jim had a number two, George Salmon, I soon discovered he was Jim's spy. I seem to recall I had organised a ballot about something or another, most probably overtime linked as this was always a touchy subject.
I'd heard a rumour about Jim and George picking their favourites to do overtime more regularly than the others. Something I was keen to stop.
Unbeknown to me, Jim didn't like my interference. He and George ran their own ship, how dare I hold a ballot without their knowledge. I'd been tipped off that things might get

heated. Oh, these pair were in for a rude awakening. How dare I interfere with their overtime choice?

So, I turn up at the outer office where a couple of the guards were.

'Through there Trev, and good luck.' My God, you could actually see the fear in their eyes?

I can honestly say I didn't give a monkey about these two clowns. They weren't my supervision, I was going in to represent the men.

I go to the office door and knock, then walk into the hub centre of security. There were monitors everywhere and all sorts of equipment. Jim was sat there like the captain of the starship enterprise.

Funny how some things stick in your mind. Jim McClure's greeting being one of them.

'Think yourself lucky we let you in here. We have a strict rule about letting civilians in.'

What a cock, civilians?

I took an instant dislike to the pair of them and it didn't take long to light the blue touch paper. The previous steward, Roy Wood was off sick with stress, so I couldn't get any pointers from him. However, I had my own source of information regarding Jim McClure.

Jim had only dealt with one of his own as a shop steward, and by the looks of it, he had him in his pocket, so to him, I was a bit of an alien and the big thing with him, he was used to getting his own way.

I won't be far out when I recall what was said at a very brief first meeting. Calling me a civilian wasn't the best of starts.

'I'll fuck off then, shall I?'

'No, I'm just saying we don't normally let civilians in here.'

'Civilian? I'm not a civilian; I'm the man you have to deal with in the future when you fuck up. And what sort of ship are you running here? Not even a cup of tea? Where's your manners?'

Jesus Christ, I kid you not. I thought Jim's head was going to blow up. Already red, I could see the veins in his forehead popping up.

'Do you know who you're talking to?'

'Yes, some trumped-up arse who thinks he's not a civilian. And who the fuck are you?' I pointed at George Salmon.

'George is the supervisor, I've asked him to be here.'

'Well next time you want to bring a sidekick in, you ask me first.' People may read this and think I was a bit over the top. But I'd done my research. I had my own source of information inside the security. I can reveal who it was now as he's long retired. Thanks, Roy Burton.

He remains a friend to this day. He'd told me all about the way this pair treated the men. Well, as the great singer-songwriter Bob Dylan would sing. "The times they are a-changin".

Plus, as I already mentioned, I didn't work for them, I was in a win-win position.

I think it's fair to say the next five minutes were spent hurling insults at each other. George Salmon tried to get in but I pointed at him and told him to shut the fuck up.

At some stage, Jim had picked up the sheet of paper that held the ballot result and ripped it up. In the end, I walked out. The security guards who wished me good luck were still hovering in the outer office. I think it's fair to say I'd gone up a notch or two in the eyes of these guys after that performance.

'Well, that didn't go too bad,' I said as I walked out. A few days later I had to accompany the *Rat* to the Human resources where an attempt was made to smooth things out with Jim and his wounded soldier George.

Much to the dismay of the H/R woman in charge of the meeting, it once again didn't take long to kick off again.

It was obvious to everybody at the meeting that Jim and George didn't want me interfering in the way they run things.

They wanted to control who worked overtime, something they had done unfairly for years.

Roy had already primed me for any shit Jim might come out with.

The *Rat* soon backed me up and eventually, they had no option but to concede. It ended with a limp handshake and a new meeting was arranged.

I seem to recall more guys were hanging around this time when I turned up for round two.

I walked in, and as I sat down, George Salmon asked if I took sugar. He most probably spat in it, but hey, a victory is a victory.

There were only a handful of guards and firemen who were unhappy with my appointment as their steward. They of course were the favourites of Captain Kirk and his sidekick.

It wasn't long before this handful of men started to give me problems.

It certainly was an eye-opener and I could understand why the former steward Roy Wood was still off work with stress. I started to receive mail through the internal post.

Pages and pages of complaints, I sat in amazement reading some of these letters.

What I found strange was these letters were long in content; it must have taken a long time to type them out?

Why they couldn't just come and see me sort of told me the type of person I was dealing with. I should mention that it came as no surprise that all the letters arrived without being signed? Today they would be known as "Trolls."

Four or five of them had written to me, telling me all sorts of stories, where I was going wrong, watch out for so and so. How this was unfair, how that should be changed. It soon became apparent that these guys had too much time on their hands.

It didn't take a genius to work out that these people writing to me were the guys who used to be Jim and George's favourites.

I did feel for the other guys, they'd been treated badly by Jim and George, or Batman and Robin as I renamed them for years. I'd had similar experiences with Jim Ferris previously.
He had his favourites and would look after them, much to the decrement of the rest of us in that department.
I'm not going to knock the previous shop steward Roy Wood. It is more difficult when you work for the man you're taking on. But, Roy and his predecessors had been in Jim's and George's pockets. It didn't take long for me to sort out Jim's spy.
I was in the convenor's office doing something and a fireman had spotted me. Now, these guys had not had someone speaking up for them for a long time. So, they had plenty to gripe about. I didn't mind and I would help when I could. Now this fireman was a nice guy, he had a genuine problem and wanted some advice.
'You got a minute, Trev?'
'Sure, what's up? Well, while this guy is asking me something, George Salmon walked in and started to bollock this guy in front of me.
'Who permitted you to leave the job? You need to clear it with me and request a meeting with the steward.'
Now, technically that was true. But I wasn't having this man throwing his weight around in front of me. I grabbed him by his tie.
'Hang on George. Don't come into this office without knocking. Secondly, if you ever embarrass one of my members again I will personally take you around the back here and beat the living daylights out of you. Now fuck off.'
'Did you hear that, he threatened me?' Cried out a shocked George.
'I didn't hear anything,' smiled the fireman.
'Trust me, George. You ever pull a stunt like that again; you'll live to regret it.'
'Jim will hear about this.'
I hope not, George. Close the door on the way out.'

What a jumped up horrible man.
Whether George told Jim about our little set to I'll never know. I never heard another word about it.
What I will say, George Salmon was a nasty shit. He had no respect for his men and thought he could do what he liked.

I have to say; on the whole, I found the security and fireman an odd bunch. They had some strange ideas, and I soon found out that I had to be very careful what I said to them.
They could recite something I said a year previously. I might say something to a couple of them and they'd say …. 'You've changed your tune. Last November when I spoke to you in the foyer, you remember, when you were going home, you said such and such.' Unbelievable.

Now, the following incident you'll read, and you'll think I've exaggerated the story. But word for word this is true. After you read the following you'll have some idea what I was up against with these security guards.
Again, let me add, most of these guys were great, but some were complete morons.
I was working away in the Hoist Crib when Tony Lynch came and spoke to me.
'Get your arse down to Thurrock, there's a major problem with the security down there. You can take the security pool car.'
Oh well, I thought this will kill a couple of hours. Now the Thurrock depot was some eighteen miles away. It was basically a packing place. Can't remember how many worked there, maybe a hundred-odd. At the time, security was made up of current and a couple of contractors. Now, the two contract guards were ex-company guards. They had worked there for years and some deal was struck so they could retire, then come back working for a contractor. I'm trying not to muddy the water here by over-explaining why there were some contract guards. It will become clearer later.

So, I drive to Thurrock, wondering what the hell this major problem was. So, I parked up and look over to the guardhouse. I can see a guard nicknamed "Little Shit."
Time has dulled my memory of this man; I think he was called Kevin Crisp. His nickname said it all.

I walk over to the guardhouse and there he is waiting for me, arms folded.
'You took your time?' He moans. I ignore the little shit and move on.
'So, what's the problem?'
'I'll tell you the problem, look at that?' He marches inside the guardhouse and opens the fridge, passing me a half-used carton of milk.
'What's this?'
'That's my milk, Trevor. And this guy has been using it to make his tea!'
Now, the guy he's pointing to is one of the contract guards. A man who only a few weeks previously, had been his shift partner before he took early retirement.
'You are joking with me, I hope?'
'I'm not joking with you; this man is a thief.' It didn't take a rocket scientist to work out that little shit had a grudge against this man and had been waiting for him to slip up.
I was a bit flummoxed for a minute; I wasn't sure how to react. It was the contract guard that put things into perspective.
'I hold my hands up, Trevor. I did use the milk a couple of times in my tea, but it's not like we pay for it.'
'What?'
'No, the canteen slips us a few cartons every couple of days, bless them. We help them out with the delivery's.'
I turned to little shit.
'Let's get this perfectly clear. You've made a song and dance about some missing milk that was taken by a former work partner of yours. Milk, that you didn't even pay for?'

'That's not the point, It's the principle, Trevor.'
I won't write what my response was to his principal, I'll leave you to imagine what was said.
See, I told you you'd think I had exaggerated. I kid you not, that is a true story.

In time things between Jim and I settled down, a fair overtime rota was set up and the letters stopped once I told a few of them that any letter coming to me via the internal mail system went straight to the paper shredder.

The reason contractors were helping out at Thurrock was the security had been outsourced to another company.
I don't want to run ahead of things so that unsavoury business has yet to come.

I guess I'm at the right stage in the book to bring in the other village idiot.
Come on down, *Pat Brown*, the time is right.
Pat Brown worked and represented the engine side of things. Five minutes in his company and you'd wonder if the shop stewards committee were participating in "It's a Knock-out." Our younger readers won't remember that show, but it was fun to watch, and at any particular time you could play your joker. Enter Pat Brown.
The first time I met Pat I thought he was going out to rob a bank. He looked like he had a stocking covering his face, it took me a while to realise that was his natural look. Obsessed with the German's, it wasn't long before I named him *Pat von Brown*.
Even more amazing was the fact that Pat was not only a shop steward, but he was also a JWC member too. He'd taken over from George Sharpe who had retired. Sadly, George passed away not long into his retirement. It's a bitter blow when that happens, you work all your life and your time is cut short. His

son Andy still works at the plant. So much like his dad, it's uncanny.

The likes of George will never be seen again, firm with his guys but fair and well-liked. I still miss his dry wit even to this day. Around the same time, we lost another recently retired shop steward, Dave Edwards, or Rupee Edwards as he was known amongst us stewards after a reggae singer.

A smashing guy, too nice to be a steward. I can always remember he called the gym …. Gymenasium?

'You off to the gymenasium then, Trev?'

'I am, Dave.' I never corrected him.

Dave had replaced the lazy tyke, Bo Varney, as the garage steward.

After he retired I'd see him occasionally in the plant. He was a part-time tour guide, still smiling away and proud to show people the wonders of the Basildon Tractor Plant.

I was shocked and stunned to hear he had passed away. George and Dave were only in their mid-fifties when they passed.

Back to Pat.

Before I renamed him, Pat was known as Postman Pat. He had been given this name for good reason.

Once in a blue moon, the factory would have a fire drill. It was always hush-hush so it made it more realistic.

The whole plant had to empty and you had to get out into the car park where your particular evacuation monitor would tick your name off.

So, after the drill and once we got back into the factory, a whisper started about the count up. Everyone was accounted for, except one person. I'm talking maybe three thousand people at the time.

I guess with Pat's face, he'd never be known as "Lucky." But what are the odds of you slipping out to the Post Office at the same time as a major evacuation drill?

The company went mad with Pat. I think the *Rat* had to calm things down. I'm sure Pat had a few days suspension over the incident. You could get away with a lot of things as a steward, but that day Pat crossed the line.

Another Pat Brown classic was when he'd hurt his ankle at home. He hobbled into work then limped over to the convenors office.
It will remain anonymous the two stewards who suggested they'd fake an accident for Pat.
Someone came up with the bright idea of spilling some oil on the stairs that led up to the toilet. So, they made Pat sit at the bottom of the stairs and phoned the medical. Some oil was trickled onto the stairs.
The buggy with the stretcher attached arrived and whisked Pat off to the medical.
It's hard to describe Pat, he was an odd-looking man, I did mention the stocking over the head look, but I guess the best description of him I can think of is …. Gormless.
So I watched as Pat was driven through the factory sat up on the stretcher waving at people with that gormless look. I'm sure he thought he was a dignitary waving at his people. In Pat's defence, there was no way he thought of this spilt oil ploy. The two stewards in question hadn't quite thought it through.
Someone from the company health and safety department arrived at the accident scene and immediately smelt a Rat. I think they suspected some form of foul play.
Rumour has it that Dennis Morley arrived at the medical to check on Pat before he was taken off to Basildon Hospital. A shoe inspection was carried out and Pat's shoes were confiscated and Dennis locked them away. Not a drop of oil on either of them.
When Pat was involved you could guarantee things wouldn't go quite as planned.

A Christmas meal and drink up for the JWC members was arranged at Boreham House. This was a huge mansion type building on the outskirts of Chelmsford. It was used for all sorts of things.

It was my first chance to meet my new manager, Keith Davies. Over a few drinks, he told me his goal was to be Plant Manager. He was a lightweight in the drinking department and his wife turned up to take him home.

This night out with the JWC and management later became known as "Fedoragate."

The day in question, the *Rat* turned up looking like Malcolm Allison, a football manager who was flamboyant and would often be seen smoking a cigar and wearing a Fedora hat. The *Rat* wore the hat and it was his pride and joy.

As the drinks flowed things started to get out of hand. The *Rat* had unwisely left the fedora on the bar. Sorry, Geoff, I'm not taking all the blame for this one. Between Geoff and me we started filling the hat with all sorts, beer crisps, cigarette butts, the drunker we got, I think the worse the hat got abused. At some point, Geoff and I saw some sort of sense and did our best to clean the hat up. Basically, I washed it out with beer and stuck it on a radiator to dry.

A few hours later we piled onto the minibus, the *Rat* was the last to get on. He was drunk and unsteady on his feet. He slurred at the driver.

'Hang on, I've forgotten my hat.'

'No, you haven't, I've got it here.' Geoff threw the *Rat's* hat to him and he put it on his head. Unfortunately, and what we later discovered was a decent Fedora doesn't take kindly to being abused. The hat had shrunk and was perched high on the *Rat's* head.

'What have you done to my hat, Geoff?'

'It wasn't me, it was Whitehead.'

I never did thank you for dropping me in it, thanks, Geoff. Well, we headed back to Basildon and all the way the Rat was whinging and whining.

'Cost forty-five pounds this hat, it's ruined.' The *Rat* was lashing Geoff then me.

'Expected better of you, Geoff.'

'Nothing to do with me. I told you, it was Whitehead.'

The Rat kept wining at me until I could take no more. I grabbed the hat off the *Rat's* head and threw it out of the window.

'There, fuck the hat.'

To be honest I can't remember much more about that night. For some unknown reason, the driver didn't drop us home, but at the Fords social Club. I vaguely remember standing there with a beer wondering what the hell I was doing there.

Of course, the next day at work the Fedoragate scandal was red hot news.

Like any good story, it didn't take long to spread through the plant. The *Rat* didn't like the fact he was the subject of a piss-take.

The funny thing now, as I think back. It was only a hat. And as much as he went on about the cost, he wouldn't have paid for it, that would have come out of some manager's expenses.

The way the *Rat* was going on you'd have thought I'd launched his pet dog out the window.

Poor *Rat*, he couldn't believe two of his most trusted stewards could behave that way.

You have to remember, the hat to him was another status symbol. A vainer person I've yet to meet. He was beyond insecure. He started to dye his hair and moustache; it made him look odd, with his pale skin and jet-black hair. I see it a lot here in Thailand, old men with jet black hair, they look ridiculous.

He'd walk into the canteen in the morning and chat one of the canteen women up for a free packet of cigarettes.

He was a big lump *Rat*, maybe six-two and thickset. He sauntered over and sat with some of us stewards; it was a bit of a morning ritual. We'd have a cuppa first thing before heading off to various locations. This particular morning, he looked like a cock.

It was the blackest I'd seen it. A grey hair or two must-have surfaced on his moustache and eyebrows because they'd been dyed the same colour.

This isn't an excuse but I used to get egged on by Alan Philips, he was the *Rat's* deputy. A fantastic character and loved the banter. As the *Rat* was getting his morning freebie packet of fags, Alan set me up.

'Trevor, look at the state of his hair?' I take a look and when he sits down I have a little dig.

'Bloody hell. What have you done to your hair? I'm a friend, so I'll tell you. You look a c*** mate. Grow old gracefully.'

I think Alan and myself would have made a good double act because he would set me up, then come out with something like this.

'Oh, listen to Whitehead. That's a nasty thing to say. It looks good.' Of course, the *Rat* loved his ego rubbed.

He had a real issue with his penis size.

As I said, he was a big lump, but he had all sorts of insecurities including his manhood.

He had a heart to heart with me one day on how he thought women would think he'd be big in that department because of his body size. I'm not sure I was the right person he should be talking to. I mean, I wasn't the most sympathetic of people.

'I see, so has someone complained then?'

'No, of course, not. I'm just saying, I wonder if they expect something a bit bigger.'

'Yes, I can see your point. You strip off and your little penis is poking out.'

'It's not little, it's average.'

'Depends on what you mean by average?'

'I mean it's normal size.'
'What's normal?'
'Well let me tell you, I've had no complaints.'
'They're not going to say anything to you, are they? No, they will hide their disappointment to save your ego. Besides some woman like a small todger, so I wouldn't worry about it.'
'I haven't got a small todger.'
'Yes, you have, I caught you in the shower that time.'

The colouring of his hair reached new heights when we were outside for some meeting or another. I can only liken it to an episode of Dad's Army. The one where Private Frazer, the Scottish undertaker does his best to make the platoon look younger. It works until they are parading outside and it starts to rain, causing all the hair colouring to run down their faces. Well, I'm not sure if the *Rat* had used a cheap brand, but it started to rain and he befell the same outcome. One of the few times I nearly felt sorry for him.

I'm being careful what I write about the *Rat*, he was a one-off, a convenor that in my opinion grew to be a monster. But in those early years, he was good at his job.
However, he became the butt of many of our jokes. He couldn't handle me; he used to complain about my lack of respect for the other stewards.
He'd bring a lot of my one-liners on by himself, aided by the ever wind up merchant, Alan Phillips.
Many a time Alan would kick it off. I walked into the office one day and Alan was sitting with the *Rat*.
'Here, Trev. The *Rat* was just telling me he went out last night and was chatted up by a lovely looking blonde.'
'Fuck sake, you still hanging around that old age people's home?'
Another time.

'Trev, *Rat's* been telling me how he resembles Engelbert Humperdinck?'
'Really? I'd say more like Elvis on the day he died.'

When I think back to this period, I guess it was my golden years. The best is yet to come in this period, but let's get back to work.
It's funny, but as I write this I realised I never really grew up. I continued to look at opportunities to have a laugh or play a joke.
Those teeth that Steve Battle got me a few years earlier I still used occasionally. Steve was into magic and had ordered the two sets from a joke and magic shop in Cleethorpes of all places.
One particular day I decided to give my old mate Pat McGowan a visit. He worked in the stores and I was after some tool or another.
I slipped the teeth in and the stood by the hatch and rang the bell.
Pat sauntered up and took the stores chit off me.
He halt walked away, then stopped. He'd caught a glimpse of the teeth. Now I'm not sure I gave these joke teeth justice earlier. They looked so real, just that they would have been more suited for a horse.
'What's happened to your teeth, Trev?' He asks as I give him my best smile.
'I've broken my other teeth, so I've had to dig these old chestnuts out.'
'Bloody hell, they look a bit on the big size, you lost weight or something?'
'No, they were my granddads, better than nothing.'
'Trust me, nothings better than wearing them.' He laughed as he went off in search of the item I needed.
While he was gone I whipped the teeth out and stuck them back in my pocket.

When he came back and saw my normal look he cursed me with all the curse words he could think of.
I had a lot of time for Pat, another guy with a dry sense of humour.

Me breaking in a set of teeth for Red Rum.

I followed Pat's path in a way. He ended up retiring to Thailand, a route I would take a few years later.

Once I settled down in the land of smiles, I made contact with Pat via his brother Danny who I was friends with on Facebook. Many a time we would have a three-way Skype call. We would laugh and joke and reminisce like you do when you look back. Pat always mentioned the teeth, that episode had obviously tickled him.

Danny was always a good picture and sound, Pat, who was less than a hundred kilometres away was often blurred and his sound was often breaking up.

I'd been here about four years when Danny informed me he was coming to Thailand to visit Pat.

I should add that Pat and Danny were married to a Thai national.

I hadn't heard from Pat for some time so I was happy to hear they were coming to Pattaya for a few days. I wasn't that far from Pattaya and we arranged for me to visit their hotel.

Danny was waiting for me in the reception; it was good to see him in the flesh instead of a computer screen.

He told me that Pat hadn't been well and was preparing me so I didn't look shocked when I saw him.

Poor Pat, he'd lost an ear through Cancer, this had happened only recently and it had affected the side of his face as well.

He was so pleased to see me and I stayed for a couple of hours as we had a beer and a right old catch up. Pat's wife was there along with Danny's two children.

We arranged to meet the next day, but the following morning Danny phoned and informed me they were going back to Pat's house in Bangkok.

It was the last time I saw either of them. It came as a shock, but no surprise that Pat passed away a few months later. He was seventy.

I kept Facebook friends with Danny but we only used to send each other birthday wishes and the odd Merry Christmas. October last year (2020) I sent him a happy birthday. Now he always used to thank me, but after a few days, I'd heard nothing. I checked his profile and although there had been no new posts for a few months, there was no indication that Danny was no longer with us.

I sent a message to a mutual friend Joe Cantwell who informed me Danny had died of cancer in May. Danny would have been around 64. Two nice guys, taken too soon.

Me sandwiched between Pat and Danny McGowan.

Now, after security had eventually settled down, I then got sidetracked by another mob. The air tool crib.
Now I should say I'm still friends with two out of the four. The other two went mad. Maybe I'm a tad unkind as one of them did end up in the hospital with some mental health issues.
The other became a foreman. Now to be fair, they were good trade union supporters and good supporters of mine.
I did often wonder why they used to play up. They were on a good thing. If that was me I would have kept my head down. How they managed it remains between them and the manager at the time. But they were getting three shifts pay for working a double day shift.
So, they were extremely lucky. But for some reason, they were always complaining about something. I have a feeling I might get some contact from two of them after they read this. But, I'm afraid to say the four of them were the classic example of the many backstreet lawyers we had in the plant.
I won't bore everybody with their numerous complaints; it got so bad once I had to bring the union's district officer in. The meeting with the officer went from bad to worse when the four of them told him they pay his wages?
What a thing to say to a guy who gave up his time to try and help them.
They'd quote things from all different sources, Internet researched they'd hit me with all sorts. With these guys and security, it was a wonder I didn't go mad as well.

Christmas time was always fun at work, with a few freebie dinner invites. I think after our last Boreham House Christmas dinner, the manager had sent a message to our Plant Manager asking that the JWC have a Christmas bash at another place in future.
The fall out from *Fedoragate* had reached many places.
The Rat had purchased another hat and he could ill afford to lose another one.

We'd always try and raise some money for a local handicap school during the festive season. The stewards would man the gates and we'd embarrass a few pounds out of the workforce. Later in the morning, we'd go around the offices catching the staff. One year sticks in my mind. Tony Wilson and I were tasked to go around the offices. We had done the previous year with Barry Mansfield and Geoff. For some reason, they weren't available so the Rat gave us another steward.

'Take George with you,' ordered the *Rat*.

Enter another George, *George Payne*. Steward for the hydraulics.

Now, George was no village idiot, he just spoke like one. He regularly got his words mixed up. George was a good runner, he'd done a few marathons. I had not long got into running and had the London marathon on my bucket list. Some lunchtime's I'd join George, along with a guy called Greek George and another good runner Tony Baker. They'd set off and I'd try and keep with them. We didn't run far, normally 5k. One day it was just me and George, and I made a big mistake trying to run his legs off. Now George was giving a good twenty-plus years away to me, plus he carried a bit of weight around the middle.

This particular lunchtime he said, 'You take the lead and I'll run along at your pace.' "Run along at my pace," I thought, cheeky bastard.

I had been running well (Or so I thought.) So, I set off, steady for the first kilometre, and then I started to pick the pace up. By the fourth Kilometre, I was a spent force, reduced to a gentle jog. George shot past and I never saw him again until I staggered back into work and he was coming down from the locker room, changed!!

'What, you fall over.'

It was a classic case of the tortious and the hare.

So, Tony, George and I set off to the admin office block on the last day before the Christmas break with a bucket in hand. These people in the offices we didn't really know that well. Occasionally I'd recognise someone from the cricket, but on the whole, they were complete strangers.

I won't use the word intimidation, but we didn't let anyone escape the bucket.

I chased a guy in the toilet once. Tony and I were old hands at this game, I let Tony and George hold the bucket and I'd watch for the runners. Trust me when I tell you there was a few of them.

You'd always get the odd tight arse trying to dodge the bullet. I watched this one make a dash for the toilet.

'Give me the bucket,' I demanded as I closed in on this runaway.

He thought he was safe, locked into one of the cubicles. I went into the cubicle next door, put the lid down, climbed up and hung my arm over with the bucket.

'We're collecting for the children at Elmbrook School, Sir. Would you like to contribute?'

There were three or for portacabin offices outside the admin. Obviously, they had run out of office space and the portacabins were for the overflow.

'Come on George, get in there with the bucket.' Tony passed George the bucket and we stood back. Now I'm not sure if the door was just stiff or they'd seen us coming and locked it. But George couldn't get the door open. This caused great amusement to Tony and me.

'Come on George, put your back into it.' He tried his hardest and the door wouldn't budge.

'For fuck sake George, let the dog see the rabbit.' Called out Tony.

I could see people in the office and they weren't escaping the bucket. Tony tried a shoulder charge and bounced back.

'See, let's leave it.' Suggested George.

Now, this was George's maiden collection, he didn't take into account the willpower of the two hardy veterans collecting alongside him.

'Fear not, George, it just needs a bit more persuasion.'

I took a run up and the door flew in with me attached to it, straight off the hinges.

I'm crumpled up on top of the door which is now on the floor, the frame as well.

This seemed to take the wind out of George and when spoke it came out something like this.

'Collection school we are Elmbrook, contribute like bucket the children?'

I stood up, wondering what the hell George was on about. The whole office was in stunned silence. We decided that this time they could escape the bucket as we made a quick departure.

I think that we escaped any punishment for wrecking the door as it was Christmas. I'm pretty sure the following year they saw us coming had had the door open ready.

Poor old George, it was a baptism of fire that I don't think he recovered from. It was certainly his only time doing the bucket collection

I can't remember what happened to him, he retired and I have never heard from him since. He'd be well into his eighties now; I hope he is still with us.

*A Christmas collection line up, I'm guessing early-90s.
Left to right.
Tony Wilson, the late Barry Mansfield, myself and crouching down Geoffrey Martin Smith.*

For some reason, my manager, the Plant Manager in waiting, Keith Davis was shipped out.
It came as a bit of a shock because he even had me believing he would be the next plant manager. But like an earlier manager, Les Clemmie, we never got the chance to lock horns before his sudden departure.
It's funny because I hadn't had a lot to do with him up to that point. Keith had a clerk who became my best friend. *Steve Jarvis*. Steve used to worry about Keith Davies and me. He knew I was a bit unpredictable when it came to dealing with management.

'Tread careful, Trevor. He is not a man to forgive easy.' Well, I never had a lot of time to test this out as one day I came in and Keith was gone.

I'll take a pause here and breathe a sigh of relief. Keith has recently become a Facebook friend and I was worried about what I had written about him four years ago.
Luckily he got away lightly, considering how some of the other guys have fared.

So, a new manager was appointed, one *Michael Newman*. Now, Michael wasn't everybody's cup of tea. But out of all the managers I had before and after, Michael was the only one I got to like.
He was a very fair guy. He'd worked his way up to that position from the tools, like a few others, but he never forgot his roots. He was always willing to negotiate with me.
First impressions you'd think he was a solemn man and very serious. He wore these half-rimmed glasses and when I had meetings with him, they'd be perched at the end of his nose. Dry sense of humour, and behind the scenes he was a nice guy. Michel will feature later on, as I feel it's time to get to the Tony Lynch era.

Chapter 6

A born comedian.

I can't remember how many foremen I had over a thirty-six-year period. Some were insignificant, some stood out and some I choose to forget.
Alf Nicholson was my first maintenance foreman. Ex-navy he could recount numerous stories of the war.
I can remember him bollocking me once about not working weekends. I was 18 and single. Working weekends would come later.
He had a sidekick at the time, John Teague: Insignificant man.
Andy Rae, a short Scottish guy who wore a perm that made him look ridiculous.
He made the mistake of not believing me when I said a tractor was pissing out oil.
I didn't think to mention the oil would squirt out at a rapid speed as soon as I hit the hydraulics lever.
We were in the vehicle repair shop when this incident happened.
'I can't see any oil?' He hollered at me as he looked closely at the back of the tractor.
Well, I thought I'd give the lever a quick pull, just to show him where the oil was coming from.
So, I started the tractor, pulled the lever and heard a scream.
Poor old Andy had taken a full headshot. He was dripping; it was that bad he had to go home to have a shower and change.
He headed off to Canada, never to be heard off again.
Dave Noble, well I thought he was a bit of a manic depressive; he was so up and down.
One weekend he told me to get in the passenger seat of his car with a fully charged water fire extinguisher.

We drive out of the factory and into the car park where one of the lads, Paul Humphrey was sweeping up rubbish.
'Squirt him between the eyes,' I was told. So I wind down the window and as we pull up I let Paul have it.
Dave never told me what Paul had done, but that was his way of dealing with a problem.
I saw Paul later and he didn't have a clue what it was about either.
Needless to say, our Dave didn't last long.
Once we were hit with the three-shift system, we had the three musketeers, Ken Lawrence, Ricky Hunt and the people's choice, Tony Lynch.
Three different characters you'd ever get to meet.

Ken, well I've said it many times, way too nice and soft to be a supervisor. I liken him to a football manager; you know when you hear the story of "He's lost the dressing room."
In Ken's case, he never had the dressing room to start with. It was because of his easy-going nature that we used to get regular visits from that shit Jim Ferris.
You should have stood up to him Ken, he never visited the other two shifts?

Ricky Hunt, well he was the dead opposite to Ken. He'd run around like a headless chicken. Played football well into his forty's. Very competitive, I lost count of how many times he wanted to race me up the stairs.
A likeable guy when he wasn't my foreman.

Now our Tony was in a league of his own. A born comedian if I ever met one.
He turned up one day out of the blue. As I mentioned it was the time we started the three shifts and he was transferred from being a production General foreman to a normal Forman in maintenance.

To be honest I didn't have a lot to do with him in his early years. He was on a different shift to me, so only if there was a problem and the steward was needed would we communicate. Tony was Irish, and he looked Irish. I think I mentioned earlier in the book that he reminded me of the great Irish comedian, Dave Allen.

He liked a beer did our Tony, and many a late shift he would pop down the Irish club for a quick pint or two.

Jolly told me a funny story about him once when he was trying to sweep the office out after Tony had returned from his liquid late shift lunch. Tony was leaning against some filing cabinets and as he went to move out of Jolly's way both feet shot up in the air. It didn't take much to get Jolly in hysterics at the best of times. Tony needed a hand up but Jolly was on all fours laughing hysterically and incapable of helping him.

As time went on, and we reduced in numbers, we were left with two foremen to look after us. Tony, and a nice guy named Paul Wellstead.

Steve Battle and I named them, Ugh and Wah. You'd go into the office and ask them something and Paul would just grunt. 'Ugh.' Followed by a Tony, 'Wah.' Which I took as a shortened version of What?

I've already mentioned the Tony Lynch weight loss programme. Cabbage soup Monday to Friday followed by a weekend of Guinness.

He loved a punt on the horses, and he'd always book the Cheltenham week off.

Paul liked a bet, but he was a dog man. Now, I'm not sure if Paul had a problem at some point with gambling.

He never mentioned it and I certainly wasn't going to ask. But his wife kept a tight control on his purse strings. He was on good money, but he never had a lot on him at any time. His dog betting was only small amounts. He was a secret smoker too. Before he went home, he had a ritual of washing his face and hands before popping in a chewing gum.

'Surely your wife can smell the smoke on you?' I asked him once.
'She does, but I blame you guys.'
It didn't take a lot of working out who wore the trousers in that house.
After Tony retired, Paul came into his own. He was a decent guy to have supervise you. Let you get on with things and always spoke to you in a civil manner.
Unlike Tony, who had a touch of Tourette's. Tony and I had a good foreman/steward relationship.
He was a bit like Dave Noble in the sense that I never knew if he was joking or not.

Let me tell the story of the Stannah chairlift saga with Marky Mark and Jolly.
This incident has stuck with me since it happened.
At the time, Tony was a bit dodgy on his legs. He had been a heavy smoker and I think he was having circulation problems. To be fair to the guy, he quit smoking and over time recovered. But at the time of this Stannah chairlift joke, he was at his worst movement-wise.
His office was up one set of stairs and it was a struggle for him to get up and down.
So Mark thought it would be a good idea to put an advert for the chairlift on his office door window.
Tony wasn't amused, at least that was the impression I got. He phoned me and told me to go to his office. When I got up there he pointed to the advert.
'Look what those pair of Kunts have done?'
'Who?'
'Marky Mark and Jolly.'
'How did you know it was them?'
'I fucking know the pair of Kunts.'
'I want an apology.'
'Alright, let me talk to them.'

So I wander off in search for the pair of Kunts as Tony aptly called them.
I didn't have to look far and they were still in laughter mode.
'Tony's not amused, he wants you to go up and apologise.'
'It's only a joke, Trev.' Remarked, Mark.
'Well, he hasn't seen the funny side. Come on, I'll go up with you, and Jolly stop laughing.'
So we waited five minutes for Jolly to compose himself. I did worry that he'd lose the plot again, but Tony was waiting so we couldn't wait for Jolly any longer.
We go up and I knock on the door.
'Come in,' Tony calls out, so I escort the condemned pair in.
Tony starts and I immediately realise this is going to end badly. To be fair to Mark and Jolly, I think Tony's opening statement contributed to the howls of laughter that would follow a few seconds later.
He sat there with his feet up on the desk.
'As you well know, I may well lose the use of my legs.' That was as far as Tony got because by then Jolly had collapsed onto the floor in hysterical laughter, enough to set Mark off. How I didn't crack I will never know.
Tony ordered them out of his office then informs me that one more outburst and he would be writing the pair of them up.
Now I'd been around long enough to know that was an empty threat. No way was Tony going to highlight his health problems.
But I said I would go and speak to them and bring them back in. Outside I explained that they needed to stop with the laughing. Jolly I had my doubts about, and the problem being if he started again it would start Mark off.
So I took Mark in first on his own. He listened to Tony and apologised. He was bollocked, but that was the end of the matter.
Taking Jolly in was like a lottery, I didn't know if he could hold it together long enough. Luckily Tony didn't use the same

opening statement and I managed to get Jolly in and out without any more laughter.
To this day I can't tell if he was serious about the incident. He never smoked again, that is no easy task.

I was working on a hoist out in the factory one day and an operative asked me a question.
'What's he like your foreman?'
'Who?'
'Scissors.'
'Scissors, who the hell is Scissors?' Then the penny dropped, he was talking about, Tony.
You see Tony would stand out in an aisle way, legs apart, hands tucked in the back of his trousers with his elbows jutting out. "Scissors," I loved that name for him.
I have many stories about Tony. His two favourite words were "Wah and Kunt."

I was working on a late shift, it must have been around the summertime as it wasn't getting dark until around nine. I'd had my dinner and was checking a hoist when "Bones" called me in a panic.
Now Mark Lewin was aka Bones. This was a name given to him by my good friend and work colleague Bob Fellows.
The name stuck the rest of his working life. Mark was short and skinny. He'd been transferred to our department and ended up working with Bob and me for a while. We didn't get off to the best of starts.
We'd been working inside a big wash machine. It was hot and sticky. We'd finished the job and Mark had gone off to get something. I climbed out and proceeded to wipe the grease off my hands on a bit of rag. I chucked it in the dustbin and Mark returned minus his shirt.
'Christ that was warm in there.'
'It certainly was, anyway it's all done now,' I announced.

'Great, shall we have a cuppa?'
'Good idea.' I start to walk off and Mark calls out to me.
'Trev, you seen my shirt?'
'Can't say I have mate.' I walk back and help him look. What colour is it?'
'Yellow.' I search around and can't see it.
'Strange, where could that have gone?' Mark then spots the yellow "rag" in the dustbin. Pulls it out and holds it up.
'You C***.' Not the best of starts!

Anyway, Bones turns up in a right old panic.
'I need help, Trev. You used to do yellow lines, didn't you?'
'Long time ago, Mark. Why what's up?'
'Best if I show you.' We amble outside and by the entrance to the factory was a large yellow lined cross-hatch square, painted to warn people not to park there. Now, this crosshatch had been there since the plant opened, occasionally it was repainted when it had faded.
Tony Lynch had instructed Mark to freshen it up. I should add here that we didn't have a late shift supervisor. Tony gave us the jobs and we were left to our own devices after 6 pm.
Now, this crosshatch had been painted with two-inch-wide yellow lines for at least thirty years. When we get there, I see a mess.
'What the fuck, Mark. What have you done?'
'I tried to paint it by hand, but it's not straight.' Basically, Mark had painted three sides of the square and the lines were all squiggly.
'Where's your string?'
'String? What do I need string for?'
'To keep the line straight, you muppet.' We go off and get some string. The time we get back, it's just starting to get dark.
'We need to straighten these three out before you do any more.' I helped Mark the best I could but because of the squiggly lines, to get them straight, the line had gone from two

inches wide to six. We just about finish the third line as the darkness beats us.

'You'll have to finish it off tomorrow, Mark. You've made a lot of work for yourself now.'

'No problem, it will look good the time I finish it.'

'Well make sure you use the string in future.'

'Will do, thanks, mate.' I walked off and thought no more about it.

The next afternoon I'm walking in and I see Tony in his "Scissors" position talking to Bones. Spotting me he called me over in his normal polite way.

'Whitehead, come here.'

Now Tony would pull a sort of gurning type of face when he was angry and close one eye. I can liken it to a "Popeye" look. This is word for word how the conversation went. Bones stood there bemused as Tony let fire.

'Tell me something, would you pay some kunt, eighty punds to paint tree yellow lines?' Because of his closed eye, I wasn't sure who he had directed the question at.

'You asking me?'

'Yes, you Kunt, I'm not asking this stupid kunt, am I?'

'Eighty pounds for three yellow lines?' I did the maths in my head.

'That's a tad over twenty-six pounds a line, yes, sounds a bit steep.'

'A bit steep, yer a kunt, Bones. And while I'm at it, why the fuck have you made them so big?'

'Just bringing them up to Government standard size, Tony.' Mark had obviously had time to prepare his answers.

'What Government standard size?'

'I went out and measured a few.' Mark tried to keep a straight face.

'Yer lying kunt, Bones.' Another one of Tony's quips he would use if he thought you were skiving. This lovely little sentence he would use regularly.

'You've been fucking the dog, Bones.' What a charming saying. 'Now fuck off and get those lines painted.' Mark walked off feeling lucky. Tony turned to me.
'These kunts will have me smoking again. He walked off, ready to throw a few more expletives at the next poor unsuspecting soul.

One thing that the guys liked about Tony was he would go out and seek overtime, it didn't matter how bizarre the task, he'd always agree to get it done. Whether it be unblocking drains at the golf course next door or clearing up the devastation left behind by the famous hurricane of 1987, where a group of us were sent to Boreham house to help clear up the mess. Jim Ferris was still with us then. He came over and said to four of us, 'Come on I'll treat you to a pub lunch.'
We walk across the road to a nice little country pub. Unfortunately, because of the storm, the pub had no power. Oh well, we did get a bottle of warm beer and a packet of pork scratchings!

Tony called Marky Mark and me into the office on a Friday. 'Right you pair of Kunts, I have a special job for you the weekend.' It transpired Tony had agreed to get the fire station's big red door painted.
To be honest, I hate decorating, but when you're getting paid it doesn't seem so bad.
So, Saturday morning, armed with a couple of paintbrushes, a paint roller and a tin of red paint, we amble up the hill to the fire station. Luckily, Roy Burton was on shift, so we're soon chewing the fat over a cup of tea.
After a while we thought we'd better make a start, fearful that Tony would show up in the little Lancia car he used to drive around the estate.
Looking at the door, it looked like a big job. But we soon knocked it out in less than thirty minutes.

'You lads want another cup of tea?' Not the sort of question you need to ask two professional tea drinkers.
So, we get comfortable and Roy kept us watered. I took a glance out of the window of their office and I see Tony pulling up in his car.
'Hey up, Mark. Stand by your bed, Lynch's just pulled up.'
Now, one thing I knew wouldn't happen, I knew Tony wouldn't be getting out of the car. He never did, so it was no surprise when he pressed and held the hooter.
The pair of us walked out, and the electric window comes down.
'Yer pair of kunts, yer fucking the dog.'
'Whoa …… Easy with the insults.' I was used to Tony's colourful language.
'We're not fucking the dog if you must know; we're waiting for the paint to dry.'
'Paint to dry, you kunt.'
'Yes, we thought we'd give it another coat.' Tony sat there with a bemused look on his face then decided we could be doing something else while we waited for the paint to dry. This, of course, we had no intention of doing.
'Follow me.'
I walked around the car and tried to open the passenger door. It was locked? Tony slid the window down about two inches then hollered at me.
'Walk, yer lazy kunt.'
Mark and I had great trouble trying not to laugh. So, Tony started to drive slowly and the pair of us walk alongside the car. He had the driver's window fully down and occasionally he would shout an order out.
'Pick that up, get rid of that, and sort those weeds out, that shouldn't be there.'
He's pointing at all different things, my head is back and forth like I'm watching tennis.

The problem for Mark and me was that Tony had now speeded up a little bit, so we're now having to jog to keep up with him. We must have looked a right pair of clowns running next to the car. Eventually, we stopped running; Tony by now was about fifty meters ahead of us. We could see the brake lights and then the reversing lights.

'Here he comes,' I muttered. However, Tony stopped about twenty meters from us. Stuck his head out of the window and shouted out his opinion of us.

'Yer pair of kunts and lazy bastard, wankers.' With that, Tony drove off. Mark and I took a good ten minutes to stop laughing.

The lovely thing about Tony, the incident was never mentioned again. As we walked back to the fire station we wondered if we had time to squeeze another cuppa in before tea break.

I had some good fun with Marky Mark over the years, he was a generation younger than me, but we shared the same sense of humour. We had a water fight one day that left us both dripping and the toilet in hell of a mess. He'd sneaked up to ambush me, but I was a step ahead. It must have been shut down time, I think I'd given him a dowsing earlier in the day. He was working on a big wash machine. He was wary of an attack so put his best man outside the machine to keep an eye. Glen Osbourne, aka Chewbacca.

Now Glen was a big man, a good six feet four, and thickset. He had a slight resemblance to Chewbacca from Star Wars Fame. Anyway, Glen was meant to be keeping a lookout, but I was teamed up with Steve Battle.

They didn't stand a chance. Glen was about as good as the lookout on the Titanic as Steve crept in close and gave Glen the eyeshot. This was our favourite target; as it temporary blinded the opposition and gave you time to get yourself out of there.

So, Steve hit Glen and he was staggering around like a headless chicken. Poor Mark, he had nowhere to run. I gave him a good soaking.
Of course, I knew Mark well enough to know he'd want revenge.
So, it was with that in mind that I hid an extinguisher in the toilet in case he came after me at going home time.
Sure enough, as I'm washing up he bursts through the door like Rambo. I run to a cubicle and grab my weapon, anybody left in the toilet scarpered and we went full pelt at each other. I don't know how much of that rank water I swallowed that day, but my God, it gave me the "Rodney Trotters," for about three days. Once we had emptied the water over each other, we had to clear up the mess. I must have been nearly forty then, so mature!

How sad that in the four years since the first edition was published that we lost Glen. I was so upset to hear the death of the gentle giant.

An incident whilst the water throwing season was on brought about the discovery of a pervert amongst our midst.
Not sure why the lads would want to throw water at me while I was in the shower? But I'm glad they did this particular day. I was happily showering away unaware of the drama that was unfolding.
I can't remember all the names who came up to the showers that day. Marky Mark, Steve Beavis and Brian Crease for sure, man-mountain Gordon Beattie was with them I'm sure. I say that because he was a notorious water chucker. I have to say, they were a bit amateurish because they arrived at the scene without a bucket between them.
Looking around, they opened the door which was the service door that ran behind the shower cubicles and toilets. Like a rabbit caught in the headlights was a fitter out of one of the

maintenance departments (Not ours, thank God) squatted down watching me shower through a spy hole. I can say with confidence he was watching me as I was the only one taking a shower.

'Trev come out quick.' They shouted at me; like I was going to fall for that one.

'Only you Muppets would come up here and want to throw water at me while I'm naked in the shower.'

I could tell by the excitement in their voices that something had happened. So, I show my face, still half expecting a bucket of water when they told me they had just seen this guy checking me out. Now, even I found this hard to believe, although I always say I'm a highly tuned athlete, I must have been mid to late-thirties when this happened, and was fondly named by Gordon, a name he still calls me to this day, "The Big Fella." A polite way of calling me fat.

'Who was it?' I demand to know.

'Don't know his name, but he works out of the P13 crib.' Revealed, Steve.

'Right.' P13 was close to the shower room, so I donned my jeans and shoes and marched down to the said crib like "Tarzan." A few guys were still milling around. Seeing me arrive without a shirt on drew their attention.

'Which one of you has just been caught wanking at me from behind the shower cubicle?' I demanded an answer.

Not an everyday question to ask, I'll grant you.

'Not me, Trev.' When I think back to that day it was quite funny, all these guys protesting their innocence.

Mark Christmas, who later became a friend sought me out the next day and revealed who the guy was.

What could I do about it? Nothing. Had I beaten the living daylights out of him I would have got myself fired.

So, I let it go. Occasionally I'd see the pervert in question, but he'd scurry along avoiding eye contact.

Mark and I had another session with Tony Lynch a few weeks later.

He took us around on the electric buggy barking out orders for jobs to be done the next day. I was sat in the front with Tony and Marky Mark sat behind.

'I want that painted, get rid of that, sort that mess out, find a home for that. Remember Marky, paint those lines again.'

Tony was pointing out things that needed doing as he was driving us around the factory.

Perhaps I should have mentioned to him that Mark and jumped off the buggy as we went past the canteen. Tony was unaware of this and was still barking out his instructions. I suppose I could have told him, but I was quite enjoying watching him talk to himself.

'Look at the state of that, you sort that out in the morning, Marky.' Eventually, Tony pulled up outside his office and went to jump off.

'Now, yer understand what you've got to do, Marky?'

Tony turned around to talk to Mark, only to find he had gone. He jumped up and pointed at me.

'Where's that kunt gone?'

'Not sure, Tony. I think he jumped off outside the canteen.'

This was all too much for our Tony; he went into meltdown with me.

'Yer stupid kunt. Why didn't you say he'd jumped off? I've been talking to him for the past ten minutes!'

'Not strictly true, Tony. You thought you were talking to him for the last ten minutes.'

'No one likes a clever kunt.' With that, he went into his office and slammed the door. A little while later Mark came strolling back. I thought it better to tip him off.

'Put your earplugs in, Lynchy is just about to perm your ears.'

Tony had a dislike of the convenor, the *Rat*. He thought he was a crook, something I was beginning to wonder myself. It was

the time of the grand opening of the gym. The carpet had just been laid, and the carpet fitters were on their way out of the plant. Tony phones me all excited.
'Get your arse over to the office, now.' Thinking one of the lads had got themselves into a pickle, I hurried over.
'Where the fuck have you been?' Tony was waiting for me outside the office.
'Last time I looked, I was Trevor Whitehead, not Linford Christie.' He threw a set of car keys at me.
'Come on, I want you to follow the van.'
'Follow the van? What van?'
'The van that's just laid the carpet in the gym. I've heard it's on its way to Benfleet to fit a new carpet to the convenors new house.'
'Who told you that?'
'Never you mind that just drive you kunt.'
The reason I asked was I had recently done a wind up on the phone with him. This was around the time you could dial a number and a prerecorded message would play a joke on you. I got a number that played a message about a man accusing you of sleeping with his wife.
One late shift I watched Tony go off to the toilet. So, I put a note on his desk and wrote, "Ring this number urgently."
I hovered about and watched him walk back into the office. I waited until I could see him reading the note then pick the phone up. As I walked into the office I did my best not to laugh.
'Wah … Hang on a minute. I don't know your wife, listen, mate, you've got the wrong man.' Tony slammed the receiver down.
'Who was that, the wife?'
'Wha? No, some kunt has given my name out to some idiot.'
He never knew he'd been talking to a message.

I get in the car and Tony jumps in beside me.
I knew about the convenors new house but hadn't been there.

'Come on, follow the van.' He barks at me again.
'Isn't the point of following the van to have the van in sight?'
'Don't you worry about that; I know where the convenors new house is.'
So, I drive us to Benfleet. It was that journey that I discovered Tony would have made a fantastic driving instructor.
'Speed up yer Kunt, next right, right yer kunt.'
'It's one way, I can't turn right.'
'I know that I mean next right after this one. Slow down, it's around here somewhere?'
'I thought you knew the house?'
'I know the road, it's on this road for sure.'
'Well that narrows it down, can only be around two hundred houses on this road!'
I drive up and down slowly until Tony shouts at me. 'Stop, it's that one.'
'What, the one without the van?'
'Well, it took you so long to get here, they must have fitted the carpet and fucked off.'
'Or they fitted the carpet before they came and fitted the gym out.'
'Of course, that's what they did.'
So, we sat in the little Lancia, pondering our next move. Or I should say Tony sat and pondered my next move.
'Go and check through the window.' Now this alleged house was, in fact, a bungalow. The road was quite hilly, so the front bay window looked quite high.
'How fucking tall do you think I am, Tony?'
'Don't be a kunt. Look, there's a ladder leaning against the side wall.' Sure enough, an old wooden ladder was laying on its side. So, Joe Muggings gets out to check if a new carpet had been fitted. I walk over, check no one is about and pick the ladder up and manoeuvre it up to the front bay window, which was a good seven feet high.
I get a hurry-up from Tony, something like,

'Get that fat arse up there yer lazy kunt.'

Now, I was a hoist man and climbed ladders every day but this ladder was an old wooden thing that had a couple of rungs missing.

Happy I have the ladder steady, I then gingerly climb up and peer through the window. Now, I had the sun behind me glaring in and with the dirty window, I could see doodle squat. So I get a hanky out of my pocket and proceed to clean an area so I can see in.

It was at this point I found out that my dear Irish foreman had made a huge mistake.

As I peered through part of the window I cleaned I could see a very old white-haired lady staring back at me with a look of horror on her face.

I can still hear the screams now. I think it's safe to say that has been my quickest ladder decent in twenty-plus years as a Hoist man.

I ran to the car, started it and accelerated away.

'Wrong house?' Asked Tony.

'What made you think that?'

'The screaming.'

Tony decided to stop for a beer on the way back. With the aid of a Guinness or two, he soon shifted the blame to me.

'Had yer not been so slow coming to the office, we could have followed the van.'

Now unbeknown to me at the time, this bungalow, not the one with the old woman I frightened in, but the one the *Rat* had purchased would lead to the undoing of his reign. That story will come later.

As I write this I guess work-wise this was my happiest time. We had a good little team and we met up socially occasionally. The banter and the jokes made the working day just a bit easier.

A night out bowling
Left to right: Mark Lewin aka Bones, the late Brian Crease, Mark Clothier aka Marky Mark, Steve Beavis, myself and Terry Watts.

Gordon Beattie vs Mark Lewin (Bones) You couldn't get a bigger miss-match. It would be like Mike Tyson taking on a featherweight. But I'm not talking fisticuffs here; I'm talking eating a sausage roll. Each morning we'd put our order in for rolls and one of the lads would pop outside the gate to a converted caravan where Mary would sell her rolls.

Now I'm talking bread rolls here, stuffed with a sausage. She must have made a small fortune the week an eating contest developed.

Now to be fair to Bones, he could eat a lot for a little un. Regularly he would tuck three or four away in the morning tea break. Not bad for a guy who was about seven stone wet through. Gordon was in charge of getting the rolls and if Bones ordered three, he'd have four. The next day, he ordered four, so Gordon had five.

'Christ Bones, where do you put it?' I asked. I knew where Gordon put it because he looked like the Michelin man.

'I burn it off, Big Fella.'

You can't eat as many as me, Bones.' Gordon threw out the challenge.

'Right, get me six tomorrow.'

'You can't eat six.' Responded Gordon.

'You'll see.' Well, the next morning's tea break couldn't come around quick enough. Gordon set off to Mary's with a mega order of rolls. He had to get a bigger box.

We sat in anticipation as Gordon returned with this big box of rolls. Eventually, six are placed in front of Bones, and Gordon put six in front of himself. The rest of us mere mortals tucked into our one or two rolls.

Thinking back, I remember Bones polishing off four quite quickly. Roll five you could see was a struggle, roll six became a bit of a mountain to climb.

Gordon just munched his way through five with ease, but roll six looked more of a struggle.

'If you match me, Bones, I'll concede. As you are a lightweight. So, the two of them attacked roll six and with a real struggle Bones managed to get it down, helped with the odd slurp of tea. As he swallowed the last mouthful, he stood and raised an arm in victory.

'What you doing, Bones?' Asked a smiling, Gordon.

'I matched you, so I'm the winner.'

'Not so fast.' Gordon stood up, went outside and returned with another sausage roll. He'd hidden one up just in case. Gordon sat there eating it as Bones had a deflated look on his face. Didn't see much of Bones the rest of the day, I think the overeating had caught up with him and he spent the majority of the day in the toilet.

Next day? Normal service was resumed.

It's only been recently that I've managed to catch up with Gordon. He left the plant soon after the sausage roll challenge and moved up Lincoln way. I hadn't spoken to him for well over twenty-five years. But one day on my Facebook his name appeared on people I might know. We became friends and then had some video chats.
My god, we laughed a lot about those years we worked together. Especially the cricket and water throwing stories. So, happy times at work, and soon I was in for some fun with Pat von Brown.

Chapter 7

The Elstree experiences.

Things started to change at work, and not for the better. I must admit it was around this time I started to get my doubts about the convenor. He was agreeing with some strange ideas and without any resistance.

I don't think I was alone in this train of thought. So, when the company wanted to implement an operation called MBU, we told the *Rat* no way. It was the new flavour of the month. Manufacturing business units to give it its full title. To the laymen out there it basically meant splitting the factory up into different units. I didn't understand the logic then, and I don't understand the logic now.

So, they needed the trade union support to implement this latest phase.

It's fair to say we didn't like it. In a bid to try and win us over, they decided to take us to a hotel for five days, and give us a seminar on how this would work in our factory.

Obviously, thinking a bit of wining and dining would do the trick?

They put us up in a very plush hotel in Elstree. Now, the first thing that made me laugh was the hotel was a tad short on rooms.

Luckily for me, I arrived early and was given a very nice room. Arriving in the room next door, the village idiot and part-time postman, Pat Von Brown.

The *Rat* arrived late, he'd been to some freebie day out somewhere. I happened to be in the foyer when he arrived '***** ***, checking in.'

'I'm sorry Mr *Rat*, we have a shortage of rooms, were just making one available in the basement.'

'Basement?' The *Rat* tried the do you know who I am, but they didn't budge.
So, he was not best pleased. While I was stood there, the actress who played Bianca in Eastenders walked past. Patsy Palmer, you couldn't miss her. Bright orange hair and freckles. I couldn't think of her real name so I tried another tactic to get her attention.
'Ricky,' I shouted out, giving it my best impression. She turned around and looked at me. Then gave me the single finger.
Not what I hoped for, but funny enough not the last time I would see her. It wasn't until later, after a few more "EastEnders" characters were spotted that I realised the hotel was dead opposite the Elstree film studios. Some of the cast came across and used the swimming pool and gym.

My first job, go and take the piss out of the *Rat's* room. I go to the basement and see a forlorn *Rat* waiting outside of a room that had obviously been used as a storage room.
I stuck my head in and could see it was a proper guest room, it just didn't have a window.
Eventually, the cleaner came out and told the Rat his room was ready.
I follow him in and he looked like he was about to cry.
I decided to poke the fire.
'This is a disgrace *Rat*, don't they know who you are?'
'My words exactly, Trevor.'
'What's your room like?'
'Not bad, nice balcony with views over the fields, a towelling bathrobe robe and slippers. Jacuzzi bath, mini bar and a big TV and not only a kettle, but a coffee making machine as well.
Of course, none of this was true; the rooms didn't have a balcony or Jacuzzi bath. It was just a standard room with a small fridge and kettle. Two teabags and two coffee sachets. However, my exaggerating was all too much for the *Rat*.
He went off in search of the plant manager.

It's a testimony to the *Rats* thinking even back then that he thought he was something special.
"Do you know who I am," What a cock.

It didn't take me long to have some fun with Pat. I mentioned to him the first evening that I was going to have a swim and a sauna before breakfast.
'That sounds like a good idea, give me a knock can you, Trev?'
So, at six am the following morning, I knock on Pat's door. Now I think I mentioned earlier that Pat looked like he was ready to rob a bank.
He had one of those rubbery face looks, he'd fit into a sketch on "Spitting Image," no problem.
Now, this hotel ran a couple of film and adult viewing channels. It wasn't cheap; I think it was around seventeen pounds per twenty-four hours. To subscribe all you had to do was punch your room number and the hash key on your phone and you were subscribed.
So, this first morning, after the shock of seeing Pat's straight out of bed look, which not only consisted of his rubber face, slit eyes but the most hideous paisley pyjamas I'd ever seen.
'Come on then, Pat. Shake a leg.'
'Hang on a minute, I need a pee.' He went into the bathroom and I quickly walked over to his phone, I picked up the receiver and tapped in the necessary numbers so our Pat was "Porned up for the next 24 hours."
I decided not to mention the porn channel until later in the day, I didn't want the others to know.... Not yet.
So, we head off to the fitness centre, and very nice it was too. They gave us a towel and we got changed and took a quick shower.
'Let's have a swim first Pat, then we'll finish with a sauna.' I suggested.

After a few lengths, Pat climbed out and went into the sauna. I soon followed and Pat was sitting in there naked and stone cold.

'What's this meant to do, Trev? I don't feel any different?'

'Well Pat, it would help if you switched the heater on.' I stepped outside and flipped the switch.

'Give it a couple of minutes and let the heater warm-up, Pat.' Now, it soon became obvious that this was Pat's first sauna experience.

'I always thought they'd be a log fire in here, Trev.'

'Don't be a clown, Pat. Who's going to look after a log fire in the middle of a fitness centre, we're not sitting on a Swiss mountain resort, are we?'

He sat and looked at the heater and wore a worried look on his face.

'But that heater, it's electric, Trev.'

'Nothing a matter with your eyes, is there?' I reached out and could feel the heat rising. With just my towel around me, I walked outside and filled the wooden bucket up with water. I came back inside and picked up the ladle.

'What are you doing with that, Trev?'

How do you think a sauna works, Pat? You throw water on the heater.

'Are you mad, you can't throw water on electric, you'll electrocute us?' As I went to throw the water Pat launched himself at me and we both flew out the door, stark naked. We ended up in a big heap on the floor right in front of a couple of female guests who were just about to enter the sauna as well.

After that bit of embarrassing excitement with Pat, I was ready for a hearty breakfast. However, a drama was unfolding in the dining room as I entered. I could see a couple of staff and a man in a suit talking to the *Rat*. Geoff was sitting at a table so I walked over to join him.

'We could be going home, Trev.'

'Why, what's happened?' Now I immediately thought the Rat had at last grown some balls and told the management to stick their MBU's where the sun doesn't shine.

Alas, it was something far more important. The kitchen had run out of eggs.

'How can I have a cooked breakfast with no eggs?' I could hear the *Rat* moaning.

'You stick me in a broom cupboard of a room, now this. What kind of hotel are you running here?'

I think *the* Rat made such a fuss; they sent somebody out to get some eggs from a local shop.

I was so glad to see our convenor focused on the important issues that lie ahead.

Of course, it didn't take long for Pat to make a complete fool of himself. You have to remember we're dining with the hierarchy of the company. A certain dress code had to be followed.

So, when Pat strolled in for his breakfast in his dressing gown and carpet slippers, it was all getting too much for the poor, *Rat*.

'Pat, for fuck sake, we're not on holiday here.' Pat scurried off to put on the correct attire.

Something Alan Phillips and myself quickly noticed about Pat, he ate as if somebody was about to take his plate away, and if a drink was put in front of him, he'd drink it. The latter we tested later that morning.

Pat was sat around a table between Alan and me. Various "experts," we're trying to sell the MBU idea to us. Of course, little did we know the *Rat* was most probably already on board and we were just being wined and dined to soften the blow. As another speaker started I filled up our glasses with fresh orange juice out of a pitcher. Pat straight away downed the whole glass. Alan and I looked at each other and winked. Alan filled Pat's glass up again and within seconds he couldn't resist, so he knocked it back. These were half pint glasses, so he had already downed a pint.

'No more,' he protested as I went to fill it up a third time.

'Who do you think that is?' Asked Alan to distract Pat. While he was turned I filled him up again.

Of course, he couldn't help himself and within a minute he was drinking again, albeit at a slower pace.

'Isn't that one of the girls from EastEnders?' I point across to the fitness centre which was in view from our conference room. Quick as a flash, Alan not only filled Pat up but changed our pitcher for a new full one.

'No, I don't recognise her, Trev.' Pat turned back and immediately started drinking again. Within a minute he'd knocked it back. He now had two pints of fresh orange juice in him. He was overloading with vitamin C. This went on until Alan made the mistake of filling Pat's glass to the rim.

'No more, Alan.' He protested.

Of course, it was only a matter of time before temptation got the better of him. However, because the glass was so full Pat had to stand up, lean forward and slurp it up. I can only describe the noise as similar to a horse. It was so loud that everything stopped and everybody looked around to see Pat once again making a fool of himself. Poor *Rat*, he stuttered and gave Pat one of his disapproving looks.

If that wasn't bad enough for Pat, he now was suffering from orange juice overload. It caused the same effect as five pints of beer. He went out to relieve himself, then found he had to go every fifteen minutes. Not helped by Alan's top-ups, Pat was up and down like a fiddler's elbow. Every time he got up it disrupted the meeting. By lunchtime, the *Rat* had seen and heard enough and gave Pat a right roasting.

'What's up with you, Pat? I heard you made a fool of yourself in the sauna this morning? Exposing yourself to two women. Turn up for breakfast in your dressing gown and slippers, then constantly disrupting the meeting?'

'It's not my fault. Trevor tried to electrocute me and Alan keeps filling my glass up!'
The *Rat* looked at Pat and did a fair impression of Captain Mainwaring.
'You stupid boy.'

That evening over dinner, Pat tapped me up about his adult channel.
'Here, Trev. Have you got porn on your TV?'
'No, Pat. You have to pay for it.'
'Really? Well, I've got it.'
'Well, I wouldn't mention it. You're not in the convenors good book at the moment. The last thing he needs is a bill for your porn.'
'Good thinking. Mind you I've not ordered it, must be left on there from the previous person.'
'Yes, that will be it, Pat.'

The next morning, I did the same routine. Knocked Pat up, then while he was in the bathroom, I ordered another 24 hours of porn for Pat's enjoyment.
This time he didn't play up in the sauna as the two women we'd exposed ourselves to were already in there and throwing water on the heater.
Pat had a short swim then headed for the sauna.
I was just getting out of the swimming pool when I saw the two women rush out of the door. I took a shower, took my shorts off and wrapped a towel around me and joined Pat.
'I thought I was in there for a minute.' He informed me.
'But as soon as I hung my towel up, they scarpered?'
Bless Pat, he didn't have a clue about sauna etiquette.
'I'm not surprised, you should keep your towel on.'
'I watched a film last night, and they were all sitting in this sauna, naked!'
'What film?'

'I don't know what it was called. It was on the porn channel.'

The next morning, unsurprisingly I'd overslept. This week at Elstree was wearing me down. A free bar in the evenings was beginning to take its toll.
The time I knocked for Pat, he'd already gone down. Deciding to give a swim and sauna a miss, I went back to my room, got showered and changed and went off for breakfast. I waited for the lift and eventually, it arrived and took me to the ground floor. As the doors slipped open, I was faced with Pat, standing in his brief speedos, with no towel and dripping wet.
'What's with the "Tarzan" look, Pat?'
'I forgot my towel and clothes, Trev.' Only Pat could do something like that, and the way Pat's luck was running, it was no surprise that the convenor walked past with one of the managers on their way to breakfast. Looking at Pat he nodded his head in dismay.

I had to be a bit sneaky at lunchtime and slip Pat's key in my pocket. I quickly went up to his room and ordered more porn on his behalf. On my way back, I did something I'm not proud of. I was in need of a poo. So, shot into the toilets next to the reception. As I entered a cubicle I could see a room key on the floor. I looked at the key fob number and smiled when I recognised whose room it belonged to. So, I had a poo. Didn't flush, nipped into the cubical next door to clean up. Then on my way out, I dropped the key neatly on top of the pile of shit. Walking back into the dining room I saw the key holder.
'****, I'm not sure, but I think you dropped your key in the toilet.'
The *Rat* searched his pocket.
'You could have picked it up.' He stood up and walked off.
Five minutes later he walked back in and gave me a disapproving nod. I didn't like to ask him how he fished it out!

That evening I decided to bring the adult viewing to a head. The novelty of getting hammered every night had worn thin. So, after dinner, I only had a couple of beers and headed to my room. I could hear Pat's TV on. I sat down and made the phone call. I decided to use a gay Scottish voice for some reason.

The conversation went something like this:

'Hello, Am I speaking to Von Brawn?'

'Pat Brown.'

'Ah, sorry, Pat von Brawn.'

'No, there's no von in my name. It's just Pat Brown.'

'Sorry, Mr Brawn, my you have a lovely voice.'

'How can I help you?'

'Ah … I'm glad you asked that Mr Brawn, you see, it's a bit of a delicate subject.'

'If it's about the sauna, I can only apologise, I thought it was normal behaviour.'

'What were you do in the sauna, Mr Brawn? I hope you weren't masturbating?'

'What … No no, nothing like that, I hung my towel up, that's all. I think I upset a couple of ladies because I was naked.'

'Don't go worrying about that Mr Brawn, we encourage guests to get naked in the sauna.'

'You do? Oh well, that's okay then.'

'Tell me, Mr Brawn, what time do you normally have a sauna, only I might join you in the morning.'

'Oh …. I think I have an early meeting tomorrow, so may have to give it a miss.'

'That's a shame, Mr Brawn, I could have rubbed some oils on you.'

'Err … Yes, that is a shame. Anyway, if that's all ….'

'What am I like, Mr Brawn, thinking of you, sitting naked in the sauna, sweat dripping off you like droplets of rain …. Oh, it's taken me right off the reason I've called you.'

'Which is?' Asked an embarrassed, Pat.

'The outstanding total of your adult viewing.'
'Oh, I thought it was free.'
'I'm afraid there's no such thing as a free lunch Mr Brawn.'
'But I haven't ordered it; it was already on my television.'
'Mr Brawn, I've worked here nearly twenty years, as if I haven't heard that excuse before, it was already on my television.'
'What I meant to say is, I've not watched any of the films.'
Now-now Mr Brawn. Do you think I came down on the banana boat? You've watched all the films over the past three days. You see it comes up on our computer who watches what. You've even watched a very good homosexual film called "Backdoor Bandits" twice?' I could maybe let you have that film free, courtesy of the management?'
'I've not watched it twice.' Protested, Pat. How I didn't laugh is a testimony of my willpower.
'Now Mr Brawn, let's get down to business, I've had your Human resources manager here. He's keeping tabs on the running costs of this seminar. He told me he has no problem paying for all food and drinks, in fact, everything except the massage service and the adult viewing channel.
Don't go worrying about a massage; I can give you a massage for free in my spare time.'
'No thank you,' answered Pat.
'Okay, well the offer remains. So, when I told him there was only one of his party using the adult viewing facility he demanded to know who it was. He said he would tell a Mr Convenor and demand a reprimand. But I told him I have to respect the guest's privacy unless of course, you don't settle your bill.'
'I see, thank you. Can I ask what is my current bill?'
'Now, let me take a look. It currently stands at fifty pounds, ninety-seven pence.'
'How much?' Pat croaked down the phone at me.
'Well three nights at sixteen pounds, ninety-nine pence comes to fifty pounds, ninety-seven pence. Now, Mr Brawn, I'm afraid

I need you to come down to reception immediately and clear this bill, otherwise, I'll have no option but to inform your boss Mr Convenor.'

'He's not my boss.'

'Well, boss or not I'm afraid I need to turn off your adult viewing channel.'

Now Pat's response wasn't what I expected.

'Err, can you leave it on for five more minutes?' Again, it took all my willpower not to burst out laughing and give the game away. I took a deep breath and composed myself.

'Okay, Mr Brawn, I'll give you five more minutes. After all, we all have needs, don't we? But I expect you down here in reception shortly to pay your bill.' I hung up laughed into my pillow so not to alert Pat, then waited.

Now, Pat had a habit of whistling as he walked. So, I soon heard his door close and him whistling away to himself.

Ten minutes later he was back. Oh, I would have loved to be at the reception when he arrived to pay his non-existent porn bill. The next morning, I gave him a knock and when he opened the door he accused me.

'I knew that was you on the phone last night.'

'What you on about, Pat?'

'I knew it was you.' He repeated.

'If you knew it was me, why did you go to reception and make a c*** of yourself.'

'See, I knew it was you, how would you know I went to the reception last night if it wasn't you?'

'Because the convenor has just rung me and told me about the embarrassment you caused at the reception last night.'

'Shit. Do you think he'll send me home?'

'Possible Pat. I'd get a quick swim and a sauna, maybe a breakfast in before he does.'

Now, Pat had this obsession with Germany. He thought they were great; he drove a German-made car, towed his caravan to

Germany for holidays, and allegedly could speak the language. This was put to the test while we were staying at the hotel. We had a young German waitress who served us in the hotel's restaurant.

Not to be unkind, but I likened her to an East German shot putter.

But being a descendant from Hitler's youth Pat was very taken with her.

It soon became obvious that Pat's knowledge of the German language you could write on the back of a box of matches.

However, we weren't going to let a little thing like commination get in the way of a good wind up.

Each mealtime, Pat would be egged on to talk to this fräulein. We tried to convince him he was in with a chance of a leg over. Even our manager Michael Law got involved when he dropped a packet of condoms on Pat's plate telling him he was representing the company and to practice safe sex.

Poor Pat, he didn't know what to do. I don't know if he ever thought he was in with a shout, but our fräulein let it be known in no uncertain terms one morning that he wasn't.

The rest of this story is better left unsaid.

I know some of you will read about Pat and have some sympathy for him.

He, despite his stupidity, was a likeable character. I recalled those stories with a smile and fondness.

However, he should never have been a Shop Steward, let alone a JWC committee member. I did often wonder if his department voted him in as a joke.

I don't know how many times he got a bollocking off the convenor regarding turning up at management meeting in the plush conference room wearing oily overalls and work boots. Pat would sit down and throughout a meeting, he'd be like a jack in the box. He could never sit still for long.

Of course, once he had gone, he'd left behind a grease-stained chair and an area of the carpet.
The convenor took me up once to try and clean it, I bought up some stuff that said it would remove grease stains.
To be fair, it certainly removed the grease, but also the dye out of the carpet. So we were left with a white patch.

He also had this habit like another guy who will feature shortly. He would invade your personal space. He was always in your face. If you turned away, he'd follow you around.
Nothing was off-limits when it came to Pat. I was upstairs having a dump once when I heard.
'You up here, Trev?'
'I'm having a crap, Pat.'
'Okay.'
A few seconds would go past and he'd holler at you again.
'Is that right they're putting the canteen prices up?'
'Can it wait, Pat? I'm having a crap.'
Bear in mind there are most probably other people sitting there listening to Pat.
Eventually, all is quiet, I finish my business and as I come out of the door Pat is standing right in front of me. He follows me to the sinks, down the stairs and into the steward's office.
'Anybody got a gun I can borrow,' I ask.

The last I heard of Pat he was stranded in Leicester. He'd moved there to be near his daughter. Then she moved away? Make your mind up about that.

Another guy I want to mention who was at Elstree is the late Richard Llewellyn.
He was another maintenance steward and quite well known locally for his council work as an elected Councillor.
A funny-looking guy who kept the mullet hairstyle all his life.

He used to drive the convenor mad at the JWC meetings when he spoke.
You see, he could talk about a subject for twenty minutes and you'd be none the wiser.
In fact, the convenor would often go out for a cigarette while our Dickie was in full flow.
He was known as "The Riddler," for that reason.
Many a time I was left scratching my head after a conversation with him.
We had to face each other in a shop stewards election one time and he'd been a steward for a long time.
Unfortunately, he didn't get many votes; he was gracious in defeat and a good supporter after.
The reason we faced each other I will get to later.
I was so shocked when I heard of his passing, another nice guy gone too soon.

The outcome of the Elstree week,
Well, Pat's adult viewing bill was paid by the company, not sure if Pat's activities were ever mentioned.
It came as no surprise to any of us that MBU's were agreed upon and shortly introduced.
As I mentioned before, I'm convinced the deal was done way in advance of this trip to Elstree.
The convenor had sold his soul by now and was sitting comfortably in the H/R department's pocket.
This treachery was only the beginning; far worse was still to come.
If I thought that was bad enough, something happened that forced me to quit my role as a union representative.

Chapter 8

Opening a can of worms!

Major changes were coming to the plant. Ford's were no longer interested in making tractors?
This came as a great shock to most of us that worked there. We had been a very profitable part of the Ford family. Now, to us on the factory floor, not only was it a surprise announcement when it came, we just couldn't understand why?
We were making a quality product, in the top two of sales. We had over the years built up a great reputation and our product was well known worldwide.
The guys were gutted and life would never be quite the same, especially financially.
Enter Fiat.
I don't think any of us realised the sheer size of the Fiat Empire, We soon discovered they were a massive company.
Not well known in the UK, so we were heading into unchartered territory.
We soon learnt that, unlike the UK companies, the Italians would always look after their own.
They'd bought a very nice ready-made factory that was producing a world-famous product.
At the time of the transfer, we thought things would carry on as normal. How wrong we were.
After a short honeymoon period, it was announced that in the future, the company would be closing the manufacturing side of the engines.
It came as no surprise when the Italians announced they were going to build the Engines in Italy then send them to Basildon. The outcome of this announcement meant we would be losing half our workforce.

You can imagine the fear a lot of the guys were feeling. It hung over the factory like a dark cloud.
It affected everybody, losing the engines made the whole plant vulnerable.
We would just be an assembly plant. The factory wouldn't be manufacturing anything.
We would become what's known as a screwdriver plant. This at the the time made for a bleak outlook.
I can remember a JWC meeting when the then plant manager Derek Neilson tried to scare us with tales that the plant wouldn't be around in a few years.
I had very little to do with plant managers, they would come and go, Neilson was a dull Scottsman who was in love with himself.
Well, he certainly was wrong with his prediction, sums the man up really when he used his position to scaremonger.
It's funny writing about this now, some twenty years later, but at the time, with the help of that cock Neilson you couldn't help but worry about the longevity of the plant.
The bottom line of all this is our previous company Ford didn't want us.
The Italians did. They stepped in and turned the place around. They were ruthless when it came to the engines, but it's a testament to their way of running the business that it still thrives today.
The other bad news was we had lost our strength of being part of a big combine of Ford manufacturing factories in the UK. We were now on our own. In time, this would give opportunities of gain to a certain person or persons of influence.

It all started with the nuts and bolts, literally.
The company wanted to outsource the small department that delivered the nut and bolt stock to the assembly areas.
I can't remember how many people we were talking about, most probably less than five. They came under the store's

umbrella, so Paul Norris was their shop steward. I was their JWC member.

Paul and I had a meeting as soon as this rumour surfaced. Up to this point, we'd never allowed contractors to do anything that was classed as in-house work.

The only contractors I knew at that point were the canteen staff and a little cowboy unit that did the steelwork for hoists. The occasional firm would come in to do specialised work outside the skill set of the maintenance department.

Apart from that everything was in-house. Paul and I were adamant; no way could we allow this. To be honest I think the majority of the stewards supported us.

It wasn't just about the nuts and bolts; it was the principle of letting contractors in to take work away from our members. You would have thought it was a no-brainer, allow it once, and as this chapter heading said, we're opening a can of worms.

Problem was, behind the scenes the *Rat* must have agreed on it.

This is where his alleged corruption most probably started. Unbelievably he managed to talk some other stewards around and it happened.

It wouldn't have happened under Ford's; he was answerable to the rest of the Ford convenors. Under Fiat, he had a free hand to do any underhand business he liked.

What the hell these other stewards were thinking at the time only they could tell you.

We could have quite easily gone to the membership, explained the dangers of opening the door to contractors, and got their support.

Not in a thousand years would the company risk industrial action over such a minor thing.

But behind the scenes, Paul and I knew the *Rat* was up to no good.

Now, I could make a statement here about the *Rat*, but I think you know my feelings about him by now. I'll leave it to you to make your own mind up.

Even though Paul and I were so bitterly against it, we got shafted.

Who knows what pressure was applied to the *Rat* of a convenor. In my view he had no pressure, just incentives that were allegedly handed out to him, after all, this is only my slant on what happened.

But against all our trade union principles, we allowed in-house work to be put out to contract. You stewards who supported the *Rat* hang your heads in shame.

The *Rat* tried to worm his way out of Paul and my hostility by telling us the guys involved would be given work elsewhere in the factory, I'm afraid it was a nothing gesture to what he allowed to happen.

Of course, the history of the plant will tell you the future fears of Paul and me soon came to fruition.

At the time, I didn't know any better. It wasn't until years later when I was on the Amicus Motor vehicle executive committee that I found out about a certain rule that favoured the convenor.

I met up with maybe fifteen members of this committee from places like Nissan, BMW, Ford's, Toyota, Vauxhall and LDV vans, spread all around the country.

The majority of these guys were convenors or Senior Stewards as they liked to be known. It was after talking and building up a network of contacts with these guys that I discovered a real flaw in our shop steward set-up.

I found out that all of these guys were elected via the factory members. They couldn't believe the system we used. We, in case you didn't know, elected the convenor from the stewards. When you think back, had the *Rat*, or any other convenor for that matter had to face the shop floor for re-election. Do you

think he would have been so easily persuaded to farm work out? I know the answer….. So do you.
No, it was left to Paul and me to get it in the neck from the guys on the shop floor.
Everybody could see the danger except the fat controller; I think he was more interested in the incentives that might come his way.

It wasn't long after that stab in the back that my favourite band of brothers came under scrutiny.
Security and fireman were next to face the firing squad.

After a rocky start, and the problem with the milk put to bed, things had started to settle down. Obviously, there wasn't a lot of love lost between me and Jim McClure and his sidekick George. We'd have a monthly meeting and deal with any problems without any shouting, so progress had been made. George kept his gob shut, which must have been difficult for him. He still had to be reminded to make me a cup of tea which by the way hadn't improved.
The guys themselves seemed to be happy with me, and despite me telling them I would shred any letter, I did still get the occasional mail in the internal post.
I would write on the back of the envelope, "Not known at this address, please deliver to security for fingerprint analysis." And send it back.

Now, for some reason, I didn't hear the security and fireman were under threat from our convenor.
No, this time he used a different tactic, he got the H/R to leak it out. I found out after I received a frantic phone call from Jim McClure.
Could I go and see him at my earliest convenience, please? Preferably, now.

I'd never heard Jim use such a word. Although our meetings were more civil these days, they weren't in the least bit friendly.
Many I time I'd look at the bottom of my shoes to check for dog shit once I walked into the inner sanctum of Jim's office.
This time I was welcomed in with open arms.
Add to this, Jim ordering George to make me a cup of tea as soon as I sat down, I knew the alarm bells were ringing. I hadn't heard a word about this outsourcing threat so was surprised by Jim's friendly manner.
'What's up, Jim?'
'Have you heard? You must have heard? Is it true?'
'I'm not sure what you're talking about, Jim?'
'Contractors, they are looking to contract us out!'
'Really?'
'Yes, you must know something. Now come on Trevor, I know we haven't always been on the best of terms, but you need to be honest with me.'
Trying not to sound like Manuel out of Fawlty Towers I replied.
'I know nothing.'
Jim sat there; face bright red, his blood pressure sky high.
'Calm down, Jim. It's most probably just a rumour. I'll go and have a chat with the convenor and put this to bed.'
'What, like the nuts and bolts?'
I ignored that cutting remark, putting it down to Jim's state of panic.
'I'm fifty-six, Trev. Where am I going to get another job at my age?'
'You only fifty-six, Jim? I thought you were older than that. Leave this with me and I'll come back and see you.'
I strolled over to the convenors office. To be honest, as much as I was angry about the nuts and bolts, not in my wildest dreams did I think security was under threat.

The *Rat* was sitting at his desk with his number two, Alan Phillips hovering. I only had to look at the convenors face to know what was coming.
'Alright, I've just had a conversation with Jim McClure. He seems to think the Security and firemen are under threat?'
The *Rat* reclined in his chair lit a cigarette and looked at me.
'Yes, they are being looked at.'
'And you didn't think to inform me, I have to find out from the guys themselves?'
'Well, I knew you'd play up.'
'Play up you c***.'
'See, that's no way to talk to your convenor.'
'You're a fucking joke. Grow some balls.' I stormed out and had to break the news to Jim. Who looked almost suicidal on hearing my report back to him.

I think it is safe to say things between the convenor and me were fractious, to say the least.
But, like the nuts and bolts scenario, behind the scenes, I believe the *Rat* had already agreed on the principle of outsourcing. I can't prove it; I can only write what I thought at the time and what shortly followed.
A few weeks later, I'm informed that a working party is going to look at some contract security firms in action. I was on a working party, along with Geoff, the *Rat* and Alan. Jim was invited along with someone from the H/R and the manager, Monotonous Michael Law.

We had three firms that had put in a tender to take over security and the fire department to visit.
They decided to leave the joke firm until last, for good reason. The first was a company that looked after a large factory. All very proficient and professional. They gave a good presentation and under other circumstances, I would have been impressed.

On the second trip, we were driven to London and taken to the BBC studios at the television centre, White City.
Again, a firm that was very proficient and they threw in a free lunch at the studios where I spent most of my time celeb spotting.
On my way to the toilet, I spotted an old friend who I'd not seen since Elstree. Once again my favourite ginger soap star Patsy Palmer walked towards me.
This time I just smiled and resisted the "Ricky" impersonation. I didn't get the finger, which was an improvement. She didn't smile either, and I can say with hand on heart, close up she's one ugly woman.

The last trip was to the Circus Tavern; yes you have read that correctly, our billion-pound company had arranged to meet the security firm that chucked out the drunks after a night on the piss.
We met up with a guy who I did wonder years later if Peter Kay had based his character, club owner Brian Potter on. Apart from the bleached blonde hair and minus the wheelchair, he could have been a dead ringer. He spoke with that Northern accent, at the time I thought he was a joke, turned out I was right.
When you think about absurd this was, for once I felt sorry for Jim McClure. Here was a man who had risen to be the head of the security, sitting in a pokey nightclub during the day looking at a bunch of hoodlums who were going to take his job.
They wanted to use a firm that only security experience was to body search the women on the way in and confiscate the bottles of booze they tried to discreetly bring in.
What was even more amazing was watching Michael Law brown nose this guy who owned the club?
I did wonder if he was trying to get a job as the resident singer? To be fair to Michael or Mick as I liked to call him, before the security betrayal I thought he was a decent enough guy. Okay,

he wasn't my cup of tea, what with his Mexican moustache and little man body. But, for some reason after my dealings with him and the way he allegedly sold the security down the river, I just wanted to punch him in the face. Along with a few others that day.

I can't explain the feeling, I guess it's because I felt they abused their positions

Mick and the convenor were getting too close for my liking; he became the enemy as far as I was concerned.

Let's, not sugar coat this, no one in their right mind would put the security of the factory in the hands of Butch Cassidy and the Sun Dance Kid.

It was so obvious who was getting the contract I felt embarrassed to be sitting there.

Not the Rat and Micky Law, they sat there like a pair of cats that had got the cream.

The whole thing was a setup; I have no doubts the decision had already been made. Two out of the three visits were just a P/R exercise.

When I hear the saying "there's no such thing as a free lunch," I always think of the lunch I had at the BBC and what followed.

So, it will come as no surprise to anybody who was rewarded with the contract. I have given you the three firms who had put a tender in. Two firms were swept under tha carpet.

Yes, the factory was now going to be guarded by bouncers!

The guy whose previous job was to look after the entertainer Michael Barrymore, was now looking after a huge factory with millions of pounds worth of assets?

I'm not sure what I can add to this. Two very professional security firms had been overlooked. I didn't like the thought of outsourcing to begin with, and now I had to face up to these security guys and try and pretend it was the best deal the trade union could get for them?

You see, what was decided, we were obliged to support the party line, no matter how much you hated it. It's the trade union way. You have to show a united front.
I'd love to know how this was sold to the Italians?
It wouldn't have been sold as an act of betrayal, which it was.

I will choose my words carefully. You do have to wonder what incentives were exchanged for such a deal!
It would have been more than a lifetimes membership at Essex's number one shit hole.
The best bit, we didn't even have a meeting with the other stewards to discuss this outsourcing of the security and fireman.
As far as the *Rat* was concerned there was no point?
He didn't even have a group meeting with the security guys.
For me, well I had grown sick of the *Rat's* antics. He wasn't answerable to anybody. He'd come out with bullshit to try and convince you it was the best deal.
'It's better to have a company you know, Trevor.' This was his way of explaining his latest deal.
'Better to be in the ring than watching from outside.' It was farcical, and I wondered who else was in on it.
Well the H/R was there? They must have rubber-stamped the contract.
Michael Law? Well, only he knows what his involvement in the whole saga was. He could well be as horrified as I was with the whole thing. Personally, I doubt it, the smile and the brown-nosing did him no favours.
I'm not sure if he's still alive?
As I mentioned earlier, there would have been no way that outsourcing to a cowboy company would have happened if we'd still been with Fords.

So, after all the good work I'd done for the security and fireman guys, it all went to shit.

I couldn't look the guys in the eye. As much as they had been a pain in the arse, the majority of them were decent guys and they were just about to be shafted big time.

Like a snowball gathering speed, the outsourcing continued. Not content with the security and fire department, with the aid of the *Rat*, and allegedly Mick Law, they honed in on the General Service department. These were guys I'd worked with before I became a hoist man.
I put up a hell of a fight, but once again I was shot down in flames. Not once did the *Rat* take any of these changes to the workforce. We had such a good case to win their support, but the *Rat* wasn't having any of it.
When I heard about his new bungalow, I started to wonder who actually paid for it?
As what happened with the security, it was a done deal before I even got wind of it. The guys were left with a shit choice, stay and work for Wyatt Earp. Be transferred to Final assembly or leave.
The majority transferred to production. A couple of older guys took the retirement option then came back and worked for the Cowboys, the rest left the company.

I was sorry to see some of my close work colleagues leave. Gordon Beattie, our stout wicketkeeper and sausage roll king headed Lincoln way, I always found it sad when a character like Gordon left, there always seemed to be a void when they'd gone.
Bob Fellows decided it was time to try his luck working for himself.
I'd known Bob since he was eighteen; so again his leaving was tinged with sadness.
He made a great success working for himself, he set up a little building company and although he experienced a few ups and downs, he is one of the few who left with no regrets.

As I write this it's hard to believe he's 60 now!

Bob and Gordon didn't fancy the option of working on a production line and who could blame them. The cowboy firm had now taken over a plush set of offices and the General Service jobs, it's safe to say I was constantly looking over my shoulder.

Fair play to the likes of Paul Norris and Geoffrey Martin Smith, they stuck it out with the *Rat*. For me, I didn't want to be associated with the likes of the convenor anymore. He was up to no good and getting greedy.
I resigned and happily got on with my life.

Chapter 9

Outsourced and another comeback

Over the next few years, I did my best to forget about all the union side of work and just enjoyed life.

One thing crept up on me, my twenty-five years of service to the Tractor Plant. Seventeen with Fords and eight with Fiat. And like my dad, I was going on a piss up. Now things had improved drastically since the Mid sixties when my dad went. By this time you were swished away to a nice hotel in London, where you were invited to a type of gala evening, you could bring your wife or partner and your manager would make sure you were kept well fed and watered. I can say that my manager, Michael Newman did an admirable job considering I was half pissed before I'd even sat down.

On arriving at the hotel, after booking in we decided to take a little walk. I haven't a clue what the name of this hotel was or where in London we were. However, fifty yards from the hotel we found a pub where a recognisable voice dragged us in.

Tony Lynch was acting as mine host and getting the drinks, after spotting me he got two more in.

I can remember a couple of guys who stood there with their wives, Tony Campagna and Mark Baldassara.

Tony was the older brother of Terry and the current mayor of Canvey Barry.

Without boring you with the details, the brothers had left the company and returned as a form of building contractor. I've known Barry since I first started back in 1974.

My fondest memory of our early years was when we were sent outside to work and it was winter.

Barry was a quiet lad back then and I was what I always was, a big gob.

I can remember Barry looking at me in amazement when I launched an attack on the general foreman Joe Payne for sending us out there without a coat. He'd not heard anybody speak to supervision like that before. However, my big gob served me well for the next thirty-odd years.

I'm still friends with Barry, and he made me feel so old recently. He posted an old wedding photo, 40th anniversary, unbelievable, I went to his stag night!

Unfortunately, his brother Tony is no longer with us.

It's fair to say, Tony Lynch kept us amused for a couple of hours and we all headed back to the hotel slightly worse for were. Luckily, it didn't affect my evening and I even managed breakfast.

Sadly, that was one of the last long service dinners. I believe there was one more and that was that. It had certainly come to a stop when I hit the 30-year mark.

This was another agreement the *Rat* let go of without much of a fight.

I'm hearing these days you don't even get a handshake when you leave the company. I've seen on the Facebook group two guys who retired, both 40+ year men who left without any form of presentation. Scandalous.

So, after giving up my shop steward's role I didn't completely give up my activist duties, because I kept myself actively involved with my local Labour Party, and exciting times were coming with the launch of New Labour.

I'm ashamed to admit, at the time I was a fan and worked hard to get Tony Blair elected. Not one of my better judgements as it turned out.

He was charismatic and just what we needed to end the Tories long run in power.

I'll continue my Labour Party activities at a later stage in the book.

The new company were ending the honeymoon period and starting to reduce the workforce. A lot of staff jobs were trimmed, as were the hourly paid. Some of my colleagues had been shipped out onto production jobs. Life in the plant was changing, and to most of us, not for the better.

The name Ford was disappearing, along with the staff discount for a new Ford car.

No disrespect to Fiat, but the cars they produced in the early 90s were not of the standard we'd enjoyed with Fords.

We could buy a whole host of vehicles, all household names, including the Panda, Uno, Tipo, Tempa and soon to be released the supermini of its time the Fiat Cinquecento!!

Now, it wasn't all bad because we could also get a discount on the Alfa Romeo range of cars. These cars seemed to be very upmarket, not cheap but they looked good. Especially the Spider, which was way out of the average working man's budget.

But as employees who unfortunately bought them, they soon found out they weren't reliable and the value of their investment dropped by about 50% in the first year.

I nearly forgot about another range of cars we could get a discount on. (Mainly because I didn't know anybody who bought one)

Fiat also owned Lancia, so we could feast ourselves on these beauties, the Dedra, the Delta, and the Autobianchi Y10 to name but a few of these classics.

All was going well until a rumour started about the maintenance personnel; we were being looked at as a possible outsourcing target.

The nightmare that started with the nuts and bolts, gathered momentum by sucking in the security and firemen and the General Service department, was now heading my way.

At first, I thought that the *Rat* was behind another dodgy deal, but as time went past, the name, Comau, came into the frame. We were told that Comau was a company that specialised in maintenance type of work.

Apparently, they were beginning to work their way into other European Italian owned plants.

I won't name the steward who represented us at the time, mainly because he didn't stand a chance of changing anything, I knew, I'd been there.

No meetings of such, just a transfer.

So, as we were fast approaching the millennium, I was now working for Comau.

The one saving factor for all the guys was that because the Italians owned Comau, we were staying in the company pension scheme. Unlike the poor nut and bolt guys and the security guards.

Now I don't want to be disrespectful to a couple of guys here. Eddie Priestaff and Richard Llewellyn.

Both very nice guys and Richard I knew extremely well via our Labour Party activities. As I previously mentioned, Richard was well-liked in the political world and respected locally due to him being a Councillor for several years.

Sadly, Richard passed away only a few months before I wrote the first edition back in 2017. Eddie passed away a few years before; I heard through the grapevine he'd contracted asbestosis.

You see the problem I soon discovered when we were moved to Comau, we were left with, in my opinion, three very weak shop stewards.

As I said, Eddie and Richard were nice guys but weren't militant or strong enough. They'd been around when I was last a steward and I knew them so well. Eddie hardly spoke, when he did it was in a whisper.

Richard could talk the hind legs off a donkey but talked in riddles.

This leads me aptly to the third person the infamous "Hoof."

I used to say I could write a book about the Hoof and his activities, and here I am.

A more despicable, tight, unethical human being I've yet to meet. A man, with absolutely no morals. A thick-skinned person and a menace to women.

Sounds like I'm being a tad harsh. Well, see how you feel at the end of this chapter.

So, I had a dilemma, I vowed that I'd never stand to be a shop steward again. I'd been badly let down by the *Rat*. I think the security still held a grudge, as far as they were concerned I was in on them being taken over by a firm of which they described to me as a cowboy unit.

By all accounts he was allegedly even more corrupt than ever, did I want to be associated with him again? I had some serious thinking to do.

It was only a few months into the Comau era when the shop steward elections were due.

The Hoof was getting a panic on; he knew I could do well in an election. He started to become a frequent visitor to the Hoist Crib.

He used the same tactics every time, telling me what a great job he was doing, then asking me if I was going to stand.

Now, this was causing me a real dilemma. I was a Transport and General union man. I signed for them when I first started, recommended by my dad.

As I mentioned, my dad was a bit of a rebel, so instead of joining the then AEEU, like 99% of his colleagues, he joined the opposition.

Now at the time of my two previous stints as steward, we had plenty of T&G members in the maintenance, so it wasn't a problem for me. But a lot of these guys had left or been moved out of maintenance. Knowing how fickle some of these maintenance guys were, I knew it would go against me in an election.

Also, it was something the Hoof would use to his advantage to try and take votes away from me.

So, reluctantly I changed unions. I did comfort myself by knowing the *Rat* had no jurisdiction with the AEEU.

It wasn't long before my changing teams came to the attention of the convenor. I can remember being called over to see the *Rat* who amongst other things had been my branch secretary up to the point I left the T&G.

I walked in and he tried to play to the audience. A few of the stewards were sat around, this was the first time I had spoken to him for a few years.

He was no Alan Phillips so he was not good at trying to belittle me.

'Oh, here he is, the T&G not good enough for you now? I'm disappointed with you, Trevor.'

'Well, I know how that feels, I've been disappointed with you for years, you C***.'

A briefest of meetings.

I sat back for a while until a few of the guys approached me. Like me, they were worried, especially now as the Hoof was apparently the self-elected senior steward.

So, I threw my name in, and the Hoof, being the snake, he was, informed me I would be going up against Richard. I thought it would be a general vote and pick the top three. He changed that format because he knew he would be shipped out. So, I faced Richard in the election and received more votes.

I felt sorry for Richard because he'd been a long-standing steward.

Why he and Eddie and let the Hoof become a self-elected senior steward is anybody's guess.

To me, it showed a certain weakness, something I'm certain the Comau management would have used to their full advantage.

I hadn't had much to do with the Hoof up to that point. He entered union life after I quit over the outsourcing issues. I heard stories about him, none that were complimentary. Geoff told me about an incident with him. A true story on how tight he was.

They'd been out to a meeting somewhere and decided to stop at a Chinese restaurant on the way home.

I can't remember how many of them, about five I think.

So, Monotonies Michael Law is in charge, he goes to pay the bill. Checking his wallet, allegedly he realised he'd forgotten the company credit card.

Not having one of his own cards with him, he asked if one of the others could pay the bill and he'd settle up with them the next day.

Geoff said the hoof flew out of his chair, as if James Bond had hit the ejector button, ran over to the till and asked for a pair of scissors? He then got his credit card out and cut it up? Unbelievable …. But true.

I asked the Hoof about this incident some years later and he told me the card had run out of date.

'If it had run out, you didn't have to cut it up; the restaurant wouldn't have accepted it.'

'Well … It had nearly run out.' Bloody tight arse.

So, I knew all about the Hoof. Now for people reading this wondering why he was known as the "Hoof," well, he suffered from *congenital talipes equinovarus.* Or in layman's terms, he had a club foot.

Now, this handicap never stopped him from being one of the first out the gate at clocking off time.

Now, one thing in my favour, no one liked the Hoof, especially Eddie Priestaff, who was still smarting over the way he changed the election procedure to save himself.

So, I went to see Eddie.

I nicknamed him Eddie Whisper; he had the same low volume voice as Les Clemmie.

For some reason, in the shop steward circles, he was known as the cat? He was an electrician, so I couldn't work out the connection to our feline friends.

In hindsight, it would have been easier to ask him.

Eddie had been a steward for a number of years, but I soon marked his card when he started on about the Hoofs self-appointed senior steward manoeuvre.

I told him in no uncertain term he needed to sharpen up, no way would the Hoof have pulled that stroke with me. Dick Llewellyn lost out because they didn't nail the Hoof down. Not being funny, but there were two of them against one? Sort of tells you what a slimy little shit I was dealing with.

I told Eddie he needed to get behind me as I was about to clip the hoofs mane.

'We should have a meeting, I suggested. Get ourselves organised.' The Hoof was a snake, always remember that. He knew what I was after and he tried his best to avoid a meeting, which was ridiculous.

'Well I'm a bit tied up the rest of this week, then I'm on holiday next week.'

This was the sort of tactic I knew he would try. People like the Hoof were easily dealt with in my book.

'No problem. We'll have a meeting when you're back off your holidays.' So, the Hoof was happy and when he went on holiday, Eddie and I went to the little office we were given by Comau to run our union business and emptied the entire office of the Hoof's stuff and put it all in a cardboard box.

On his return, I went to see him first thing.

'Nice holiday?'

'Yes, great.'

'Good. Now, I've emptied all your stuff out of my drawers and filing cabinets and put it all in a cardboard box for you. Can you ship it out of the office today, it's in the way.'
'You can't-do that, I'm the senior steward, that's my office.
'No, you *were* the senior steward. Unfortunately, Eddie and I didn't want you as our senior steward, so Eddie backed me.'
'You can't-do that, I wasn't at the meeting.'
'Well, I've organised a meeting for ten this morning, you can speak about it then.'
Simple. So simple it's a pity the stewards didn't adopt the same tactics with the *Rat*?

At the time, we didn't know how long we'd remain with Comau.
Although I thought we were doing okay under them, I couldn't see it being a permeant arrangement, no money to be made. I had the usual suspects that were never happy. One, an electrician named, Dickie Burton. He used to bend my ears regularly.
'It's not right, Trevor. We should have someone from the H/R here permanently.'
There were less than one hundred of us and he wanted some poor sod to be in the plant permanently just so he had someone he could gripe to.
'If you have a problem, tell me, if I can't sort it I can ring and they will send somebody down. Trust me; we don't want H/R here.'
What a cock.

I'd joined the AEEU just at the time it was merging with the staff union the MSF. This merger of unions produced a new name, Amicus.
I went along to my local branch meeting; the secretary was a full-time union officer. The Hoof had wriggled himself into being the chairman.

So, I sat through the business and stopped and had a beer with the officer afterwards. The Hoof, not wanting to open his wallet used to slope off. This continued for about six months until one night the officer asked me if I'd ever considered being a bit more pro-active?
Well, of course, I did. Within weeks of that approach, I found myself in the role of the new Branch Secretary.
This, of course, put the Hoofs nose out.
'I've been coming to this branch for years, I've never been asked?'
'Yes, and for years you've not put your hand in your pocket and bought the secretary a drink.' I soon straightened the Hoof out.

This little promotion opened some more doors for me. I received a strange phone call asking me if I was interested in getting a position on the executive committee of the newly formed Amicus union. They wanted me on the Eastern Region Committee.
I was a bit sceptical, but I thought I'd go to this meeting and see what's what. It was held in a pub in Ipswich. I didn't know a soul there but introduced myself. Contacts details were swapped along with phone numbers.

A month later I get an invitation letter to go to the first meeting of the Amicus Eastern Region. This meeting was to elect members to the Regional Executive Committee.
It was held on a Saturday, again in the Suffolk area. By the time I was driving home, I was now a member of the Eastern Region Executive Committee.
Within six months of moving away from the T&G, I was now in the union's hierarchy.
I guess I was in the right place at the right time.

I should thank the old T&G convenor for his help in forcing me out of the T&G union. But I wouldn't piss on him if he was on fire.

The perk of these added responsibilities was more paid time off from work. Something I don't think the company were overjoyed about but were obliged to release me.

If the sudden change in fortunes caught me off guard, it was nothing compared to the changes that came in my Labour Party activities.
For years I'd been a member of my local party, Basildon & Billericay. I used to go most months to the meetings and during any election period I would step up and help out, albeit delivering leaflets or the dreaded door knocking.
I guess it's fair for me to admit I wasn't overly keen on that task. Especially when you're campaigning in a Tory stronghold. But it had to be done, and I went at it with my normal enthusiasm. That's why I hold Richard Llewellyn in such high regard. He would always hold his own in an argument about politics.
As I mentioned he was known as the "Riddler," amongst the shop stewards. He could ramble on about something for an hour, at the end of the conversation you'd forgotten what the question was. But face to face on a doorstep, he was in his element.
Now, I'd heard whispers about some boundary changes but didn't for the life of me think it would have any effect on me. How wrong was I?
I lived in Wickford, and because of that, I was shipped to the new constituency of Rayleigh & Wickford. The Hoof lived in Wickford, but he wasn't as active on the political front as me.

It's funny how my fortune changed by certain events I wasn't in control of.

I felt forced to change unions to stand a chance of winning the stewards election. This led me to become the senior steward of Comau, this opened the door to the branch secretary job for Amicus in Basildon, which came with a huge membership. This led me on the path to be on the Executive Committee for the Amicus Eastern region.

Now I found myself moved to another Labour Constituency. I didn't know it at the time, but another door was shortly to be opened.

A few months had passed and I hadn't heard anything about this new Rayleigh & Wickford constituency.

In the end, I phoned up the Labour Party head office and was informed they'd already had a couple of meetings?

'I haven't been informed of any meetings?' I stated. To cut a long story short, the girl I spoke to said she would contact the Rayleigh & Wickford CLP secretary and get him to contact me about the next meeting.

Sure enough, through the post came a large envelope with the previous meetings minutes and the time and date of the next meeting.

I read through the minutes and I couldn't believe what was written, it was unbelievable. I'll give you a couple of examples:

"Election of Chairman:
As nobody stood, John ******** Said he would reluctantly carry on.
Election of the secretary:
As nobody was willing to take on this role, David**** Said he would carry on."

I sat and read through the remaining minutes. Nothing about fundraising, guest speakers, advertising. No treasury reports. Basically, it was a crock of shit.

At the bottom of the minutes was the location and time of the next meeting.
A stroke of luck, it was going to be held not far from me in Wickford.
Time for some action. I had to get the Hoof active. So, I phoned him and told him what had happened. He didn't seem too interested, he was still smarting after he had watched my speedy rise through the ranks, plus taking the senior stewards job away from him. However, I mentioned the chairman's position and he softened.
'Sounds like there crying out for an experienced chairman. Think about it, Chairman of your local Labour Party is a prestigious position.'
'When did you say the meeting was again?' I had him hooked.
I agreed to pick him up, the first time I'd been to his house, and one I'll never forget.
It had been raining and the Hoof's wife Brenda answered the door.
'He's just getting ready Trevor, come in.'
I was wearing a nice pair of Nike trainers, I'd only just got them. But I kicked them off in the hallway and followed Brenda into the lounge. They had one of those ugly dogs, a British Bulldog Terrier. He kept trying to jump up at me. Brenda grabbed him and chucked him into the hallway.
'Sorry about that, he can go up and torment Hoof.'
She made me a cup of tea and said she would go up and hurry him up.
Five minutes later he came down.
'Right are we fit?'
'Yes, let's go.' I walk out into the hallway and my trainers are no longer there?
'Where're my trainers?' I ask.
'I don't know, maybe Brenda put them away somewhere.' The Hoof opened the understairs cupboard, but no trainers were to be seen. So, he called up the stairs.

'Brenda, have you seen Trevor's trainers?'
I look up and see Brenda coming down all embarrassed carrying the remains of my trainers. Remains maybe not be the right word to describe two rubber soles.
'I'm so sorry, Trevor, the dog has had a go at them, they looked expensive.'
'They were, Brenda.' The Hoof takes a look and comes out with a rather stupid statement.
'Leave them here, Brenda can fix them.'
'Well, I'm not sure there is much I can do.' Remarked Brenda, being realistic about the situation.
'There's glue under the stairs. Have a go.' Called out the Hoof, desperate not to have to open his wallet.
'Borrow a pair of my shoes for now.' He disappeared under the cupboard again and came out with a pair of white trainers.
Now, although they were my size, there was a slight problem. I didn't have a hoof, so the right trainer had been built up. So, when I walked, it looked like I had a limp. Because we were now running late, I had no choice. We trotted out to my car like a couple of thoroughbreds.
Of course, no mention of paying for a new pair of trainers entered the conversation as we drove to the community centre.
As I pulled up, I sensed something was wrong. There wasn't another car in the car park, although I could see someone standing by the entrance door.
'That looks like Diana Taylor.' I tell the Hoof.
'Wait here.' I got out of my car and hobbled over to her. Now Diana was a very active and outspoken member of the local Labour Party. I'd known her for years. She was another one like the Hoof and me who had been moved from the Basildon & Billericay group.
Unfortunately, she'd had a heart attack and wasn't in the best of health. She stood there holding her walking stick as I approached.

'What have you done to your foot, Trevor?' Not wanting to discuss it I quickly dismissed the question.
'Just a slight sprain. What's going on here, Diana?'
'Those bastards from Rayleigh have moved the meeting back to their place.'
'They never notified me.'
'No, they wouldn't. I've just rung their secretary and he said because of the lack of interest from the Wickford members they decided to keep the meetings at Rayleigh.'
'Did they now. Come on Diana, well track these c**** down and sort it.'
The pair of us headed over to my car. As I'm getting in, the Hoof is trying to bundle Diana in the back. My car only had two doors so it wasn't an easy task for a limping elderly woman.
'Let Diana sit in the front, for fuck sake.'
The Hoof, absolutely no scruples at all.
I drive to Rayleigh like a man possessed; to say I'm pissed off is an understatement. What with my trainers and now these clowns playing silly buggers I was just about ready for a showdown.
Maybe it was my red hair, but once the switch was flicked, that was it. Nothing got held back.
I eventually find the village hall, pull up and the three of us walk in, or I should say limp in. If you've watched a three-legged race, double that and you'd get an idea of what we looked like entering the hall that night. I stopped and kicked off the white trainers.
'I can't wear these anymore.'
I leave the trainers in the porchway of this village hall.
Diane offers me her walking stick, thinking I had an injury, bless her.
I can still see the setting now. Two men at the back of the hall, sitting behind a table. One about seventy, bald and was a double for the little guy Benny Hill used to slap on the top of his head.

The other, a man of about sixty. Thickset and heavy-rimmed glasses. Four others were sat, three elderly women who would have looked more at home in the snug of the "Rovers Return" and another bald man, but this one had a bushy beard. He looked like he had his head on upside down.
Our entry had killed any conversation that was taking place at that time.
We sat down and the evening's entertainment took only seconds to get underway. The bald man behind the table pointed at me.
'The meeting started thirty minutes ago. Coming in here disrupting us without a bye or leave. Who the hell do you think you are?'
Well, that was the ignition switched flicked. I stood up, walked over and grabbed him by his jacket collar.
'Listen c***. I'm a member from Wickford, if you ever move the meeting venue without notifying me again, I promise you, you'll live to regret it.'
Well, you could have heard a pin drop.
'Who are you?' Asked the man wearing the glasses.
'I'm a member of this constituency. Who are you?'
'I'm the secretary.'
'Oh, so you're the pair of clowns who hold these two positions because no one else wanted them. Well, let me tell you something now. You have these positions because you kept the first meeting hush-hush. You never notified any of the Wickford members of the inaugural meeting. Well enjoy your brief reign, because next month we will come mob-handed, we'll put a vote of no confidence in for the pair of you, and trust me when I tell you, you'll be history.'
I went to sit down. The bald man threw the strangest of questions at me.
'Well, where were you in 1953?' I turned and looked at him.'
'I wasn't even born then, cock.'
'Precisely.' He called out.

I never did find out what he was on about. We sat through the rest of the now subdued meeting until it came to any other business. I shot my hand up then stood up and delivered a damning speech about what had gone on. How did they expect to get new members carrying on the way they did? I won't bore you with the details; let's just say for ten minutes I lashed them. Eventually, they closed the meeting and the chairman and secretary hurried out without a second glance. The three old women came over and you'd have thought the lottery had come up.

'My God, we've been waiting years for those two to be put in their place, well done. You'll get our vote.'

'Well I suggest we put the Hoof up for chairman, he has a lot of experience in that role, and we'll try and find a suitable secretary.'

'You need to be the secretary. You are the type of man we want.'

'You'll get my vote, Trevor.' Diana smiled.

Oh well, it looked like I had a shot at being the new secretary. I had a month to drum up support and get them to the next meeting.

As I started to contact Wickford members, it all fell easily onto my lap. I received a letter from the current secretary telling me that the chairman and himself were resigning from their roles. Due to ill health, according to the letter.

It was a shame; I didn't go to that meeting to take his job. Just shake the tree a bit. But if I'm honest, the pair of them shouldn't have been holding those types of positions. As far as I was concerned, New Labour was the future. These old dinosaurs had to go.

A few days later at work, the Hoof was walking around in sunglasses.

'What's up with you? Is it a tribute to Stevie Wonder night?'

'No, my dogs died.' If he was looking for sympathy, he'd come to the wrong guy.

'Well that's no surprise; it will be those trainers of mine he ate, that will teach him. Most probably the glue got stuck in his intestines, was he in much pain when he died?' The Hoof hobbled off distraught.

The sorrow didn't last long for he was soon hobbling around with a smile on his face.

'What, you get a refund on the vet's bill?'

'No, we got a new dog, a puppy.'

'What type?'

'Same as the last one.' So, the Hoof had put his hand in his pocket for a new dog. A dog that would soon enough leave his mark on me.

I should have known better than to go around to his house after seeing him walking around with a black eye.

'Christ, what's happened to you?'

'Well, I went to my daughters for Sunday dinner, she lives at Burnham on Crouch.

I thought I'd take the dog for a walk. Well, all was going well, I took him off his lead and he was having a great time. All of a sudden, he spotted a cat in a garden, and he was away. The bloody dog chased this cat for miles; I was running behind trying to keep him in sight. Eventually, the cat ran up this lamppost. I managed to get the dog on his lead when this man walked over to me and shouted.

Is that your dog?'

'Yes, he is my dog, why do you ask?'

'Because that's my cat up there shitting himself.'

'With that, this bloke thumped me.'

I couldn't help but laugh, but as the old saying goes, he who laughs first laughs last.

About two weeks later I'd arranged to pick the Hoof up for a Labour Party meeting. As per normal, I drove; Mr Tightarse would never volunteer to drive.

It was my first visit since the trainer's episode and I should have had more sense. Brenda opened the door and immediately advised me to leave my shoes on.

Made of the same stuff as the Hoof, she never mentioned my trainers or any financial offer to pay for a new pair.

'He's just getting ready, come on through, Trevor. So, I follow Brenda into the lounge and could hear the dog barking and scratching at the kitchen door.

'I heard you got a new dog.'

'Yes, and he's a bit of a handful.' Well, I wasn't on the ball because as she opened the door, this dog flew past her, leapt at me and locked itself onto my forearm. I kid you not, this dog was mad. The Hoof appeared and between him and Brenda, they prize the dog off my arm, which now had six puncture holes and blood running out.

'For fuck sake, you pair shouldn't own a fucking dog. The last one wrecked my trainers, which by the way you owe me seventy quid for, and now you have a dog that draws blood to your guests.' I stormed out.

'What about the meeting, Trev?'

'You go, I'm off to the hospital, the way my luck is with you I've most probably contracted rabies.'

'You don't have to worry about that, he's had all his injections.'

I won't write the reply I gave him. I'll leave that to your imagination.

So, after two visits to the Hoofs, I've arrived home once on a wet night in just my socks, and this time with my arm bandaged up and a course of tetanus injections to look forward to.

There was something about the Hoof; I guess the best way to sum him up is he was an unsavoury character. Like Pat Brown, he was one of these people that would invade your private space.

You'd talk to him and he'd keep edging nearer. Notorious if a woman was around and had some perverted ways. I can remember Geoff telling me they'd been to London with their wives and while waiting for the train, Hoof handed Geoff some of what he thought were business cards. When he looked, they were call girl cards; he'd been picking them up out of the phone boxes.

'Here, put these in your wallet, you never know when you might need one?' Remarked the Hoof.

I never saw his collection of porn, but allegedly he had the biggest collection of porn for a private collector in Essex. He got barred from our "Tug club," early on for so-called losing a film?

Anyway, he was behaving himself as my chairman of the union branch and the local Labour Party.

I thought a miracle had happened one night when we'd gone to a meeting in Chelmsford.

It was a union meeting and the branch secretary's and chairman were invited. So, we go and as we walk in I'm called over by a couple of Ford guys from Dunton who I got to know from my involvement in the Eastern Region set up. Les McDonald and John Scarola, a couple of decent guys and good union reps. Hoof disappeared inside and I walk over and have a bit of a networking chat.

Well, I looked over and could see the hoof hobbling towards me with two pints in his hands. He was gurning like a good one, It was one of those double-take moments.

'Here you are Trev, got you a pint.' He gave me the drink then ambled off.

'Fuck me,' I tell the Ford reps.

'I don't know if I should drink this or have it framed. It's the first pint he's bought me.' The bubble didn't take long to burst.

'It's a free bar, Trev.'

After this next incident, I'm going to talk about, by rights, the Hoof should have been stood against a wall and shot. He let the trade union down in a big way. He brought shame to our Labour Party constituency and our local branch.
I should have known better than to think I could trust him.

We had to pick a candidate to represent Rayleigh & Wickford at the next General Election. These meetings were called hustings.
Now, the timing couldn't have been worse, the meeting date was set at a time I was abroad on holiday. I put my trust in the Hoof, I mean he'd been involved before when we were members of the Basildon & Billericay constituency. What could possibly go wrong?
I reluctantly went to his house a few days before I was due to go away. This time only after he promised to have the dog in a cage.
Sure enough, when I arrived, the dog was in this large metal cage in the kitchen. When I looked in their lounge, it looked different.
'You had a change round in here?' I ask.
'We treated ourselves to a new three-piece suite.'
'Oh, I didn't think you'd had the other one long?'
'Eighteen months. We left the dog in here while we went shopping, came back and he'd eaten and ruined the lot.'
I couldn't help a wry smile.
The chances of getting any new trainers from the Hoof had gone out the door along with the furniture.

So, I go through the selection procedure, let all the would-be candidates have five minutes to introduce themselves and speak about their vision of representing us at the next General Election. Then hold a vote.'

'No problem, Trev. You go and have a nice holiday.'
So, I did, I mean, what could go wrong?
I forgot one golden rule when dealing with the Hoof, I didn't check if we had any women candidates, it was a schoolboy error that came back to bite me.
I arrive back from holiday and check my answerphone, the usual array of messages until one came out that spelt big trouble.
'Mr Whitehead, I'm calling from the political office of Amicus the union. I have to say not only me but the general secretary is appalled at your choice of candidate at your hustings meeting for the next General election.
We put forward who we thought was the ideal candidate, only to be overturned by one vote in favour of a university graduate. Call me back as soon as you can.'

Now, in my defence, I never knew any of the candidates, I wasn't at the meeting, I'd stupidly left it to the Hoof. So, I phone him and tell him to lock the dog up as I'm on my way round. I purposely don't mention the phone message. I arrive and play it cool.
'So, everything go okay at the hustings?'
'Yes, it was a close-run thing between two in the end.'
'Good, have you got copies of their resume?'
'Err …. Somewhere.'
'Find them, I want to see who we have representing us.' Hoof brought his battered briefcase out and hands me a sheet of paper.
'This is who we elected.' Smiles the Hoof trying to hide his fuck up.
'A woman.'
'Yes, Trev. But what a good speaker.'
'I see. Comes from Scotland, and knows nothing about our local problems. University graduate and never had a job. She must have been a hell of a speaker.'

'She was, Trev, she was.'
'Who were the other candidates?'
'Well, there were five candidates to start with, then it just came down to these two, this was the other candidate, it was a close-run thing I can tell you.'
Hoof passed me another sheet of paper, and it soon became clear why I had an angry message left on my answer machine.
'When you say it was a close-run thing, how close?'
'Errr …. Really close.'
'How close, Hoof?'
'The votes were level, so, I as chairman had the deciding vote.'
'What a surprise, you picked the woman.'
'But she was a good speaker, Trev.'
Luckily Brenda, who knew my language could sometimes be a little colourful, was in the kitchen making a cup of tea.
'You're a stupid C***. You have dropped us right in the shit. I've got the hierarchy of the union on my back because of your fucking stupidity.'
'That's a bit harsh.'
'Fucking harsh you c***. Look at this guy's resume. Twenty years a trade union member, an activist who has loads of experience in the Basildon area. He was put forward by the union, our union, you stupid prick. And you have the deciding vote and don't pick him; you pick a fucking schoolgirl?
'But …'
'If you mention she's a good speaker again I'll kick your arse and lock you in that cage with that fucking dog you stupid c***.'
Brenda walked in and caught the tail of me shouting at her perverted man.
'I'm sorry for the shouting, Brenda. But your husband has done something really stupid.'
'What have you done?'
'I picked who I thought was the better speaker.'

'Well, if I get summoned to head office, you can come with me. Then you can explain why the chairman of our local trade union branch voted against one of our own in favour of a girl.'

In the end, I dealt with the problem. I could have blamed the Hoof, but I tried to save face for the branch's benefit. If you read this Hoof, I hope you hold your head in shame. You have the morals of a sewage rat.
I wouldn't mind when I met the woman she was a plain Jane that looked like she was auditioning for the lead role of the Prime of Miss Jean Brodie.
Ugly wouldn't deter the Hoof.

Now, there's a funny ending to this story. I'd like to say justice was served, but the Hoof is so thick-skinned it just bounced off him.
Let me just say the candidate he had chosen got well and truly hammered in the election and was soon on her way back to Scotland.
And trust me when I tell you, she was a crap speaker. But she wore a skirt and that was enough temptation to get the Hoofs vote.
Let's jump forward five years. It's heading towards hustings time again. After the last embarrassing disaster, I make sure I am not on holiday.
I get an approach at work from Richard Llewellyn. Now Richard knew his politics, he was a councillor and I always had time for him. He asked me how the candidates were shaping up at the forthcoming selection meeting.
I told him I had a couple that looked interesting.
'I have a guy who I'd like you to meet Trev. I think he could do well for you. A local man, and a good trade unionist.'
So, we arranged to meet over a beer in a local pub in Basildon. I ring the Hoof and ask if he wants to come and meet a prospective candidate.

The offer of a free beer is just too much for him. So, he says yes, as long as I drove.

He had a car, but only bought it out of his garage to wash it? So as per normal, I drive to the pub, and the four of us meet up. Richard introduces the guy and we get a beer and sit down. Five minutes of general chit chat and then we get down to business. For the life of me, I can't remember the man's name. He was a post office worker, I can remember that.

So, I asked the guy what experience he had.

'Well to be honest Trevor, this is my second attempt. I don't think you were around five years ago when I last stood.'

'I must have been, I've been the Labour Party secretary for seven years now.'

'I don't remember you being at the meeting? I don't know if you remember me then, I was unlucky, I was pipped to the post by the chairman's deciding vote. Some young girl, a university graduate.'

I looked at the Hoof who was now starting to perspire and wriggle on his seat.

Oh, deep joy, I wasn't going to let the Hoof off this one.

'You mean this c***. He was the chairman at that meeting and went against you to pick a school girl.' The three of us looked at the Hoof who avoided eye contact and supped his beer.

'But she was a good speaker.'

The end result of this story was we picked a very good candidate in a guy called Mike Le-Surf, who went on to bigger and better things. I'm still in contact with Mike and can I say what a very good MP he would make. Now here's a man I can say is a very good speaker and works extremely hard for the Labour Party.

Chapter 10

Brussels

The Hoof was becoming a liability. Well, to be honest, he'd been that all the time I'd known him. I thought it was time to ease him out to graze.

I'd known Mick the Munch for several years. He was quite vocal at meetings and I liked the guy. However, he was one of these guys who sometimes didn't engage the brain before talking. Hence the "Could be worse, could have broken a leg," gaff.

He knew how slippery the Hoof was; he worked right next to him for many years.

I encouraged him to stand for steward at the forthcoming shop steward election. We were still working for Comau, although the rumours were beginning to filter in that this move wasn't working as well as the Italians had hoped.

Stories were coming in that some of the other European plants, that had also outsourced maintenance were going back in-house.

Now, as much as I used to get the backroom lawyers telling me how crap it was working for Comau, we'd never lost a penny in our time with them. What New Holland achieved in a pay deal, we'd get. As far as I was concerned we had it good. We'd stayed in the pension scheme, so we were doing okay. The one thing the backroom lawyers never considered, while we were Comau, we couldn't be fodder for the production line. In other words, when the line was short of bodies, they couldn't come and take any of us.

Michael Newman was a manager who would listen and I could do business with him.

Now Michael wasn't popular with a lot of the guys because he favoured his son Justin.

Justin was an electrician and let's just say, he was looked after. Nepotism I think is the word I'm looking for. A word was thrown at me from some of the workforce. I must admit the first time I heard the word I had to look the meaning up!
It didn't bother me; it was something we all would do given the opportunity. But it got the backs up on a few of the guys, and they'd regularly bend my ears about it. Jealousy, a terrible trait.
All the years Michael was my manager, I can only remember him losing his temper once. I can't remember the problem, something in my mind recalls we were organising a ballot. I think the word "Ballot," would set something off in the minds of a manager.
My first meeting with the Security manager Jim McClure blew up over a ballot I was organising.
It was something to do with Tony Lynch and us three stewards wasn't having it. I should rephrase that. Eddie Priestaff and I weren't having it; the Hoof was in his usual position of sitting on the fence.
Anyway, the word ballot had reached our manager and we were summoned to Michael's office to sort this problem out.

Michael had phoned me and said they were waiting for me. Now, always one to mix things up a bit I told him I was on my way. But I stopped at a vending machine and had a coffee. Michael rang me again.
'Where are you?'
'I told you, I'm on my way.'
'Where are you coming from ... Wickford?'
'Two minutes.' I told him. So, I waited for five and then walked in.
Now the maintenance office was a rather large affair. With Michael's office at the far end. It was a full-length glass affair so when the blinds were open you could see right in. A row of desks was positioned for the various foreman. Trevor Evans,

one of our foremen was sat at one. A nice guy and like me a Southend United supporter.

'Hurry up, they're waiting for you.' He tells me as I enter the outer office. So, I knock on the door and walk in.

Outside, Trevor Evans sat back and watched the fun begin.

I'll set the scene. Michael sat behind his desk; glasses perched precariously at the end of his nose. Tony Lynch, one eye shut and gurning was sat to one side. Eddie and the Hoof sitting directly opposite Michael.

I could see Tony, chomping at the bit, he knew I'd purposely dragged my heels and he wasn't happy.

'Where the fuck have you been?' He asked, in his usual polite manner.

'I had work to do, I can't just drop everything because of you.' My tactic of letting them simmer for a while had worked a treat.

I could see things were about to get lively, Tony didn't like it if he didn't get his own way, and he didn't like backchat, especially from me.

Michael, seeing the tension rising tried to keep the meeting in an orderly fashion.

He'd make a good poker player, Michael. He didn't show any signs of what was about to come.

'Now lads, what's all this nonsense about?' He asked.

Well, what happened next has stayed with me forever. Eddie, a man of few words and gently spoken looked across at Michael stared him in the eyes and said.

'What the fucks it got to do with you.'

Well, it was as if a powder keg had been lit, the room erupted into mayhem. Michael, I'm not sure to this day what started him off; maybe he'd not been spoken to as a manager like that before. He stood up and threw his glasses at Eddie.

'What's it got to do with me, I'm your manager.' All I can say is for the next five minutes the room was just full of shouting, pointing the finger, there was pushing and shoving going on.

Tony and I set about each other, at one point I had to get between Eddie and Michael. I think I had Tony by the tie at some point. And through all this chaos sat the Hoof, not saying anything, but getting whiter by the second.
At one point I knocked him off his chair as I grappled with Tony. In the end, we were sent out; a calming down period was called for. The three of us walked out past a smiling Trevor Evans.
'What time are you meeting again? I'll make sure I'm in here.'
'I bet you will, give it twenty minutes, the Hoof needs a laydown.'
No truer word was said in jest.
We ended up going to Eddie's electrical crib where we did our best to calm down over a cup of tea. The Hoof sat there white as a ghost and quiet. Things needed to be said.
Eddie had a go at him first.
'You need to get involved, sitting there like a bloody mannequin.'
My views on Eddie changed after that day, he was the type of guy that was quiet and polite, but if you pushed him too far, he'd explode.
Eddie's remark to the Hoof didn't quite hack it with me, I felt a stronger approach was needed.
'Hoof, you need to go. You are too old and gutless to be a steward.'
'I'm a year younger than Eddie.'
'You might be a year younger, but you're a liability, as Eddie pointed out, you sat there like a tailor's dummy when you should have been getting stuck in. You let us down and you let our colleagues down. I'm not going back to them until we have the agreement to hold a ballot.'
The Hoof sat there, like he always did, with that stupid smarmy face. This time he wasn't going to get away with it. He'd ducked and dived for the past ten years as a steward, but for once he hung himself without any further help from Eddie and me. Once comment sealed his fate.

'I don't like confrontation!' He hung himself. A shop steward, who didn't like confrontation. He didn't know it at the time, but his time was over.
I told him to stay where he was and let Eddie and me go back in and sort out an agreement.
He was a liability that was getting found out.

A few weeks later, he was booked in for an operation on his foot. While he was away recuperating, they pensioned him off. Now, surprisingly for a man who never spent a penny without breaking into a sweat, he had bought a luxury caravan in the South of France.
By doing that, it meant he would be gone a lot of the summer months. Mick the Munch came on board and I soon made him the branch chairman.
I replaced Hoof from the Labour Party chairman's position too. He was missing a lot of meetings with his new holiday home. However, he still came to the branch meetings when he was home.

It was at a branch meeting that I read out an invitation to visit the European Parliament in Brussels.
You needed to be a Labour Party member and the trip included travelling there on the Eurostar and two nights in a hotel. The second evening would be a bit of a gala dinner with one of our MEP's.
The cost was sixty-nine pounds a head. We were a bit flush in the branch so I said if anybody at the meeting would like to go, the branch would pay.
Like the three amigos, Hoof, Munch and I stepped forward.

If I thought the hotel business with Pat Brown couldn't be beaten, I was in for a shock.
The Pat Brown entertainment show was just a matinee for the main event.

I can only describe this trip as going on an excursion with Laurel and Hardy.

It started well enough. I travelled with the Hoof from Wickford station, and we met up with the Munch at St Pancras.

I spotted my two fellow committee members from the Eastern Region, Fords reps John and Les.

We then meet a girl who is in charge of the group for this trip. She works for the union in the political department. She was pretty and as per normal, the Hoof is all over the poor girl, introducing himself and hanging on to her hand way too long. I had to step in and prise her away so she can introduce us to the rest of the group.

It was a mixed bunch, to say the least. One, whose name I can't remember was a turban-wearing Geordie, who had a wicked sense of humour. Turned out to be a very nice bloke. There were some older women and a couple of would-be trainspotters.

As what was required by now in the Labour Party the group had to have a fair representation of the LGBTQ brigade. Two people turned up who without a shadow of a doubt represented the Q. Say no more. We had the Turban wearing Geordie, so I think our group was well represented to the politically correct minded mob.

I'm guessing there was about twenty of us on this trip all told. We had about forty minutes to kill before the train was due, so the three of us and the Fords guys decided to get some refreshments in. We hit the bar and the Hoof did his normal hanging back approach.

Munch stepped up, 'What do you want lads?' We order up a pint each and the Hoof asked for a cup of tea.

I then read the hoof the riot act.

'Don't you embarrass me on this trip; you put your hand in your pocket.' The Hoof did his usual innocent plea along with his stupid face.

'I was just about to ask but Munch beat me to it.' If dodging buying a beer was an Olympic sport, the Hoof would have a whole collection of gold medals.
Munch returned with a tray with five pints.
'Teas off, Hoof.'
Just as we are finishing up, I tell the Hoof to get a round in. Honestly, he was nearly in tears. The smile that came on his face as our trip guide came over and told us the train was boarding was unbelievable.
'Oh, that's a shame; I was just about to go to the bar and get you, boys, a drink.'
He calls out as he gets up close and personal with the guide as she heads to the train.
The Fords guys weren't impressed with the Hoofs antics with this girl. Something John Scarola pointed out to me.
'You need to have a word with your mate Trev before he gets hit with a sexual harassment charge.'
'I'll have a word, don't worry.'
Yet again the Hoof is embarrassing the union.
Once we were on the way I marked his card.
'For fuck sake Hoof, leave that poor girl alone, will you. You're in your sixties and she is no more than twenty-two. You're making a fool of yourself. People are making complaints about you and we're still in England. Fucking behave yourself.'
John and Les were sat opposite looking like the Kray twins.
'I was just being friendly.'
'Well, go and be friendly to our friends over there.' I pointed at our two Q representatives.
'Maybe later, I need to close my eyes for a while, I was up early.'
I pointed to the Buffet car and John and Les followed.

The trip on the train went quickly. The four of us were soon settled in the buffet car and the journey was, let's say enjoyable. The Hoof hadn't budged from his seat since I

threatened to send him over to make friends with our Q guys. To be honest, after a few more beers I was past worrying about him. A coach picked us up at the train station and dropped us off at our hotel.
It was late afternoon by the time we arrived.
I hadn't been to Belgium since I was a kid and I'd not been to Brussels, before. So was keen to visit a few places as well as listen in and watch the European Union in action.
Now, we had the first evening to ourselves.
John and Les had done the trip before and told us they knew a nice restaurant in town. So, we arranged to meet in the bar at seven and get a taxi to the restaurant.
As per normal, the Hoof did a swerve.
'I'm going to eat in the hotel.' He announced.
Hotel food was expensive which the Munch would find out shortly.
Hoofs statement about eating in the hotel most probably meant he'd done himself a packed lunch and would scurry away somewhere to eat it.
We collected our keys and headed to our rooms , it turned out the whole group were on the same floor. The Hoof was between Munch and me.
I decided to grab a couple of hours sleep and set the alarm on my phone for six-thirty.
After a power nap and a shower, I felt great. I head down to the bar just before seven and I find the Munch tucking into a beer and a large plate of chips?
'I'm starving,' he announced.
'But we're going out to eat in a minute.'
'Don't worry about that, this is just a starter.'
'Let's have a chip then,' I ask.
'Make sure it is one at this price.'
'Why, how much?'
'Seven euros.'
'What with the beer.'

'No seven euros for a plate of chips.'
I can't remember what the exchange rate was back then, but I think it's fair to say the Munch had paid over five pounds for a plate of chips.
'Why don't you put some tomato sauce on the chips?' I ask.
Munch points to the menu, fifty cents for a small sachet of sauce!!
John and Les turned up with another guy from the group.
'Where's your mate, the Hoof?'
'He didn't want to come; he's up in his room eating cheese sandwiches.' I joke.
'Yes, and watching the porn channel knowing him,' piped in the Munch.
I must admit at that point I did think of Pat Brown, another porn addict.
I prayed the Hoof wasn't going to cause us a problem when checking out.
I'd looked at the film channels and a message flashed up that if you were on a pay per view channel for more than five minutes you would be charged for the whole film.
Like the price of chips, it wasn't cheap.
I sort of relaxed when I read that message; there would be no way the Hoof would be forking out for Porn.

We end up going in two taxis and after a less than ten-minute drive we arrive at a very nice-looking restaurant. Now, can I just state at this point, the only other time I'd eaten out with the Munch was at a McDonalds? So I wasn't prepared for what was to come.
We go into the restaurant and get a large table for the five of us.
I sit opposite the Munch and we browse over the menu and eventually order up. The beers come and we are in good spirits.

I suppose in the Munch's defence, the menus were written in I believe Dutch and French, but unbeknown to me at that time, it was all Double-Dutch to the Munch.

So, the food arrived. I had played it safe with a nice pate dish for starters.

I look in amazement as a huge bowl is placed in front of the Munch. I'm talking fishbowl big.

'What you got there, mate?' I enquire.

'Soup.' He announced, with a look of "What the fuck have I ordered."

Now, apart from the sheer size of the bowl, I thought that was a wise choice for a skinny man who had tucked away a large plate of chips some thirty minutes earlier.

I start on my pate and toast and it was very nice. All of a sudden the Munch spits out a large mouthful of soup back into the bowl.

'Aghhh,' he shouts out. Causing a lot of the restaurant patrons to look round.

'What's up?' I ask.

'It's this soup, Trev. It's got fish in it.' He proceeds to chase a bit of fish around the bowl till he gets it on his spoon. He stands up to show me and the other guys.

'Look.' Sure enough, sitting on his spoon was a fish head, a big fish head that explained the large bowl.

'They should have served that with a fishing rod,' remarked John, making the rest of us, minus the Munch, laugh.

'Jesus Christ, Munch. What did you order?'

'Fish soup!!'

Now, I know we were in a different country, but I would imagine wherever you go in the world if you order fish soup, there is a strong possibility you might find fish in it.

I live in Asia, fish head is a delicacy here.

Of course, this little pantomime scene had the others and myself very amused.

Next up, the main dish.

I had ordered a chicken dish and once again it looked and tasted very nice.
The Munch, who again is served last, gets a large steak and salad plonked down in front of him.
'I don't believe it,' he moaned in his best Victor Meldrew voice.
'What's up now? Has that steak got meat in it?' I jokingly ask.
'No chips. Bloody salad, do I look like a rabbit?'
He called a waiter over and demanded chips.
'French fries, gracias.' I didn't like to tell him we were nowhere near Spain.
He picked at the steak and eventually gave me about three-quarters of it. Plus, most of his late delivery of chips were shared amongst the rest of us.
A dessert trolley was wheeled around and he seemed to get a second wind. He picked two different desserts and made a right pig of himself.
Washing it down with more beer, he started to look a little pale.

The Fords guys, past masters of pacing themselves were off to sample the nightlife.
I looked at the state of the Munch and knew I wouldn't be sampling a lot of anything.
I thought I'd better get him back to the hotel.
We settle the bill and walk outside and hail a taxi.
We were on the road for about two minutes when he screams at the driver to stop. He jumps out and projectile vomits everywhere. Luckily he'd not honked up in the cab. However, the cab driver wouldn't let him back in and we ended up having to walk back to the hotel.
A two-mile walk with a drunken sick man is slow and tedious. I haven't a clue what the time was when the hotel, at last, came into view.

As we approached the entrance, I could see the hoof hovering about. He looked suspicious with his long coat and cloth cap on.
I crept up behind him and tapped him on the shoulder.
'What are you up to?' He jumped out of his skin. Then I saw what he was looking at. Across the road from the hotel were a few ladies of the night.
He just couldn't help himself; he wouldn't pay for sex with one of them, no, he would Rather watch and perv for free.
'Go to bed, Hoof before they think you're Jack the Ripper.' I suggested.
'Yeah, I will in a minute, I'm just enjoying the fresh air.'
'Up to you, John and Les were telling Mick and me about a guy who got stabbed by a prostitute outside this very hotel only last week.'
'Maybe I will go to bed. What's up with Mick?' He asked on spotting the Munch slumped down on a chair in the reception.
'He fell out with a fish, come on.'

The next morning at breakfast we were told we had the morning to ourselves, then early afternoon we would be taken as a group to the European Parliament for a sit-in and a tour around, plus a chance to meet a few of our MEP's.
The three of us go for a walk around and ended up at a beautiful and very popular landmark. The Grand Place, we literally stumbled across this beautiful building by luck. So a look around and a couple of other buildings in this famous square took us to lunch.
We'd passed what looked like a nice pizza place on our way to the square. After The Munch's last eating performance I thought Pizza was a safe bet.
We order a very large Pizza for the three of us and a soft drink each.
We nearly had to shake the hoof upside down by his ankles to get him to pay a third of the bill.

Luckily the large pizza arrived and there wasn't a fish head to be seen.
In the afternoon, we were taken to the European Parliament building and we sat in for an hour to listen in on a debate. We were given headphones and I take my hat off to the translators who could translate many different languages.
The previous late night had caught up with the Hoof, the Munch nudged me and I looked at the Hoof who was sat next to me.
He was sound asleep. Not for long as I leant over and pressed the button that would turn his headphones up to full volume. His shout made everybody jump.
'Wake up Hoof, your snoring.'
'I wasn't asleep, I was resting my eyes.' He pleaded.

We ended up in a room with a couple of MEP's, neither had I heard of, then or since.
Once back at the hotel we were told to meet in one of the hotel function rooms at 7 pm, where we would be wined and dined by one of our local MEP's, Richard Howitt.
I'd met Richard a few times at Labour Party Conferences.
To be honest, I thought he was gay, however, he was married with kids, so I got that wrong.
He was a tall man, at least six feet six. So, the high soft voice didn't quite go with the rest of him.
The three of us sat at a table. The Fords guys decided they didn't want another night of Munch's eating disorder or be in the presence of the lecher from Wickford and kept away, as did our tour host who kept a safe distance from the Hoof ever since that first encounter at the train station.
There was a bottle of red and a bottle of white wine on the table. Hoof announced he only drank white wine. Munch and I weren't fussed as we stuck to the beer.

The evening was a bit of a bore, to be honest; Richard Howitt sat with us for at least two minutes before he wandered off to another table.

By now, Hoof had sunk the white wine, however, his statement of I only drink white wine wavered as his love of red wine had started?

Might have had something to do with it being free.

So, after another hour, Munch and I went off to the hotel bar. We had met two women from Ilford.

Nothing in it, but we joined them and had a laugh. Later I'd gone up to the bar to get some more drinks when I looked out and spotted the Hoof staggering in. Two bottles of wine were obviously taking their toll.

In a language unbeknown to me, he ordered a drink. The barman surprisingly understood and put a large glass down which when I smelt I discovered was a neat whiskey.

'Easy Hoof, we have to travel home in the morning.'

'Don't worry about me, I'm pacing myself.'

Spotting Munch, he staggered over and plonked himself down between the two women.

It was hard to understand him because he was slurring his words. Unfortunately, the women understood him only too well and the next thing we knew he'd got a slap. Munch pulled him up and sent him to bed.

After apologising for his behaviour, they settled down. A good hour must have passed and I was getting us a nightcap when I spotted Hoof wandering around the foyer.

Now, because of his Hoof, he had a funny walk anyway. But he was staggering around defying the laws of gravity. I was worried he'd hurt himself.

I walked out to see what he was up to.

'What you doing? You went off to bed an hour ago, go to bed for fuck sake.'

Hoof looks at me with his glassy eyes and said something that made me laugh.

'I can't find my room?' He announced.
'Your room is between Munch and mine.'
'I know, but where is that?'
'Wait here.' I sit him down then go and tell the others I'm calling it a night.
I go back, help him up and escort the Hoof to his room. I shove him in and throw his key on his bed.
I get into my room, I'm feeling a bit worse for wear, but I still knew what I was doing.
I have a quick shower, drink a bottle of water, set my alarm for seven.
We'd been told to be at breakfast for seven-thirty as we were being picked up at eight-thirty. I checked my watch, It had just gone 2 am.
Feeling knackered, I climb into bed and within a minute I was drifting off.
A loud knocking on my door made me jump. I check my phone and it's 3 am. I slip on my jeans and open the door.
Standing there, swaying was the Hoof.
In his hand, a TV remote control.
'What the hell do you want?'
'I've got my TV stuck on the porn channel and I can't switch it off. My batteries are dead. Can I borrow yours?'
'No.' I slammed the door.
As I get back into bed I can hear some shouting and gather the Hoof had woken the Munch with the same request. This all ended with some loud banging of a door and someone shouting to keep the noise down.
I'm past caring and drop back into a deep sleep.
The next morning I'm woken by the alarm, I get showered and packed and enjoying a coffee and complimentary biscuit before I go to breakfast.
A sudden knocking on my door, again made me jump. I open it ready to blast the Hoof when I'm surprised to see the Munch standing in just his Y-Fronts.

'Come on, we need to be at breakfast.' He informs me.
'You going down like that, are you?' He looked down at himself and realised what a fool he looked.
'No, hang on.' He ran back to his room and within seconds he is back out in his jeans and t-shirt.
'Better give the Hoof a knock.'
So, while the Munch is trying to get his shoes on I knock on the Hoof's door.
There's no answer.
'I bet he's already gone down for breakfast.'
'Cheeky fucker, he could have waited for us,' moaned the Munch.
We get the lift down and as we walk into the dining room we can see the rest of our group, but no Hoof.
This was all getting too much for Mick; he was hungry and could see all this food. Now he had to go back to the Hoof's room.
'Let's leave him,' he suggested.
'We can't do that,' I tell him, as much as I was tempted to.
So, back we go and I knock really hard on his door.
This time we hear groaning and eventually, the door is opened. I look through and can't see him. I look down and there he is on all fours.
'Come on, it's breakfast time.'
'I don't feel well.'
'I'm not surprised. Two bottles of wine and a large whiskey. You need to get something down you, it will sort you out. You can't travel on an empty stomach.'
I can hear moaning in the background and as I walk in it's coming from his TV.
'Bloody hell, you've still got the porn on.'
'I told you last night, I can't switch it off, my remotes not working.'
Munch walked over and pulled the plug.
'That was difficult, wasn't it?'

What a palaver getting him dressed, he was worse than a toddler, all waving arms and legs.
Munch didn't help the situation by putting Hoof's shoes on the wrong feet.
'I thought you were hungry?' I ask as we piss about putting them on the right feet.

We end up wedging the hoof between us and escorting him down to the dining room. After getting him some tea and toast, I go and join the Munch in getting Belgium's version of a full Monty breakfast.
We're all sat around this big table.
The guy with the turban calls over to me in his broad Indian/Newcastle accent.
'Hey, Trev lad. Did you hear all that commotion outside our rooms last night?'
Before I could answer, the Munch stepped in. He didn't care that there were women at the table; he told them how it was. He pointed at the Hoof.
'That would be this C***. Banging on my door asking if he could borrow my remote because he'd got the porn channel stuck on his TV.'
Well, you could have heard a pin drop. All eyes were fixed firmly on the Hoof.
'I put it on by mistake.' He remarked with that smarmy grin he had.
Mick wasn't having any of the Hoof's bullshit.
'Yes, he thought he watching a film called *Another Queen*. Turned out it was called *Anal Queens*,' wasn't it, Hoof?'
I looked across at our two Q representatives and I wanted the floor to open up and swallow me.

Good old Munch, never backwards coming forward.

I never saw the Hoof check out of the hotel, I would imagine he got stung heavily when the hotel worked out the number of films he'd watched and the price of a large whisky at the bar.
I half expected him to turn up at the next branch meeting with a receipt and try and claim it back.

The Hoof must be closing in on eighty as I write this. I've been in Thailand for over eleven years now and never heard a word from him. Thank God.
I did ask Geoff about him and he'd not heard a word about him either.
I've met a lot of people in my time, but never anybody remotely like him.
If you've read that chapter and think I have exaggerated, I can assure you I haven't. People who knew the Hoof would tell you I am spot on.

Chapter 11

Gone, but never to be forgotten.

Well as we know, all good things must come to an end.
I was summoned to Michael Newman's office and told the news. Our time with Comau was coming to an end.
For once the rumourmongers had got it right.
For me on a personal level I felt a bit sad, I thought we'd done well under this so-called maintenance specialist company. As for Michael, well I guess he knew the exit door wasn't far away. This is only my view on things; I might be completely off track here.
I think, well I know actually that Michael upset the CNH hierarchy and once we were heading back in-house, a few scores were to be settled.
One manager at the time, who I got to know, later on, was a very vindictive and nasty piece of work. I could imagine the frustration he had in not being able to get at Michael because we were with Comau.
He never told me at that meeting, but I think we both knew it was the beginning of the end for him. He was in his mid-fifties at the time.
But, unfortunately, his days were now numbered.
The *Rat* phoned me, he couldn't wait to tell me the news. I went to see him. Now, because he was so unpopular with the workforce, he'd moved the convenors office out of the factory and into the Admin building.
Have you ever heard of such a thing? An hourly paid convenor who was based in an office block away from the factory.
I'd not seen him for a long time. He'd rarely be seen on the shop floor.

I knew he wanted to see me and gloat. Plus of course, he was still angry that I'd changed from the Transport and General union to the AEEU, or Amicus as we were now called.

Now, this chapter is going to be very difficult to put any humour in. This was the time of big change.
As I went into the convenors office I was surprised to see how bloated and ill he looked. Ridiculous comes to mind when I think back to how he looked as he sat there.
Bloated, puffy-faced, pale and dyed jet black hair. Here was a man who had a heart attack in his early thirties, smoked like a trooper and did no exercise. How is he still alive?
I have a message for him. Keep moving *Rat* before they start throwing dirt over you.
Any respect I had for this man had long gone. I knew what he'd been up to. Things had happened in the plant that was a bloody disgrace. But we'll come to all that shortly.
What I remember it was as normal the briefest of meetings with him.
He told me nothing that I didn't already know.
I knew I'd always remain a junior steward now. I wasn't Transport and General anymore, so all the plum roles would stay with them.
I didn't care; I was doing well without all that crap. I was a branch secretary, a member of the Amicus Eastern Region executive committee and the secretary of the local Labour Party, plus I'd recently been put onto the Amicus political committee which guaranteed a place at the Labour Party conference each year.
All these positions were untouchable to the likes of the *Rat* and the Transport and General stewards.
I should mention at this point that the rest of the guys I got on well with. The likes of Geoffrey Martin-Smith, Alan Phillips, Paul Norris and a new steward, Warren Gibson, I think I can say we had a healthy respect for each other.

I knew they would always stick together, but I think they were happy to have their numbers bolstered a bit.

Before the transfer back to the company happened, a major shock was announced.
The *Rat* had gone. Rumours were rife, but to be fair to the remaining T&G stewards, they kept a lid on the reason for his sudden departure.
I knew something must have happened because he wouldn't have gone voluntarily. The *Rat* would have been around the fifty-five mark when this happened.
I recently contacted Warren Gibson who I knew would tell me the truth about the real reason for the *Rat's* departure. He was more than happy to put the record straight.
I'd suspected for years he was on the take one way or another. The way he rolled over on letting contractors take the work away from our men, was a disgrace. I could fill this book up with his dodgy deals

You have to go right back to the nuts and bolts outsourcing. It just didn't add up, why let it happen? We had the support of the men. Everybody knew that if you open the door to one, it didn't matter how small the department was. The door was permanently ajar.
The security takeover was downright criminal. Farcical when you think of one of our allegedly better managers, a representative from the H/R department could be swayed by the *Rat* to outsource to a company that had no experience. That was the straw that broke the camel's back when that happened.
As I mentioned earlier in the book, I couldn't be a party to that sort of thing, so I resigned.
So, Warren told me exactly what happened, and I will use the word **allegedly** happened to save any comebacks.

It was the time when the *Rat* had bought the bungalow in Benfleet. The bungalow Tony Lynch was trying to find when we played *follow the van*.

Now the *Rat* obviously at this point of time had a lot of power, so he got a few of the stewards to help him move some stuff from his house in Canvey Island to Benfleet, during working hours of course.

Luckily his laziness and abuse of power led to his downfall. Warren and two other stewards who I won't name were removing contents from the house when they came across a tin of old payslips. A lot of them are unopened. Curiosity and the mistrust they must have felt at the time led them to open a fairly recent payslip.

What they found was incredible. **Allegedly** the payslip showed that the *Rat* was no longer hourly paid, but paid as a staff member. They worked out that the monthly rate he was getting paid was around what a grade ten manager would earn. He was earning more than Michael Law, **Allegedly.**

Could this scandalous accusation be true?

Well, I'll never really know, I wasn't there. If it is true, then it all makes sense. The outsourcing, the cowboy type of firms that were coming in. The poor results of pay negotiations. If it is true, my God the H/R personnel at the time must have been rubbing their hands together. They had the convenor in their pocket.

They got away lightly when you think about it. If they did get him to agree to a low pay rise, it would save the company millions over the years, not just the reduction in wages, but your pension too.

I know we weren't Fords anymore, but I kept a vested interest in their pay and conditions. It only took a few years for their production employees to be earning more than a pound an hour more than our guys. Like I said, if this was true then the knock-on effect was saving the company millions long term. Warren had no reason to lie about what **allegedly** happened.

Two things I will say about this. It brings me back to the way a convenor is chosen in the plant. It's badly floored when a convenor is protected and doesn't have to face the guys on the shop floor.

No way would the **alleged** activities of that man happen if he had to rely on the workforce to get re-elected.

A few of the stewards who were long-time supporters of the *Rat* should be hanging their heads in shame for letting it continue for so many years. I won't name you, but you know who you are.

Unlike the previous convenor, George Catton, who took the underhand way he was removed like a true gentleman. The *Rat*, true to his nickname, scurried away to count his money. To embarrassed to ever show his face back at the plant again. I've been told that he tried to get support by saying he'd never let these company incentives affect his work as the convenor. Thank god, the rest of the stewards had some backbone and shipped him out.

So, there he is, some twenty years later, still living allegedly off a manager's pension. Bloody disgraceful.

I often wonder who in the H/R was involved in this alleged skulduggery.

I have my suspicions of course; one left all of a sudden, maybe the guilt was causing sleepless nights, I hope so.

As I said earlier in the book, I didn't have time for this new breed of H/R specimens that we, unfortunately, ended up with. I'm friends with Dennis Morley, eighty years young and still sharp as a knife.

He, along with the likes of Ken Pocklington and Carl Curbishley, were decent guys who treated you with respect. They were streetwise and knew the working man's problems.

Not like the university graduates that wandered in straight from graduation day and sat in positions that they didn't have a clue about.

I won't lash Dennis over his involvement with the cowboy firm that took over the security and General Service guys.
Even then, he treated people with respect and understood the issues.

Chapter 12

New Beginnings

Out with the old and in with the new. Well, not new by any stretch of the imagination.
Enter Geoffrey Martin-Smith as the new convenor.
At the time, I would think Geoff had been a shop steward for a good thirty years.
I have to admit I wasn't a huge fan of Geoff in his early years as a convenor. But since my recent discovery of the man he took over from, I have nothing but admiration for the guy.
He had to take over and inherit all the shit deals the *Rat* had agreed to over many years.
All this happened while we were at the dregs of our time with Comau.
Things happened fast when we did come back in-house.
As predicted, heads started to roll almost immediately.
My manager Michael Newman was soon shown the door, along with a few of our foremen, including our scissors impersonator Tony Lynch. Trevor Evans waved goodbye, which was a damn shame.
Whispering Eddie Priestaff called it a day.
He was in his early sixties and I think his health was starting to deteriorate.
This left just the Munch and me to come back into the fold as stewards.
We had a new manager appointed, Philip Harris. Strange choice, Phil had progressed from the tools to an engineer and was now promoted to take care of the maintenance. We were a sinking entity; the engine side of the business was disappearing fast. Within eighteen months the back half of the factory was empty.

Now, Phil looked like a choirboy, and to be fair to the guy he was in my eyes a decent enough manager.

However, his boss was a different kettle of fish. I was now faced with a man who made my old manager from way back, Bomando look like a saint. Tough times were coming for the guys in maintenance.

Enter *Bill Sikes*. Now, this is not his name. I won't reveal it, I didn't in 2017 and I don't think it's right to do now.

One reason I don't want to make him famous.

I'll come to this piece of work later.

I must admit I was in for a bit of a shock when I joined up with the old stewards.

I'm not sure how long it had been since I was last with them as a steward. I'd resigned when the security was taken over by Wyatt Earp and his gang. Add on to that the three years with Comau, it must have been a good decade.

To be honest, I wasn't prepared for the shock of seeing how things had slipped.

Gone were any scheduled meetings with the company.

There was no such thing as a Joint Works Committee. Shop steward's meetings were ad hoc and no minutes were taken. There were no records kept. To be honest, the convenors office looked like it had been burgled.

The only good thing I can say about the whole thing is the steward's office was now back in the plant.

I don't know, but I guess it suited the *Rat*, after all, he'd removed the office out to the back and beyond. Unfortunately, Geoff was happy to let it continue. Of course, once you let things like that go, the company would never let you get them back.

What a turnaround, from the days of Bill Cleary and George Catton. Everything was organised, the meetings were set in stone, minutes of the meetings would come out on the factory floor at regular intervals. The guys were kept informed.

The stewards held some respect back then. I do remember bringing it up with Geoff and Warren who was then the vice-convenor.
They did hold their hands up with embarrassment, but nothing changed. Such a shame.

It didn't take long for the maintenance moaners who were regularly berating me about how bad it was working for Comau, to be singing a different tune.
They started loaning us maintenance guys to production. If an area was short, we'd be obliged to send two or three guys over to work on the line.
It was tough for many, it's not easy work, and if you've only done maintenance work for thirty years, trying to keep up with a moving assembly line wasn't an easy task.
I can remember being loaned out myself with a fitter named Andy Sackett.
Christ, that was a long week. We'd been given the fairly easy task of fitting the steps on, we couldn't believe it when the guy showing us said we were doing a job that one man normally did.
We thought we had it sussed one morning, we didn't have to fit steps to every tractor, some didn't have the steps so we could relax for a minute. Andy walked up the line and returned smiling.
'Stand down; we have a gap of ten tractors.'
In my head, I worked out that we had a good thirty to forty minutes to relax.
'I'm going for a poo,' I announced.
Luckily the toilets are next to the line, so I go in, sit down and relax with my paper. Just as I'm finishing off I get Andy shouting at me through the door.
'Hurry up, I got it wrong, we've missed a couple.' My God, I came out and we were now in the shit, literally.

We had to chase down the line and for a good hour, we did our best to catch up. The guys further down the line weren't happy with us. Getting in their way while we had to borrow airlines to plug our guns in and all sorts.

I think I lost half a stone that week. Better than any slimming club.

If work was getting more difficult, I was at least enjoying my time away at different facets of the union.

I was attending many conferences. I'd somehow got myself an invite to the TUC conference.

Now I was there representing the Amicus motor vehicles executive committee. I was asked to do a 3-minute speech on the decline of the UK motor industry. So basically, apart from these 3 minutes, I had five days to relax and enjoy the conference, and of course, in the evenings do some networking over a few beers. I was put into a nice hotel in Brighton and was having the time of my life.

On Thursday, I was due to speak. Now people who know me will vouch that this is something I don't have any trouble with. I reported to the administrator's office first thing and they gave me a beeper.

My instructions were simple; when your beeper goes off, report to the side of the stage. Show them you're ID, and they will tell you what to do. What could possibly go wrong?

I had my speech in my pocket and was looking forward to delivering a damning account of how the motor vehicle industry was in a downward spiral.

I'd done my research, timed the speech and was feeling confident.

That morning I was listening to various speakers and suddenly the bleep vibrated in my pocket. It made me jump and suddenly I was feeling a tad nervous. I made my way to the side of the stage and produced my ID.

I was told to wait until the next person stood up to speak. Then go and sit on the side of the stage. So, I waited, and as soon as the next speaker made his way to the lectern, I made my way up.
Now, there was a man already sitting there who was next to go, I sat down next to him and I could feel the shaking coming from him.
'Nervous?' I enquire.
'Bricking it, mate. I've never done anything like this before. And that doesn't help.'
When I looked at where he was pointing I could see a huge screen staring at you from the back of the hall.
Basically, as you spoke, you could see a giant headshot of yourself looking back at you.
'I see what you mean. I bet he's regretting eating a black seeded roll for breakfast.'
That little funny from me settled the guy down a bit. I told him I'd been on a public speaking course and the best advice I could give him was to think everyone in the audience was naked. A thirty-second warning beep could be heard and the guy on the stage wrapped up his speech.
'Fancy a beer after?' He asked.
'Go on then, I'll see you in the Aussie bar next door.'
I can't remember his name, but I didn't make the bar for a drink as a catastrophe was heading my way.
For as he walked out onto the stage, the man behind me sat down. Not any man, the bloody Prime Minister. Yes, Gordon Brown had plonked himself down. Not knowing the correct etiquette, I just hit him with, 'alright Gordon.'
To be fair he said hello back, and I was now keen to show off my hard-hitting but with a touch of humour speech.
I think the nerves were beginning to get to me, which caused me to keep talking. I don't know what I was rambling on about, but it drew attention to Gordon's bodyguard who I could see staring at me from the side of the stage. He gave me the two-

finger gesture, not the one that you stick up, the one where you point to your own eyes and then to the other person. It was his way of saying "I'm watching you and shut the fuck up."
Next thing I'm being tapped on the shoulder.
'Excuse me, Mr Whitehead, do you mind waiting. We want Gordon to go on next.' Some flunky had put me behind the Prime Minister. I was angry, so said back.
'Of course, no problem.'
Well, what else could I say?

Now Gordon Brown wasn't my cup of tea I have to say. His popularity was on the slide at that time. But one thing he could do, he could deliver a great speech.
So, for ninety minutes, I sat and listened, and started to sweat. Not helped by the bodyguard still scouring at me. Imagine what it feels like when you've been persuaded to get up and sing at a karaoke night. You can't sing, but you'll give it a go. Suddenly a guy gets up and sounds like Frank Sinatra. You pray and hope, but to no avail, your name is called out to follow that guy.
So, by the time Gordon had finished, all my confidence and self-belief in myself had long gone. In fact, I was becoming a jabbering wreck. My heart was going ten to the dozen and I was feeling breathless.
Gordon walked off to sumptuous applause. He looked at me and ignored a handshake.
I stood up, walked out to the lectern and pulled my speech out of my pocket, and it was as if I'd used invisible ink?
The ink had disappeared in my sweaty pocket.
'What the fuck.' Maybe not the greatest opening line of any speech, but a certain attention grabber.
I'd forgotten about the microphone and my deep voice was now booming across the auditorium. If any of the delegates weren't paying much attention, they certainly were now. I looked up and could see my giant head staring back at me.

My advice to the guy about imagining the audience naked backfired because I looked at myself on the screen and I thought I looked stark bollock naked. I take a deep breath and try and compose myself.

'He's got a cheek that Gordon, making me wait ninety minutes to come out here. Some bugger has nicked the ink off my notes while I've been waiting.' I held my blank paper up and got a laugh.

To this day I couldn't tell you what I spoke about for the three minutes.

Obviously, I must have somehow mentioned the motor industry, but trust me when I say I must have waffled on and was praying for the thirty-second warning beep.

I think I was mediocre to poor, judging by the limp applause at the end.

Funny enough, I was never asked to talk at a conference again? Not sure why?

I preferred the Labour Party Conferences, I built up friendships with guys that I still have contact with today.

For some reason, the Welsh contingent took a liking to me. I'd go out and have a drink with them at night and they were great fun.

They smuggled me into their gala evening, it was in some hotel and they had a spare pass as one of their group hadn't made it to the conference.

'You need to get rid of that cockney accent, Trev and try and speak a bit Welsh sounding.'

Sound advice from one of their group. Well, that was no problem for me boyo.

I had a great night, got drunk and ended up dancing with Glenys Kinnock.

The only Englishman amongst a thousand Welsh, what a night. My last Labour Party Conference was in Manchester in 2008. They saved the best till last. It started badly as I never received my invite. I was going as part of the Amicus trade union delegation. Someone had dropped a clanger and left me off the list of delegates.

So, after contacting the union I received a very apologetic phone call from a woman from the Trade Union.

Now, because it was late in the day, all the hotels were booked up. The only one with rooms was the Hilton, and it wasn't a room, it was a suite. I didn't know about any of this until I arrived.

I took the train to Manchester and sat opposite quite a well-known political reporter Nick Robinson.

Baldhead and glasses.

He was doing the Times crossword and now and again he'd call out a question and looked at me.

I tried to look like I was thinking of the answer, but he was asking a man who struggled with a *word search*.

Leaving the train station I grab a cab who gets me within two hundred meters before we become gridlocked.

The cab driver advised me to walk the last bit.

So I strolled into this very impressive hotel.

After a thorough body search by two rather large men. I went into the lobby. I stood in a queue waiting to book in. A very nice young lady asked to see my booking details.

'Oh,' she looked at me with a tad of amazement.

'Your VIP, you don't need to queue, come with me.'

She led me to a very plush lounge area and I got booked in.

'I'll take you to your room,' she announced. We go over to a lift that has emblazoned, VIP guests only. This lift I found out later was manned 24/7. So, we go up to the one from the top floor and I enter the world of the rich.

God knows what this suite cost a night, but we're talking serious money I would imagine.

It was floor to ceiling glass. A lounge, a bedroom with an eight-foot bed. A bathroom with everything including one of those showers that squirts you everywhere and a huge jacuzzi bath.

I then get taken up a floor where I'm shown a lounge area reserved for VIP guests. I was informed that this lounge was open from 11 am to 7 pm. Now here's the thing, this lounge had food, beer, wine, all sorts.

I had to endure this treatment for five days.

Now if I didn't think things could get any better, the following morning I came out of my room at the same time as my new next-door neighbour. Old Mr 2 Jags himself, John Prescott. I introduced myself and we shook hands.

And what a nice bloke he turned out to be. We went down for breakfast together and he asked me to join him. He was on the way out at this time, he'd been Deputy Prime Minister but he was getting past his sell-by date.

Although he had a Yorkshire accent, he was in fact, Welsh. He was funny and had a real dry wit about him.

He didn't suffer fools gladly and he had me in stitches with his antics.

He had the waiter running around for him, and one incident that first morning sticks in my mind. Some guy in a very smart suit came over to our table.

'Good morning John, my secretary phoned me and said you wanted to speak to me urgently.'

'Not now, Richard. Can you not see I'm having my breakfast?'

'Oh …. Sorry, John. I'll wait in reception.' The guy walked off and John waited for him to disappear and then pulled his phone out of his pocket. Putting on a thick set of reading glasses he played with the phone and then stuck it to his ear.

'Hello, Sylvia. What the hell did I ring you about this morning? I had Richard here just now saying I wanted to speak to him urgently?' Smiling at me he listened.

'That's it, for the life of me I couldn't think what it was.'

Putting his phone back in his pocket he looked at me and said something my dad would often say.

'No fun getting old, Trevor.'

The conferences were a time to make new contacts and do what is known as a bit of networking.

It was also an excuse to get bladdered every night. The Hoof would have fitted in well because if you were that way inclined, you could get into most functions and grab a few free drinks. My other Amicus colleagues were in modest accommodation, and I didn't feel the need to brag about my VIP upgrade. After the conference finished for the day, we would normally have a couple of drinks before going back to our respected hotels.

Maybe with an arrangement to go to some function or another. Obviously, I was keen to spend a couple of hours hobnobbing in my VIP freebie lounge.

Unfortunately, John Prescott blew my cover one night. A few of us had gone to some function; we came out slightly worse for wear. Now because of the high level of security, there was never any danger to you. Everywhere you looked you'd see armed police. As long as you had your ID hanging from your neck, you were fine.

We were walking back in the direction of our respected hotels when one of my colleagues pointed across the road.

'Isn't that John Prescott over there?' Indeed, it was, and he was being surrounded by some young girls who were trying to get a photo with him. All of a sudden his bellowing voice boomed our way.

'Trev, come over here and take a photo will you lad?'

'You know John Prescott?' One of my colleagues asked.

'Err … Sort of.' I mumbled as I walked over. A girl gave me her camera and I took various photos of these girls hanging off John. Eventually, they walked off.

'Not bad for seventy, am I lad? Come on I'll walk back to the hotel with you.'

I said goodnight to my colleagues and knew I would be getting an inquisition in the morning.

Now I should say that we went back straight to the hotel, but John had a lot of stamina for a seventy-year-old and he took me to a certain kind of club.
I'll park that story there and save the rest for my memoirs.

I have hundreds of stories about my conference experiences; I met loads of nice people, many so-called celebrities. My favourite, Kate Garraway, was an odd choice maybe, but I liked her. It was soon after her exploits on Strictly Come Dancing. She was lovely and down to earth. Chatted away to me, so much nicer than the ginger minge from Eastenders.
I had a great night in the company of Anthony Booth, of Death us do part, fame. What a nice guy he was. He was Cheryl Blair's father; I never held it against him.

One story I will share, once the Munch and I were back with the T&G stewards I received an invention to go on some protest meeting in London, I spoke to a few other stewards and they were keen to join me.
So we end up hiring a minibus and about six of us go. I know Alan Philips and Warren Gibson were with us.
We get dropped off somewhere in London and we have to head for a Townhall that for the life of me I can't remember. What I can remember is we reached Westminster Abbey and we sort of got separated. Munch asks a guy where this Town Hall was.
He tells us the quickest way is to cut through the Abbey. So, being a couple of half-wits we start marching through the Abbey, ignoring the queue of people waiting to purchase tickets.
So we're now inside this famous building and once again we're totally lost.
'Ask that guy over there,' I point to a guy who looks a bit like a school teacher, all gowned up and looking, official.
'Excuse me mate, how do we get to the Townhall from here?'

'Can I see your visitor pass please?' He asks.
We tell him we don't have one, this causes him to blow a whistle and suddenly we're escorted out smartly.
Eventually, we find the Townhall and find the others. After about an hour most of the group have slipped off leaving Warren and me sitting at the front.
The protest was about building more council houses, not something I was overly interested in but it was a day out from the factory.
Tony Benn got up on the stage and delivered another one of his dynamic speeches. It was worth the trip just to listen to him.
As I listened, another guy came and sat next to me, fresh off Celebrity Big Brother, the one and only George Galloway.
Now, I don't agree with the majority of what George stands for. However I will say this about him, he can deliver a speech. If I thought Tony Benn was good, unfortunately, he was second division compared to George.
Warren was impressed too and we waited for him to get off the stage before we ambushed him for a photo.
We went to the pub all smug.

Now, this book is really about the factory, so let's get back to work.

It seemed every few weeks *Bill Sikes* would call me to his office and give me more bad news.
Look, I don't want to be unkind to the man. At the end of the day, it was the nature of the beast. He was being told to cut down on the headcount, and that had to happen. I could sit with him all day and argue the case for keeping our guys, but it wouldn't make any difference.
It didn't win him any polls on the popularity charts. Even to this day, I can't find anyone who has a good word to say about him.

Of course, a new tool had been introduced along with the thousands of other politically correct changes.

Since year dot the way we would lose people was by the last-in, first-out rule.

But now, thanks to a new system called Matrix. That rule was no longer applied. In fact, it became illegal to use.

You were discriminating against someone for not having long service? Absolute bullshit and madness.

So basically, the manager would give you points for all sorts of skills and attitudes.

It's in my mind completely flawed. If your face didn't fit, it was good night Eileen.

The company were doing nothing wrong, they were abiding by the laws that were now in place.

But it was hard to explain to a guy with thirty years' service that you're surplus to requirements and no longer needed,

however, you're young mate with two years' service is staying?

It was an awful time, and I dreaded the phone call from *Bill Sikes*, it was never going to be good news. I had to sit there and watch him destroy people's lives.

For me, well I thought everything was going to shit.

I know the maintenance guys were fed up with me and the Munch. But there was nothing we could do. Trust me, had the Munch and me not been stewards at the time, I'm certain we would have been top of the hit list and both been shipped out.

On the union front, Amicus were in a merger with the T & G. I was going back to my roots.

Unfortunately, the T & G had a much larger membership, so I knew my time on any union executive committee was not going to last much longer.

We became UNITE. And within a year I'd lost all my former amicus positions apart from carrying on as the branch secretary.

The shop stewards in the plant were down to a handful. We had become a laughing stock, I'm not going to point out the blame, they'd let things slip to such an extinct that we had no support.

Warren Gibson had gone. It sort of tells you how bad things had got when a young popular deputy convenor jacks it in.

If we had a mass meeting to discuss a pay deal, I could see the real anger in the guys.

The respect had gone and we were targeted to some real abuse. How Geoff kept a level head at these meetings I'll never know.

Sometimes I was worried about his safety as the meeting got really heated and threatened to boil over. All sorts of accusations and abuse were thrown at us. We were literally hated by the majority of the membership.

We can thank the previous convenor for that.

I was fifty-four and I'd had enough. In the space of a year, everything had worn me down.

The constant shrinking of the maintenance headcount was making me ill, mentally ill.

I'd had enough of sitting in with guys who were being kicked into touch. It was a horrible feeling and I used to take this entire worry home with me.

We'd lost a huge amount of hoist work due to the engine side closing. Each week there seemed to be another Health and Safety rule that made our life looking after hoists more difficult. It wasn't fun anymore.

Phillip Harris was another casualty, another manager I waved goodbye to. Phil could have only been in his early forties, replaced by a former contractor who none of the guys liked.

As I mentioned earlier, I knew *Bill Sikes* was keen to ship me out; it must have been very frustrating for him as I was protected by my shop steward status.

In the end, I jumped before I was pushed. It was 2010 and it was game over.
Sadly I left the company. Within a week I was on a plane bound for Asia. I didn't know it at the time, but I never returned.

The author at Pattaya beach, with one I made earlier.

Author's summary

Well, I've read through this book twice and can now say I'm happy with it.
I've named a few which I didn't the first time around; I still won't name the convenor or one of the manager's.
They know who they are, that's enough for me.
I think the majority of you know who they are too.
I found it more difficult to remember certain incidents, but I hope I've stayed accurate.
I did put a disclaimer in the front of the book, as I like to say, some of the things I write about are alleged.
I left eleven years ago and some of the guys I mention I don't know if they are still with us.
I hope you had a good chuckle as you read about certain events and characters.

Thank you for taking the time to read about factory life.

If you enjoyed the book and like my style of humorous writing, I hope you try some of my other books.

I'd also welcome any feedback, feel free to email me.
trevorwhitehead58@gmail.com

Trevor Whitehead's author's page:
https://www.amazon.com/Trevor-Whitehead/e/B01N5NNZ3E